My Father Had a Daughter

a Daughter

Judith Shakespeare's Tale

GRACE TIFFANY

BERKLEY BOOKS, NEW YORK

B

A Berkley Book
Published by The Berkley Publishing Group
A division of Penguin Group (USA) Inc.
375 Hudson Street
New York, New York 10014

PRINTING HISTORY
Berkley hardcover edition / May 2003
Berkley trade paperback edition / August 2004
Berkley trade paperback ISBN: 0-425-19638-0

The Library of Congress has catalogued the Berkley hardcover edition as follows:

Tiffany, Grace, 1958–
My father had a daughter : Judith Shakespeare's tale / Grace Tiffany.—1st ed.
p. cm.
ISBN 0-425-19003-X (alk. paper)
1. Shakespeare, Judith, 1585–1662—Fiction.   2. Shakespeare, William, 1564–1616—
Fiction.   3. Stratford-upon-Avon (England)—Fiction.   4. Fathers and daughters—
Fiction.   5. Dramatists—Fiction.   I. Title.

PS3620.I45 M9 2003
813'.54—dc21
2002036028

PRINTED IN THE UNITED STATES OF AMERICA

10   9   8   7   6   5   4   3   2   1

To Tom

Viola   My father had a daughter lov'd a man
As it might be perhaps, were I a woman,
I should your lordship.

Duke   And what's her history?

Viola   A blank . . .

—William Shakespeare, *Twelfth Night*

My Father Had a Daughter

Chapter One

My brother and I played on the riverbank, four streets from my mother's house, where the water narrowed and the field-stones we threw could reach the other side. The river pooled in the shallows, and sometimes it smelled bad from the offal dumped willy-nilly by housewives upstream, but if you pinched your nose and stared down hard at the pools you could just see your own self, muddily reflected, holding its nose and staring hard, till you and it laughed and blinked. When Hamnet and I looked together and stayed still enough, it was easy to imagine that I was he and he was I, and that truly we were four.

Bad smell or no, rushing or sluggish water, the river was our best place to be on spring and summer and fall afternoons, and many were the cuffings we got after coming home muddy and wet and scratched from the sharp-bladed grass that grew thereby. Our mother was a merry or furious sort, never much in between, and at such times we felt the bent of her rage on the backs of our legs. I do not blame her. I think her wrath had less to do with our filthiness than with the plates uncleaned, the floors unswept, the beds unmade, and our four hands that should have been working now mired with river-dirt. And also, perhaps, with some wild envy she couldn't name but which threatened to choke her when she saw the two of us holding hands. Even then I sensed it and forgave her.

Of course it was she who punished us, just as it was she who scrubbed us clean and then hugged us and gave us apple slices and set us to work. In the early years, Uncle Gilbert would often be there with his pot of ale and his reddish nose, seated humming on a kitchen bench, but his way with us was a pat or a pinch and a wink and little more to hinder our play. And the same with the grandparents, and with the other uncles and aunts and great-aunts who crowded in for Sunday dinners in the bigger wing of the house. All of this was of course before we moved to the biggest house in town, where there was too much room entirely.

I thought Uncle Gilbert was my father until I was three and something blossomed in my head. Until then I had thought the scribbling one a mere visitor, a family friend and sometime lodger. He always paid his money, handing silver coins to my mother to drop in her pocket the minute he came in the door. He was affectionate and distracted, and had the odd habit of acting as though he owned the place. He was the strangest person I ever saw. Hamnet and I would sit at his feet and pull at his bootlaces because we could do it without him changing a thing he was doing. He would still mutter and scribble and shift in his chair, and if he jumped up suddenly it was not because of us, but because of some strange thing in his head that made him bounce and roar. When we learned to tie, we more than once bound his laces together just to see him lose balance when he tried to stand, and even then he seemed not to notice us. One time, so hobbled, he hopped to the window shelf for a new pot of ink and hopped back and sat without bothering to free his poor feet, which caused us high glee. We waited in suspense to see him do it again. The next time, however, he fell over.

When the visitor was there my uncle Gilbert wasn't. Or if Gilbert came in for a minute or two, to bring my mother some cut lilies or us some gloves from my grandfer's Woolery, he was a different uncle, not lazy and affable but closed-faced, gazing sidelong at the scribbling man with an expression it took me years to name. Worse it was that our mother would be quiet and tense at such times, until Uncle Gilbert left. With Gilbert alone she spoke constantly, but with the other man she spoke little; sometimes sharply, sometimes gently, but always little.

Yet mostly in our childhood she was calm, and the house was cheerful, with the five of us always busy. Five, I say, because we had a sister, Susanna, older than us by two years. She was a prissy bossy cat who sang to her dolls and had to have her hair plaited just so, and her dolls' hair plaited just so, and knew nothing of the pleasure of smearing boot-blacking on one's face to look like a Moorish warrior. She also knew nothing of the beating that came afterwards for having stolen the boot-blacking.

My brother was no Susanna. He was open-faced and bold and he did what I wanted, and for that I loved him. That he was a boy and ten minutes my elder did not lead him to run riot over my desires; he was gentle and listened and laughed out loud at all and any of my ideas and plots and was the willing reflection of my spirit. We would hang from the ash trees like monkeys, though the first time we did it my smock fell over my face. From then on he lent me his second pair of trunks and hose, and in those I climbed high as a squirrel. We played mumblety-peg in the garden and then, when we were six and he went to school and I had to stay home, he lent me his hornbook to show me what he had learned each day, so we learned to read together.

After that our games began in earnest. It was then that we would buy the penny ballads at the bookstalls by the Market Cross and take them to read by the riverbank. Hamnet would dress up as Patrick Spence or the Virgin Mary or Tristram and I would be Isolde or Christ on a cross, and all was merry as could be. The costumes were mostly of our imagination, but our imagination was sufficient.

As I have said, it was before this, when I was three, that I came to know that our sometime visitor who mumbled and wrote in his chair for hours was my father. Here is how that came about. I was singing and rolling about on the floor displaying all there was of me to see, and the fellow looked up from his writing long enough to say, "That is all right now,

Judy, but a little less of that later. Else you will end up like your mother." That brought a gale of laughter from me because it caused me to imagine my stout mother waving her naked legs and bottom in the air and it was a wondrous image. At the same time my mother poked her head in from the kitchen with a look of rage, and saw me laughing and waving myself in the air. There she was then, doubling me over and beating my hind parts with her hand and me howling, and then it suddenly stopped. I sat upright to see the visitor standing by her, holding her wrist in his hand, and as mildly as milk he said, "Let her be. You know your anger is not for her." Her face was flushed but she stayed still, on her knees and staring up at him with her eyes bright blue, and he gazed down at her, his face all pale and his eyes an unfathomable grey. And then he dropped her wrist and went back to his chair and his pen, and she rose to tend her stew.

So I knew. It was not that I had not called him Dada before, as Susanna did, but that I had not known that the word meant he was married to our mother, and that he was like the other fathers in town who lived with their families in their own houses. I had never seen my father go upstairs to sleep in my mother's chamber. Every night when I climbed the stair he was still bent over his paper, and every morning when I rose he was there as well, writing or else reading one of the books he bought or borrowed (though I do not think he ever read one of them all the way through). So I didn't know where he slept, but now I knew he was our father, because he had held my mother's wrist in that way, as though it were his own wrist and he could grab it if he liked, and she had not shaken him off. I ran upstairs to tell Hamnet, who was as surprised as I, but who believed me because he believed everything I said.

When my father was not there my mother sat with Uncle Gilbert and talked about her sisters, and her hard-dealing farmer brother, and the queen's red hair and whether it was real, and wool prices, and winter gloves. Gilbert would drink and squint and sometimes he would wipe his eyes and speak in a low voice and our mother would look worried and pat him on the shoulder. But most times he would chuckle and eat pasties. Sometimes our skinny aunt Joan would join them, and the three of them would be louder than the three of us, Susanna and Hamnet and I, as we wrangled in the next room. There Hamnet and I often tried to rub Susanna's dolls in the dust and Susanna would kick us silly, for she had a strong leg.

When I was older and learned to write, I would join the throng in the kitchen and scribble recipes of my own making as the big folk chattered. I would sit on my mother's lap and sometimes Gilbert would lean over my head to whisper something to her that I would not try to hear because I was busy writing. My recipes were terrible, with titles such as "Horror Soup" and "Death Juice," calling for ingredients of human toes and rat's bane and papists' tongues and cooking times of upwards of a thousand years. I would hide them in the kitchen beneath the buttery bar and my mother would find them later and show them to my aunt Joan, and the two of them would laugh very hard and tickle me.

I began to attend more to my grey-eyed father when he came home then, because I had many questions about what he was writing. And so he would hand me the pages and tell me to blow on them so the ink would dry, and I would blow and read and blow and read. That is how I discovered that on those pages were people talking to each other about murder, love, and so on, and I was thrilled so to learn he was doing something useful with his time.

Bit by bit my father took Hamnet and me into his confidence, and told us the stories of the plays he was writing. There was one about a murderous moneylender and one about two star-crossed lovers and one about a poor young English king who got stabbed in a prison cell. He told us he had friends in the big city far to the south who would say the lines, and that he himself would get on a big stage and say a few of them too, and folk would pay money to hear.

My father and Hamnet and I and sometimes Susanna would hover together by his writing table and trade lines back and forth. He taught us how to say them, and after we did, he might change something, a word or the place in the line where the word fell. He showed us the special gestures that the players used to show this or that emotion on the stage: fists clenched for anger, arms thrown up for fear, head bowed for grief. He said that when he himself stood on a stage he scanted these gestures whenever he could, since he thought them foolish enough. "When a man is scared, he does not shoot arms skyward as though he would presently perform a handstand!" he said. "More like he bites a lip and turns pale. And a fellow player can ask him, *Why lookest thou pale?* Words will say what skin will not."

Still, my father told us, he would never have been able to

get player's work without showing he knew the proper faces and motions. And he knew them well, since by the time he had come hat in hand to the players, he had studied their ways from the yards of the public playhouses for many months, paying his daily penny to shove through a narrow door and then elbow through a stinky crowd under an open sky; stepping over nutshells and ash and piss (we giggled), past ale-vendors and orange-hawkers and market-women with garlic breath, past gowned law students and yelling wool-capped apprentices of all trades, all of them fleeing studies or work for an afternoon.

That is where our father spent his time during the long months of his absences. Of course, once we knew, we begged to go with him to the playhouses. We had hardly seen a play in our lives, because the town only allowed licensed players to perform in the square or the guildhall, and such players came only once or twice a year and we rarely were let to go. My mother did not like us to see men and boys with painted faces, or hear all manner of ranting about king-killing and bloodshed and *adultery,* a word I didn't understand, but which made my mother redden every time she uttered it. How amazed, then, was I to find my father the creator of such stage rant, and how far that discovery went to explain the way my mother frowned and shook her head at his figure bent scribbling over the table! Though it did not completely explain it.

In any case, Susanna, Hamnet, and I wanted to go to London, and our father would only say that we could come if our mother would bring us. But our mother said she would not bring us, and she wouldn't say why. Great were the wails in the kitchen then. Susanna and Hamnet moaned and screeched that they must see one of our father's plays *or else*. Hamnet said he would die. I stayed quiet because I knew that my mother would like what I had to say even less than she liked the moans and screeches and the threats of present death.

I did not want to see one of my father's plays.

I wanted to be in one.

Chapter Two

OF course, I had no notion that such a thing would ever come about, and no plans to make it happen. What I began to want in those days, when I was seven, was for my father to let us act a play of his at home. Or for him to walk to the river with us and tell us his wild stories and watch us imitate the odd playing-gestures he had shown us, or carry us on his back in the garden and take us to the bowls on the green. And all of those things he would do now and then, but mostly he would sit and be quiet and write.

When I think on those times, I cannot describe how much Hamnet and I came to love him. When we understood what he was doing with his quill and parchment, we could not imagine anything better in the world, except for him to tell us what he was writing about. Because anything wild and fantastic or magical or otherwise intriguing that could be thought of might be growing on that paper. I had only to tell my father that I had seen a fairy queen in the Arden Forest, and he would put her on the page and give her something interesting to say. My mother and Aunt Joan were much more likely to smack me for lying in such a situation. I am not an idiot and so I learned quickly who to talk to about fairies, though in truth I had never seen one. My father knew it didn't matter whether I had or not. The thing was to imagine her.

My father took all our ideas about fairies and whatnot and spun them on his pages and when he was done, or sometimes even before, he would begin mumbling to himself and making odd, jerky hand gestures, and then he would jump up and say something incomprehensible like "Kempe?" or "Dick!" or "It wouldn't fit in the inner-stage."

And within a day or so he would be gone.

And we were bereft.

At night, in the room above, where we all slept, I whispered to Hamnet, "When do you think he'll be back?"

"Lent," Hamnet said mournfully. "It is always Lent."

"Because the London playhouses close at Lent. But we could make him come sooner, if we would. We could make him stay longer."

"How?"

I furrowed my brow in the darkness. "When there is plague in the city the playhouses close."

"Judith," Hamnet said, "even you could not send a plague to London."

I sat up on the bed abruptly. "Dost thou doubt my power, vile worm of earth?"

Hamnet snickered, and across the room Susanna tossed impatiently in her sleep.

"Do you think I could send a plague on Susanna?" I asked.

"No," Hamnet whispered fearfully. "I mean, do not speak of it."

"I wouldn't," I said. "We might catch it."

"But what of our father? How can we make him leave the city?"

"I will think on it," I said. And I lay awake many hours doing just that.

It was the spring of 1592, and there were so many things to be done—from churning butter to carding wool to sweeping leather bits from the Woolery floor—that I stopped thinking about how to bring our father home early. Hamnet still often spoke of it, though, and hoped he would return at Christmastide. One day, just as my brother was due home from school, our mother told me that our father had become very grand and might have to appear before the red-haired queen at her holiday revels, instead of coming home to us. When she said this, her voice was dry, and Uncle Gilbert, reading a ha'-penny broadsheet behind her, gave a snort and a roll of his eyes. Then he pretended to have laughed at something in the broadsheet, and the corners of her eyes smiled. I glared at my uncle and made sure I stepped on his foot before I left the kitchen. For this I was swatted, I don't know by which of them.

By this time, Hamnet was already studying his hornbook

very seriously on the oak bench in the parlor. When I stopped in front of him he looked at me and I looked at him and it was as though we'd swapped eyes. Then I made a face and he made the same face at the same time, and I made a gesture and he made the same gesture exactly. We had gotten so good at this that it frightened the adults, especially when we stayed glassy-eyed and expressionless, as we strove to do. It was our mirror game.

"What am I thinking?" I asked Hamnet, while I stared at him. Our hands were clapped together as in a suspended game of pat-a-cake.

"The *devil* if I know!" said Hamnet. This was something my grandfer John said often, and Hamnet had taken to repeating it. "The *devil* if I know! You'll have to tell me."

I dropped my hands in disgust. "Why can you not read my mind? I can read yours."

"You can?" Susanna or any of my cousins would have sniffed, but Hamnet was interested. "How do you do it?" he asked.

"Well." I sat next to him on the bench. "First I hold your hand tight, like so. And then I squeeze my eyes shut, like so. And then I say: *Hamnet, Hamnet, doober doo. Hamnet, Hamnet, I know you.*" I opened my eyes. "And then your thoughts are like words printed in blazing letters in my mind."

Hamnet gazed at me admiringly. "In blazing letters!" he said. "And you can hardly read yet. What do they say?"

"*And she can hardly read yet.*"

Hamnet's eyes grew wide. In truth, he could be a dunce. "Be you a born sorceress?" he asked.

"Yes."

"Being your twin, I should have some powers too."

"It seems it is only for girls."

Hamnet accepted this serenely. He nodded. "Then it is you who must spin the spell to catch our father," he said. "To catch him and return him to us."

"And so I will," I said. "I have thought on it." In the walk between the kitchen and the parlor I had already formed a plan. It was not precisely a plan to bring my father home, but a plan by which I could pretend to influence my father's comings and goings. I knew that he would surely return at *some* time. It would be sport to play the witch who brought him here, and I could grow nothing but more glorious in Hamnet's eyes for it.

I sat next to Hamnet on the bench and whispered in his ear. "Tonight we must creep down the ash tree by our window and run to the river bend. There I will say the spell."

Hamnet shivered, but his eyes lit up. "What spell?"

"Clotpole, could I say it now? If I said it now you would perish of plague on the spot."

Hamnet quickly made the sign against the evil eye. "Do not, Judy!"

"Fear not. Only do this: bring three petals of our mother's peonies and the skull of the cat our uncle Edmund buried beneath the apple tree."

"Mama will throw me in the buck basket if she catches me tearing her peonies."

"Then she must not catch you! Hsst, a moment." From the kitchen we could hear our uncle murmuring, low and sad.

"Nuncle Gilbert will be weeping into his cup any moment now, Ham," I said. "She will stay and listen. Go now, quick. I'll keep watch."

So Hamnet went, and stole the flower petals. Later, near dusk, I helped him dig under the tree for the bony remains of Uncle Edmund's cat. We threw the skull and the petals into an old cloth and I tucked it inside my sleeve and off we went to supper and then to bed, where we lay for an hour until we heard Susanna breathing evenly. And then we were off, through the window and down the tree, me in a pair of Hamnet's old breeches to make the climbing easier. We ran, evading the town crier's lamp, zigzagging through the streets of Stratford to the darkness of the river.

Our heart was pounding. I could tell that Hamnet was about to cry from fear, but he would not show me that. He did not have to. "Calm thee, Ham," I said, and put my hand on his arm. It was shaking. "You have only to do what I say."

"All right," he whispered.

I dropped to my knees on the grassy bank. "First we dig a hole, as round as we can make it," I said. Obediently, he knelt by my side and together we scrabbled until we had opened a small, shallow pit in the earth. The moon shone on the water, and I could half-see Hamnet's pale face.

I handed Hamnet the folded rag. "Now, empty the sacred objects," I said. Hamnet cast the cat's skull and the wrinkled petals into the pit, and I hastily covered them up and smoothed over the top.

"What next?" he asked anxiously.

"*Hsst!*" I said. Hamnet froze. "Stay there, on your knees,"

I said. I rose, reached my arms heavenward, and turned three times, slowly, so I would not get dizzy and ruin the solemnity of the ritual. Then I recited the poem I had written in my head that afternoon.

> *Plaguey come and plaguey go*
> *Plaguey high and plaguey low*
> *Plaguey London, plague come down,*
> *Make our father flee the town.*

I dropped my arms and stood silent. I was shivering, not from cold but from the fear that I had put into myself. Hamnet was breathing quickly behind me and I knew he was terrified, but I knew he would stay still for me because he really feared that if he did not then something would go horribly wrong with my spell. And for my part, I stayed still the better to convince him, and perhaps myself, that I was not really afraid.

After a long minute I knelt down. " 'Tis done," I said, and Hamnet let out his breath in a long gasp. "Come." I grabbed his hand. "We can go home now."

In the morning we were very tired, but we rose when we had to and were not caught and flogged for our late-night dealings. We had learned long ago how to combine our night-stained clothes with our day-stained clothes in the buck basket and so attract no special suspicion. At home I yawned and helped my mother spin and dust until Hamnet came home from school.

He looked worried. When I got him to myself I asked him why his face was so long, as my spell was bound to work soon. I said this with confidence because just that afternoon I had overheard my aunt Joan reading a letter from my father in London. The letter said that a group of players would likely be traveling to Stratford within the month, and that perhaps he would come with them.

"I am afraid of the plague," Hamnet said.

"But why? My spell was for London, not here."

He looked at me with an odd expression. "But if the plague comes to London, folk will die."

"But not our father," I said quickly. "I put that in the spell. The plague will make him flee the town, but he will not catch it. He is plague-proof, know you not that? Do you not remember Gammer Mary's story?"

"What story?"

"That our father was born in a plague year, with children dying up and down the street, but he laughed in his cradle and would not catch it!"

Hamnet shivered. "I do not like children dying."

"But they will be London children. We do not know them."

Hamnet looked at me then in a way that was new to me. It was as though he looked not at me, but through me, or inside me. His look was almost disapproving. That stung me to the quick, and I spoke angrily. "You are a blockhead," I said.

He looked wounded, and began to walk off.

"Wait," I said. I grabbed his arm. "The plague smites evildoers. Do you not remember what the rector said three Sundays ago?"

Hamnet shook his head. "I cannot understand him. I never listen."

"The rector said when plagues and deaths come they are a punishment on the wicked. Do not worry about my spell. If plague comes and children die it will be only the wicked ones, like Samuel Sadler, who stole your biscuit after the homily."

"But I would not wish Samuel Sadler to die."

"He will not die. Wicked *London* children might. They are acres more wicked than the ones here."

Hamnet nodded slowly. His face was happier. I was glad it did not occur to him to ask me what the rector thought of children who stole peony petals and chanted spells in the moonlight by the river.

THREE weeks later the players came to town, blowing their horns and waving their banner and marching in red while the children and dogs ran yelling and barking behind them. Despite my spell, our father was not with them.

Hamnet and I and even Susanna wanted to run with the crowd of children and dogs, to see if just maybe he was there indeed, disguised in a marvelous false beard that fell past his knees. Our mother got angry and told us we were foolish. Our father was in London hunched over a table in an ill-lit room jotting away, a thing he could just as well do at home but had chosen not to. She would be fried in grease with two eggs, she said, before she would let her children make fools of them-selves—and of her—by running screaming after a gaggle of players who could do no honest work, but finagled pennies out of poor folk and gave them nothing but a pack of lies in exchange. A bunch of beggars who, however so gorgeous their costumes, did nothing but act out a lot of wild stories about things that never happened.

Or, if they had, should not have.

Hamnet ran upstairs and cried when her ranting convinced him that our father had not returned, but Susanna and I still harped to see the play. Hamnet's tears softened my mother, and she relented. She gave us each a penny to go with Aunt Joan and Uncle Edmund to see the play in the town square, and a penny to buy muffins as well. So off we went, leaving her cradling poor Hamnet's head in her lap and looking as though she might cry herself.

The play was wonderful, about a magician, and a fair lass and her lover, and a friar who casts spells but is soundly pun-ished for doing so. When it was done the lass took a bow and off came her wig and we saw she was a boy, and a young boy at that, not older than me but by two or three years, his face all painted up. When he saw me he gave me a wink. That made my face glow, and it glowed all the way back to our house in Henley Street, and I sang a song with Susanna and Aunt Joan and Uncle Edmund. I almost liked Susanna that day. But I lost my glow when I came in the house and saw my mother's worried look. She said that Hamnet was feverish and that we should be very quiet and that Susanna must get supper.

Susanna dished out cold turnips and leeks and salt mutton, but I had little appetite. My mother stayed upstairs and held a cold cloth to Hamnet's forehead, and after supper she told us that we must sleep with my grandparents in the other house that was connected to ours. So off Susanna and I went, and my grandfer John told me a story and offered me a sweet, but I could not eat it.

The next day Hamnet was better, though he coughed now and then. My mother was afraid I would catch whatever chill he had, so she kept him upstairs and me in the garden pulling weeds. I threw a ball of string through the upstairs window and Hamnet caught it and sent it down with a message penciled on paper I had taken from Grandfer John's account book. I sent a message back, and so we had a merry afternoon. And in two days' time Hamnet went back to school and all was well. Only now I began to worry because I did not know what would bring my father home before Christmas. We would see him *at* Christmas, of that I still had hopes. He rarely missed Christmas with us. But if he did not come before then, what would Hamnet think of my powers?

And yet, mark what happened next.

Within a week of Hamnet's fever I saw my aunt Joan open a letter given her by a rider who said he had come from London. When she read it, her face grew pale and she shook and threw the letter in the fire. Then she hurried to take counsel with my mother. When I pulled the half-burnt paper from the flames and saw what it said, I must have paled myself. I threw it back in as quick as I could, knowing my dark prayer had been answered.

The plague was in London.

In two weeks the daily death toll had risen above one hundred. That night, a cup to the floorboards and my bottom in the air, I listened to my mother and Gilbert and Joan speaking in the parlor below. They spoke of quarantined houses with crosses nailed to the doors, and people perishing within. And of the plague carts rattling through the streets, and of pits outside the city walls where men dug with their faces wrapped in cloth and then burned their own clothes.

"He'll not come," my mother said, in a near desperate voice. "To throw away his life, with barely a thought of me or the three babes to feed, and him not yet thirty!"

"Anne, he is thriving there now, and so are we here," Joan said.

"Aye," my mother said bitterly. "One petty triumph with those *history* plays and now he thinks of nothing but more kings, more battles, more silly combats to put on that dirty stage. He thinks himself immortal."

Gilbert spoke then. His voice was so low that I could not hear what he said. But then Joan spoke again. "And they're like to *stay* closed until autumn," she said. "Till St. Dennis' Day or later. The city will not open the theaters now. I'm sure 'tis all they can do to bring folk to church to pray for themselves. They fear contagion in the sanctuary."

"At least I need not fear he'll show his face there," my mother said, with a short, hard laugh. "I know him. He's not saying prayers. He's in his room." Her voice grew sad. "Or in someone else's."

"Oh, Anne." My aunt's voice was soothing. "Oh."

I heard my mother rise and close the shutters. Gilbert said something low again, and then fell silent.

I crept back to bed. *Please,* I prayed. I heard Hamnet's slow breathing beside me. I had not yet told him about the letter, and his sleep was undisturbed.

Please, Da, I prayed. *Get out.*

THREE days went by. Our mother did her best to keep her worry from Hamnet, Susanna, and me. But I was beside myself with fear. I told Hamnet what I knew, but I kept him from knowing how scared I was. I assured him that this plague was but the workings of our spell, and that our father would be safe out of London in a fortnight. I spoke so firmly that he believed me, though he still shed tears for the wicked London children behind their cross-marked doors. I pitied them too, and felt a pang of guilt for having wished such troubles on a city full of folk I had never seen. Yet I was more than half-sure that the spell I'd chanted was only some gibberish I'd made up. Plagues came and went as they would and I could not fairly be blamed for them.

At Hamnet's request I chanted another spell to conjure my father safely out of the city. This one we muttered together in the storeroom as we knelt inside a pentagram. I had drawn it with chalk I'd convinced him to pocket from the schoolroom over the guildhall. We chanted and then knocked the floor three times with a sheep's leg bone. The night before, I had taken Hamnet to the graveyard at Trinity Church. I had buried the leg bone there myself, under a foot of soil, while he was at school. When we dug it up, I convinced him that it was from the leg of a notorious Warwickshire murderer. He was scared nearly silly, but proved willing to brave the ghosts and the darkness for me—and even to hold the murderer's bone for a moment when I climbed back over our garden wall.

After we cast the spell we were most careful to rub the chalk pentagram out completely, and I threw the sheep's bone in a rubbish pile at the end of Henley Street.

I was sick with anxiety four days later when the message came. It was delivered by a passenger from a southern coach, who left it on the doorstep and walked quickly away. I was playing in the yard, and I ran over and saw my father's hand on the paper, and itched to open it, but I had to wait for my mother to return from the baking ovens at the end of the street. When she appeared with Joan she snatched at the letter and the two of them disappeared with it into the kitchen and bade me and Hamnet go back out and play. Through the kitchen window I saw Joan open the letter and begin to read, and saw my mother's eyes grow wide and her expression turn from fear to confusion to anger. But I could not hear either of them.

It was at supper that she told us. My father was not in London—indeed, by Joan's reckoning had already been gone from London on the day we first heard of the plague there.

"Then he will come home?" Hamnet asked excitedly.

"Nay," said my mother. "Not he. He's a lordly fellow, your father."

My mother often spoke in this way that was both barbed and oblique. Though I would have known neither of those words at the time, I knew the tone, and knew that the story would not come from her. Hamnet was looking pale and ghostly and would say no more either. So I turned to my aunt Joan. "Where is he, Aunt?"

"At a fine place," she answered, sipping her broth. "Do not worry on his account, children. He's at a splendid mansion with a splendid earl and he's writing poems for him."

"For the splendid earl?" My mouth hung half-open.

"Yes, my dear. Poems for a splendid earl."

"But I thought poems were written from men to ladies."

My mother once more gave the short, hard laugh I had heard through the floorboards nights before. "Yes, my Judy," she said. "And so they should be."

I looked at Hamnet, who looked at me, and neither of us knew what to say, but my mother's voice seemed to suggest we should say nothing more. And so we didn't, but after we finished our cheese and pears, when we were clattering our dishes into the washing tub, I whispered to Hamnet, "Do you see, Ham?"

Hamnet looked perplexed and sad. "He's writing poems to a lord and he will not come home. Perhaps he'll not even come at Christmas."

"It was the *words* of the spell," I said. "I conjured him *out of London*. That's what I said, and that's what came about."

Hamnet looked at me wonderingly. "We should have conjured him *farther* than that. Not just out of London, but homeward."

"He will come," I said firmly, though I didn't say when. "In the meantime, he's safe."

"So he is," Hamnet said, more cheerfully. He looked at me admiringly. "You are a fine spell-caster, Judy."

I basked in his praise, yet his words frightened me.

I almost believed them myself.

Chapter Three

OUR father did not return for Christmastide.

It was a dark and disappointing time, with the Yule Log forbidden by the aldermen, and public celebrations discouraged, and the rector with his flat cap telling us the festivities of the year's end were pagan mischief. Still, my mother and my grandmother and my aunts laid a table with roast mutton and eel pie and conies and raspberry tart and Hamnet and Susanna and I received oranges studded with cloves. Grandfer John sang and we all drank wassail and tried to be merry. My mother and my uncle Gilbert and my aunt Joan really were merry, but I could feel my brother's disappointment and it weighed on my heart, as did my own.

Great was our surprise and joy, then, when within two months of the New Year's beginning, my grey-eyed father strode into my mother's kitchen like a young Saint Nicholas, clad in a hooded cloak and holding a tin full of sweets. At first Hamnet and I clung to our mother's skirts and stared; then, as one, we ran to him and hugged his waist. Afterwards I left him speaking to my mother because I couldn't wait to pull shining-eyed Hamnet upstairs to remind him that my magic, though slow-acting, was potent.

My mother was laughing and happy to see my father again. They stayed in her chamber for much of the time of the following week, with Hamnet and I rapping on the door and being told to go away, but not in an angry way, and so we kept up our rapping. After suppers our father would sit by the fire with his cambric shirt unlaced and the strange yellow ring that made him look like a pirate glinting in his ear. Whenever we asked him where he had been he would tell us stories ever more fantastic: that he had wandered vast deserts in the East; that he had been shipwrecked among cannibals and seen monster-men whose heads grew underneath their shoulders; that he had sailed on the Spanish main and boarded a galleon with a knife clasped between his teeth. We shrieked in mock fear and not even Hamnet believed any of it.

Eventually from listening through floorboards and hiding under tables I learned that my father had left the lord's house where he had been employed because something painful and bad had happened there, and that he never would go back to that fine estate.

We thought now we would have him forever, which was good news for all, except perhaps for Gilbert, who trudged grimly between the yard and my grandfather's Woolery and said little enough. But it wasn't long before my father fell quiet again, and began to mutter and scribble at the table in the parlor and sometimes on the floor of the big room upstairs, with his papers spread all around drying.

"Do not walk on them," he would caution absently, not looking up. "Keep apart. Get away, now."

In truth, he was a great slobber, leaving crumpled pages and broken quills and open books on the rush mats, and filling drinking flagons with ink. This was one of the causes of my mother's displeasure with him. There was a night when she slammed a bowl on the table in response to something he said, and from the brittle tone of the words that followed I knew that our holiday time was over. I could hear little of their dialogue, only my father saying "Money" many times in different intonations, and my mother once raising her voice to say, "There is no shame in the Woolery."

And then there was much silence for a day or so, and one morning we woke to find the table in the parlor empty of all but some bent and pen-marked paper and our mother grimly brushing snow off the windowsills so it fell below into Henley Street.

He was gone.

I grew in understanding, of course, and by the time I was nine I understood far better than my mother what kept him in the bustling city of London. To me no great argument needed

making. When he came home two or three times a year, before he settled down to write, he would tell us such stories of
the playhouses that I ached to be there myself.

I wanted to be in the tiring room, in the midst of the panic
and powder and paint, watching my father calmly instruct the
players, seeing his own costume as he rose from the trap as a
grey, ghostly ghost, hearing the musicians play the drums that
meant war and storms and shipwreck. I wanted to see and
smell and hear the yelling crowd and the vendors with their
oranges and hazelnuts and beer. I longed to face down the
impudent roaring boys in the yard, the groundlings who inter-
rupted all plays with rude shouts and questions. I wanted to
yell clever things back at them. I wanted to brandish a wooden
sword so that the onlookers applauded and everyone laughed—
players and rude boys and lords and ladies in the galleries—so
that all of us, hundreds on hundreds on hundreds, cheered each
other on to make a play.

By the fire I would dream such scenes, and outside in the
snow or the summer's heat by the frozen or muddy river,
Hamnet and I would fence with sticks in the way our father
had taught us, feigning to stab, feigning to die, with terrible
bloodcurdling shrieks.

"It is a dream," my father said of it all.

And my dream was then but a reflection of his, a dream
of a dream.

My mother could not understand why he or any of us
should long to be part of a dirty crowd that spread disease
amongst itself, or wish to live in a city full of noise and stink,
where you could not walk from one end to the other in less

than a full afternoon. Her contempt, I know now, was fueled by something else, a darker suspicion and personal hurt.

But her disdain for the playhouses was well bolstered by the rest of my family. Though they welcomed the money my father sent, buying new cushions and rugs and expanding the Woolery, still they shook their heads in embarrassed amusement when neighbors asked of my father's doings. I could see how greatly my grandfather would have preferred to answer his friends by boasting of my father's success in the law courts, or as a merchant funding voyages to the Indies. As glamorous as my father's life sounded to me, the Shakespeare men were only bemused by the fact that my father frequently appeared in costume at Queen Elizabeth's court. That he went there not to sell anything useful, like corn or grain, but to recite poetry, wearing powder on his face and hundred-year-old armor or some sort of odd wizard's robe, was unseemly to them, and in fact, to all the businessmen and laborers of Stratford. And then for him to dance the morris with clowns for the entertainment of courtiers dressed almost as outlandishly as he! The thing was absurd. My uncle Gilbert made high sport of it when my father was home.

Gilbert's needling was the only thing I ever saw pierce my father's skin of amused detachment. "Will," Gilbert would say, in front of my mother and Joan and assorted family members. "*Sweet* William. Did you kiss the royal seat of the gorgeous Earl of Southampton at our queen's Christmas Revels?" Then he would give a great smack of his lips.

"He was not there." My father's voice would be dry. "He was fighting with Essex off the coast of Spain."

"Did you dance the *morris* for the queen?" Gilbert would rise and hop about so foolishly that the rest of us had to laugh, except for my father, who would stare broodingly at his younger brother, his long, ink-stained fingers tapping the table, his mouth twitching, not with humor, but with frank impatience.

It was then I clearly understood that my father and Gilbert hated each other.

And so they all spent the money my father made, but shied away from the subject of the plays he wrote unless it was, like Gilbert, to make nervous or scoffing remarks about them. It was only Uncle Edmund, very quiet and only five years older than me, whose eyes would glow like mine when my father spoke of the playhouses south of the River Thames, where the public entertainments of London were allowed to flourish. Hamnet loved the stories of London too, but they did not mean to him what they meant to Edmund and me. To him the stories were the thing itself, not the mirror of another thing as far off as it was desperately wanted. What Hamnet yearned for was that my father's storytelling would go on forever, with the rest of us, my grandparents and Susanna and Edmund and my mother—and especially me—all gathered in the garden or the parlor, as a family.

Or he wanted our father to come outside and teach us how to fight with sticks.

I was different from my twin. I wanted to sneak into my father's traveling bag and pop out of it on a stage in Southwark. There was no lord or lady or king or wizard or witch I could not imagine myself becoming once I was able to parade in front of a crowd. When we played by the river, Hamnet stood for the crowd, crowing and clapping with delight when I gestured and recited the lines I'd learned peering over my father's hunched shoulder.

I was nearing the end of my eleventh year when my father showed me the play that was to change my life utterly. A blustery wind blew outside, and late snow came in through a crack in the wall. It was February of 1596.

Hamnet had gone to bed, and though I usually went with him and whispered tall tales till he slept, this night I stayed in the parlor in my nightgown, because my father had said I could sit with him by the fire for a special treat. The treat was some ink-spotted pages that he handed me to read.

After some minutes I looked up from them at him. "You made her," I said breathlessly.

"To be sure," he said. "And why should I not?"

"I thought you had forgotten."

His laugh was a short bark. "I?"

I bent my head again, and began to read. "*These are the forgeries of jealousy,*" I said. "*And never, since the middle summer's spring, met we on hill, in dale, forest, or mead, by paved fountain—*"

"Pav-ed," said my father. "Pav-ed."

"*By pav-ed fountain or by rushy brook, or in the . . .*"

"Beach-ed."

"*Beach-ed margent of the sea, to dance our ringlets to the whistling wind, but with thy brawls thou hast disturbed our sport.*"

"Very good, child."

My mother put her head in from the kitchen. "What do you have her reading?"

"A poem about the forgeries of jealousy," my father said.

He had taken back the pages and was correcting something with his quill. I saw her look hard at him, then disappear inside the kitchen an instant before he looked up hoping to catch her eye. We could hear Gilbert singing a catch as he came in the door of the adjacent house. My father sighed. "Read, Judith," he said formally, returning me the pages.

"Therefore the winds, piping to us in vain, as in revenge, have sucked up from the sea contagious fogs."

His hand cupped my chin, and he raised it so he could see my eyes. "Do you understand what you read?" he asked.

"The fairy queen is angry at her husband and she is going to make him pay."

He laughed. "You have it well enough." He stretched out his legs and arms and spoke through a yawn. "And well can she do it," he said more loudly. "She has all nature at her disposal. She can throw spells on him from the witchy wood . . . she can send her sprites to bake mischief into a custard coffin . . ."

I was thrilled. "And will this play on the stage?"

He dropped his arms. "It will. And I will tell you how it went. Go to bed now."

I dragged myself up the stairs, excited but so frustrated I thought I might explode. When I crawled into bed next to Hamnet I told him the news.

"Our da has made a play of the fairy king and queen! The

ones who cavort in the wood with sprites and make magic spells! It's to go on the stage, and we will not be there to see it!"

Hamnet pulled his blanket around him. He was shivering slightly with cold, and his forehead felt warm as it brushed my hand. "But he will tell us of it later," he said. "And we can play the parts down by the river."

"Hamnet, you could die without ever leaving Stratford and you would not care," I whispered angrily.

"If you are here it's as good as a London play to me," he said.

Chapter Four

WHEN Lent ended in March and the new year began, my father celebrated in his usual way, by riding back to London on a rented nag. I wanted to climb into his saddlebags, but contented myself with making him swear to write me every week about the progress of *A Midsummer Night's Dream*.

His oath, of course, was no guarantee that I would get thus many letters. As faithful as my father was in writing to us, it would sometimes be weeks before he would come across a traveler who was planning to stop at Stratford, and weeks also before he could tear himself from scenery paint and script scribbling and playing practice to look for one. In the intervals between his letters, I entertained myself by imagining goings-on at the public theaters in Southwark and elsewhere, indeed at the command performances at nobles' houses and the queen's palace at Greenwich. For it was as my mother had said: my father was grown very grand in London.

When the weather grew warmer after Lady Day, I borrowed an old yellow linen apron from my mother and tied its strings about my neck so it hung down my back as a billowy cape. Hamnet and I found two pairs of discarded embroidered slippers in my grandmother's house, and we wore them down to the riverside, where we painted our faces in streaks with the reddish mud that banked the rushes. The anglers downriver laughed to see us, but they were used to our antics. It became a common event for them to watch us disappear through the ash trees into the Arden Forest, where I had hidden a treasure.

This treasure lay in a box that our sister Susanna had used for keeping scraps of colored wool in some foolish game of making doll hairdresses. I'd dumped the scraps and taken the box and feigned innocence amid her complaints and accusations, because I knew this box must be consecrate to our more sacred purpose.

It was also just the right size and I couldn't find another one.

I had buried it under a spreading oak tree by a forked path in the forest, then marked the spot with a pile of stones. Day after day as the weather grew warmer, in our silver-threaded slippers and face-paint, Hamnet and I would scrabble with our fingers to unearth our treasure, and I would slowly remove the tin top while chanting another spell of my own making.

Spirits of Arden, enter now,
Spirits of Arden, bow wow wow!

My father, not I, was the poet. I was only his spritely minister.

I would make Hamnet keep his eyes squeezed shut while I reverently raised the wrinkled pages from within, saying, "*Excalibur Nebuchadnezzar Mugwort!*" Then, "*Open!*" I would whisper, and Hamnet and I would huddle together and read aloud.

I am sure my father had no inkling that I had kept the foul copy-papers of his plays. He never heeded what happened to the discarded pages that he crumpled and dropped to the floor, after every last open space on them was scribbled on. And in general there were fewer of these wasted pages than I would have liked to find, because paper was costly, and because my father tended to write at breakneck speed and to make, as it seemed, very few mistakes.

But with regard to this new play I had been lucky. My father had written it so very fast he had determined that the first manuscript was too illegible to take back to London and show to his actorly friends. He had copied almost the whole play over onto a fresh roll of paper and left the scraps behind. They vanished very quickly.

Perhaps he thought it was fairy-work, if he thought about it at all, which is unlikely.

WE played that play every day after Hamnet was done with school, as soon as we could escape from our family's clutches, and the chores our mother imposed. Saturdays were glorious because then the grammar school released its pupils after only half a day, and those free afternoons gave us hours to play and replay scenes, and change places and parts, handy dandy.

At times I was the fairy queen Titania, and at other times Hamnet was she and I was Bottom the Weaver in Titania's fairy bower. Or he was Puck and I was Oberon, or he was Hippolyta and I was Theseus. Or he was Demetrius and I was Helena chasing him madly through the forest, although unlike poor Helena with her Demetrius, I could always catch Hamnet and wrestle him, laughing, to the ground, because I was faster and stronger. *"Run when you will, the story shall be changed,"* I would pant, tickling him; *"Apollo flies, and Daphne holds the chase!"*

At such times we would roll around in the leaves together like an eight-limbed monster, laughing and hugging and spilling out lines of verse as if our hands, our sides, voices, and minds had been incorporate.

But the best scenes were the enchanted scenes, the spell-casting scenes. Hanging from a tree, I would command spotted hedgehogs and weaving spiders to do my will. My true will was that these small beasts would arrange for me a trip to London, or transform me to a boy so I might climb walls and trees with greater ease, and hear what real boys said of girls behind their backs. Hamnet assisted my conjurings, bowing at appropriate moments, wearing a wizardly crown he had made out of oak leaves threaded together with stuff from the Woolery.

When we were done with our day's worth of magic he would slowly doff the leaf-cap and lay it to earth, transforming us both back to ordinary children by chanting a line from my father's play: *"Be as thou wast wont to be; see as thou wast wont to see."*

After a week or two we were able to speak all the lines without the help of my father's pages, and we left them moldering in the earth in Susanna's tin box.

Perhaps they lie there still.

OF course, we made our father's powerful spells suit our daily life as well. We prayed for raspberry tart, or for our uncle Gilbert to take us angling or to the fair, or for our grandfer John to carve us new toys. To be sure, to increase Hamnet's awe and interest in the game, I would make sure of these things' probability in private. Before I embarked on a special incantation, I would spy out ingredients my mother had already set forth in the pantry, or extract a promise from Gilbert or Grandfer.

Once I took one of my own hoarded pennies and without Hamnet's knowledge hid it in a hollow ash tree. Later I made him pretend to sleep right in front of this tree while I said this spell: *"What thou seest when thou dost wake, do it for thy truelove take. There will be a penny there!"*

This was a very clumsy version of the fairy king Oberon's spell, but it worked for my brother. No sooner did he open his eyes than he searched in the hollow tree and found the penny and yelled in delight.

I marveled at his simplicity.

. . .

THAT year my father wrote us that when the weather warmed he would leave London, but not, alas, to come to Stratford. Instead he would tour with a crew of players, walking the southern route from London to Maidstone to Wells, and thence along the coast from Hastings to Dover. After that he would return to London. My mother relayed the news with a resigned sigh. Hamnet looked stricken, but said nothing.

"May we go to London to see him, then?" I asked. "Please, Mama?"

My mother frowned at me. "I have told you that London is no place for children."

"But our father says—"

"That there are scores of children in London, yes. And very fine children they are. Dirty-faced ragamuffins who scour the streets to find props to sell to the players—old pots and pans and cast-off clothes and, no doubt, human bones. God in Heaven knows where they find those things; doubtless they steal them. Doubtless they dig up graveyards."

I glanced sidelong at Hamnet, who looked guilty.

My mother railed on. "I know not why he finds them so amusing. Little pickpockets who sing bawdy songs and dance around the death carts every time plague hits, which seems to be once a week in that city. And then they get run over by cart-horses and are dead as can be."

I stormed to the top of the stairs and threw myself down on our bed. I was wise enough to know that my mother's fear of London was something unreasonable. My grandfather went there at times on business, to sell wool or gloves, and he thought it a splendid town. He had offered to take me if my mother agreed, but she never, ever would. And I, splitting at the seams with curiosity, to be chained to the will of such a woman! She thought Stratford the universe; Stratford, with its ten paved streets and its smug wool-trading aldermen and its one church and its communal baking ovens where the gossips gathered and chattered.

And Uncle Gilbert.

I sat up, troubled.

I could hear my uncle downstairs now, my mother talking to him with angry vigor, he responding with slow humor, and finally the two of them laughing. I felt an inexplicable pain. I thought how rarely I heard my parents share laughter now, on the ever-fewer occasions when my father was home. And suddenly my anger at my mother changed to anger at my father. Unwillingly, I felt the beginnings of an understanding of her hatred of the great city. If Gilbert was his rival, London was hers.

Now I know that the truth was much more tangled than that. I know that my parents' lives, like all couples' lives, were a mingled yarn. Still, despite the things I did not know and could not then have understood, I think that as I sat that spring day on my straw-stuffed bed, grubby, tearstained, and eleven years old, I grasped the nub of it indeed.

·   ·   ·

I became purposely indifferent to my father's doings then, and did not listen to the readings of his letters. But I could not transmit my indifference to Hamnet, try as I would. The night my mother told us that my father would spend the summer footing the southern road and never come near to Stratford, my brother would not eat. Even weeks later I heard him weeping as he lay in bed, though he turned his back to me in an effort to hide it.

ONE rainy morning, Susanna and I were sweeping the rush mat in the dining parlor when I saw Hamnet's face like a ghost's at the window, pale above his black jerkin. I started and yelled, "*JesuMaryJoseph!*" This made Susanna likewise jump and stare, but by the time she turned to the window Hamnet had ducked and was totally gone.

"What in the world made you screech?" she challenged me, and I told her it was absolutely nothing and thus drove her near to a frenzy, she shaking me and asking curious questions as to what it had been. "A spirit all rotten of face, come to haunt the living!" I finally said, and that was sufficient to make the fool girl clap her hands to her mouth and run to tell our mother, who only sent her back to work with a swat.

When the rush mat was done, I hastened through a warm drizzle to the spreading oak by the forked path in the forest, for I knew Hamnet would be waiting for me there.

"Why are you not at your lessons?" I asked him. "How did you flee school?"

"I slipped down the road when the master paraded us to the privy," he said. "I cannot read or recite or do anything. I sit there as dull as a clod of earth." He sniffed. He was seated hunched on a dead, fallen tree. Water dripped from his bonnet, and he kicked the dirt with the toe of his scuffed shoe. After a moment he said, "I want you to cast a spell."

It would have been far better if I had told him then that I had no magical powers at all. That I had spied out our mother's baking plans, and used my own head to guess at our father's calendar, and pulled my spells from our grandmother's fireside tales or invented them entirely. I could even have told him that the Warwickshire murderer's bone we'd found years before was only the remains of a sheep leg left to molder in the town tanner's yard. Perhaps that would have made him laugh. Perhaps it would have lifted the gloom that had now settled over him. But I was afraid it would not.

The fierceness in his eyes frightened me. In the past two years my father's visits had been rarer and shorter, and I saw that Hamnet was rightly afraid we would never see him again. Against this void I was his only hope. Were I to shred that hope, I feared, my brother might stop eating entirely, might despair and even die.

And I will be honest. My fear held something else besides a worry for Hamnet's welfare. I was afraid that if I unveiled myself to him as a fraud, and he did not laugh, he would despise and turn from me. It was the thought of that I couldn't bear. For I did not know then how to walk or breathe outside the mirrors of my brother's eyes.

I dropped to my knees on the damp earth and grasped his hands. "What you ask is perilous," I said in a low voice.

"Why perilous?"

"The spirits in the south of this land are strong, and they will plot against our plans. They will strive to keep our father with them as he travels through their realms. I cannot promise that we will win, brother."

He squeezed my hands tight, and his eyes looked brighter. "We must try, though Hell itself should gape!" he declared.

I frowned. " 'Hell gape'? Where did you hear such words?"

"Our father muttered them once as he sat in church. I think he was thinking on a poem."

"An odd poem." Our gazes were locked, like our hands. I stayed on my knees and he on his fallen tree, and our heads were level. Then, as one, we got to our feet.

"The magic you seek is not woods magic," I said as we walked homeward.

He turned to me in excitement. "I know it. It is river magic, is it not? We must go to the river tonight. We *must* go."

"Yes." I nodded. "Tonight when the crier calls twelve, we will climb down the tree outside our window, and follow darkness like a dream to the bend in the water."

THAT night began with a hint of stars and moon, but soon grew cloudy. This made things hard, because we could not see well as we scurried along the darker streets at the town's edge, avoiding the watchman's lantern. We tripped once or twice over dust heaps and skittering cats, but we had been this way so often that we had little difficulty finding our place by the rush-grown riverside. Indeed, we heard the river long before we saw it, so swollen and fast did it move with the strange summer rain. When we got there we stood dismayed to see that our hollowed-in bankside spot was covered with swiftly moving water. Branches of bushes poked through the currents, and the river bend, usually narrow enough that we could throw stones from one side to the other, was almost twice its normal width.

"The river god is powerful," I whispered to Hamnet, and he nodded in awe.

I looked up at the sky, where the moon still hid her face. "This augurs ill," I said.

"What?" asked Hamnet breathlessly.

"Our moon, our goddess Hecate, the governess of floods, helps us not. She is cloud-covered. What's more, we are past the solstice."

"What of that?" Hamnet said. "Does not God listen to children's prayers on any night?"

To this day I am not sure what mingled, parti-colored deity Hamnet had in his mind when he said that: a thing part nature and part spirit and part fancy. Yet I sometimes think that had he stayed in our bed and prayed alone to his children's god, that god might have pitied him.

But he thought I had power, and so instead we were here in the dark, in the damp chilly air. In the end, it was me he worshiped.

I nodded. "Go we to the river's edge," I said, and we stepped down to the rushing water.

"What now?"

"Strip off thy garments. We must join the river."

Obediently, Hamnet unbuttoned his breeches and pulled his shirt over his head. I took off my smock. We left our clothes on the grass at the top of the bank.

We had done this before many times, on hot days, and sometimes in the dark, when we'd run home giggling and let the summer night dry us before we reached the climbing tree by our bedroom window.

So we thought it would be a small matter, even in the fast water, to find the flat rocks to stand on and recite our spells. But the current was strong, and we slipped and grappled for some seconds before we could steady ourselves with the poking branches that scratched us underneath. Even then our stance was precarious. Below the water's surface the river threatened to push our legs from under us.

With one hand I firmly grasped a thick branch that thrust from the water, and raised my other hand to the sky. Hamnet's head was dimly outlined before me, and I could hear his quick breath, but I could not see his face in the dark. He was clutching a clump of tall river grass. "Say it quick," he panted through chattering teeth. "The rock is slippery."

> "O river god," I chanted.
> By the musk-rose buds and the reremice,
> By the midnight bats and the grubs and lice,
> By the clamorous owl and the river reed,

By Cobweb, Moth, and Mustardseed,
By the elves that through the forest roam,
Bring thou our errant father home.
Parsley, sage, rosemary, thyme,
Bring him within one month's time.

I lowered my hand. "And now," I said, "we must join the river god in his element."

"What be that?" asked Hamnet.

I did not truly know, but I thought it should have something to do with water, and so I told Hamnet we must duck our heads three times beneath the surface. "One," I said, and we ducked. "Two," I said, and we ducked again. But when I came to the surface the second time I did not see Hamnet's head.

Instead I felt his legs scrape against mine as the current carried him downriver.

I ducked underwater and felt frantically for him. I managed to grab a hand that was still clutching the blades of grass that had broken in his grip when he slipped on the slimy rock. I could barely keep my footing on the rock's slick surface. I held tight to Hamnet's hand and stepped off the rock onto sharp pebbles and river mud, submerged myself, and pulled his arm. Both of his hands now clung to me desperately, and I could feel him jerking as he kicked, but his body did not budge, and as I felt down the surface of his smooth skin I discovered the cause.

His foot was caught in the cleft of an underwater branch that had been downed by the storm.

I struggled to free the foot, but I could not. He kept kicking, but he was not strong, my brother, or nimble, and could not push free of the branch's grip, and the foot stayed, and his kicks grew more feeble. I came up for breath and then plunged down again to pull and pull, feeling nothing but sick desperation. I tried to lift the branch, and then to break it, but it was too slippery and heavy and thick and I knew I would fail.

I returned to struggling and pulling at Hamnet's foot until long after he stopped kicking.

It was ten minutes' run to the nearest house on the edge of the town and I do not remember much of it. Nor can I recall the mad conference I held, standing naked and dripping on a stoop, with a goodwife who stood openmouthed in her nightgown, holding a candle. They tell me I was wrapped in a blanket and brought to the riverside where our clothes lay, but I do not remember that either, though I do remember the look of Hamnet's face by lantern light, when they pulled his naked body and the treacherous branch from the river with a rope. His face held no expression at all, as though he were sleeping.

I tried to throw myself on him and cover him with kisses but they stopped me, thinking perhaps I would jump again in the river. Then there was another journey in a cart during which I sat numb and motionless in the lap of a man who held me firmly and did his best to hide the fact that my brother lay dead in the cart beside me.

And then there was my mother.

At first she did not wail. She only looked frozen, standing by the cart for what seemed like a very long time with her head bowed and her hand on Hamnet's chest. Everyone else stood still and looked at her, including me. Then slowly, as though she or we were dreaming, she turned and walked to me where I stood, crying and shivering in the flannel gown they had put on me. "By God in Heaven, what did you do?" she asked in a low voice. Behind her I saw Gilbert run from the big house to the cart and cry out at what he saw and then sink to his knees with his hands on his face.

"*What were you DOING?*" My mother's voice was loud now, and her eyes were beginning to look wild. I was very much afraid, and all I could do was stammer the truth. "Only a game, Mama," I sobbed. I wanted to hide in her arms, but she had raised her hand to strike me. "A magic game!" I said. "To bring our father home!"

At that she dropped her hand, looking as though I had struck *her*. She stared at me. "So help me God, I'll not lay a hand on you, Judith," she said. "For if I did I would kill you. And I will not lose two."

And then she sagged to the ground and began to shake with dry sobs. Gilbert came and put his arm around her back and lifted her and carried her into the house.

Chapter Five

WHEN my father walked into our parlor three weeks later he found the rhythms of his house unchanged. My uncles were cutting and stitching gloves in the Woolery, and my mother was cleaning windows upstairs. My grandfather was reading to his wife and Aunt Joan from our big Geneva Bible, upstairs in the other parlor. Susanna was seated at Joan's feet sewing a button. I was crouched in the storeroom with the door closed, rocking back and forth on my heels.

I could hear my father's tread as he crossed the parlor floor and walked into the kitchen, where I could see him through a knothole in the storeroom door. He wore muddy boots and a traveler's cloak and a flat leather cap. His beard was ragged and his face was burnt from the sun of his southern walking.

He stood there by my mother's wallboard with its knives, graters, and pothooks and looked at nothing. Our cat jumped from the stool where she had been sleeping and rubbed his ankle, and he looked down at her. "Why should a cat have life?" I heard him murmur softly. "Why should a cat?" Then he crouched to pat her.

Steps sounded on the stair, and he stood and left the kitchen. I heard my mother greet him formally.

"Anne," he said. "Anne. I came as soon as Joan's letter found me. I bought a horse."

I heard the measured creaks of the staircase as my grandfather entered the parlor. "Ah, lad," my grandfather said. "Ah, ah." Grandfer crossed the room to my father, and after a moment I heard the strange and frightening noise of two men weeping.

Behind the storeroom door I rocked on my heels.

EVERY morning that he was home my father walked by himself to Trinity Churchyard to visit Hamnet's grave. Every afternoon he was gone for two hours or more, riding the horse he had bought in London to the fields outside the manor where one of my gammer's cousins had lived, before that cousin was jailed and executed for being a Catholic and for plotting against our queen. *Falsely jailed and falsely punished,* my family said whenever they spoke of him, though they said very little about any of it in front of us children. I knew my father was riding toward the old manor because I would sometimes follow far back from him alongside the path that wound there through Arden Forest, until his horse outstripped me as it galloped into the fields and I went home.

Another time I trailed behind him as he walked on foot to the spot in the river where Hamnet had died. I hung back in the rushes and peered at him, while he stood on the bank for a long time and then slowly crouched and touched the water. If he knew I followed him, he never said so.

He wrote little this time, though some evenings he sat and stared dully at a blank page, holding an idle quill in his hand. After a few minutes he would push his chair back and come to find me or Susanna. Then he would walk with us in the fields, naming flowers for us, harebells and oxlips and primroses, or playing word games, spinning us lines of poetry to rhyme with, or having us invent absurd words to which he would give meanings. Susanna played and sometimes laughed at him, but I would only listen. I knew that he wanted me to invent some words or say anything at all but I could say nothing to him. And he did not press me to.

One morning I followed him to the churchyard. He walked down the High Street and the people who passed him touched their hats and looked grave and sorrowful. Sometimes they stopped and clasped hands with him and spoke, and at those moments I would duck into doorways until he continued on his way. At the churchyard I hid behind an ash tree and watched as he approached the grave. Someone had been there before him that morning, I knew, because I could see a bunch of cut lilies on the new dirt from which grass was already starting to spring. I could guess who had laid them there.

My father knelt and placed a clump of honeysuckle next to the lilies. He stayed there for several minutes with his head bowed, praying, it seemed, and I stood still and watched him. I did not pray.

Then he stood and looked toward the river, and it suddenly seemed that he grew completely still. I followed his stare and saw what he saw: Uncle Gilbert, sliding down the hill through the brushes, then disappearing from view along the river's edge.

My father turned, and began to walk home much more slowly than he had come.

THAT night I was awakened by the sound of angry voices from my parents' bedroom. I lay looking at the ceiling, my heart beating quickly. My father was speaking very fast and low from the far side of the room, and my mother, close to the wall between us, was crying. I heard something turn over, a book or a stool, and then all I could hear was my mother sobbing and gasping to be let go. Then she seemed to fall to the floor, still crying, and my father walked out of the room and down the stairs. The front door slammed behind him, and I heard my mother weeping ever more softly. Then she stopped.

Hours later my father returned, and mounted the stairs with a step that was not steady. I heard bedsprings creak in the other room, and then nothing.

The next day, neither of them passed more than a few

bare words. My mother told us that my father was leaving for London on the morrow.

That night my father came into our bedroom, and stroked Susanna's brow, and then mine. Susanna was sleeping sweetly; I kept my eyes closed and pretended.

He knelt and kissed my forehead, then touched my cheek while above me he whispered, "Little fawn, arise." I was jolted by the words. He said them just as though he were uttering a magic spell. I opened my eyes and looked at him.

He was gazing at me intently, his eyes all grey and fathomless. His hand still touched my cheek. "Little Jude," he said softly. "Love is most terrible. Yet you will not grieve forever."

At that I shook off his hand. He looked perplexed and hurt. I turned my face to the wall.

After he left the room I lay for a time staring at the inside of our thatched roof. I wondered just what god my father served, and whether he or she was the same dark power to whom I myself had prayed, all unknowing, on the night that Hamnet died.

When I awoke the next day he had gone.

I changed utterly without Hamnet at my side. I spoke less and I forsook my wild games. I could not keep from imagining him with me, or above me, always watching me. The notion would have been comforting had I believed it to be anything more than fancy. At times I seemed to feel him close to my elbow, yet in my heart I doubted he was really there. Ghosts were a game we had played. I could not trust that his presence was anything more than a dream I conjured in my loneliness.

Still, I could not stop dreaming it.

On the night of the drowning my dread of punishment had been almost as great as the shock and grief of my brother's loss. I knew myself at fault. Thus I was dully astonished to find that neither in the days or the weeks, months, and finally years after Hamnet's death did my parents and grandparents and uncles and aunts treat me with anything but charity. My father, of course, had always been sweet; he was gracious to all, except, at times, to Gilbert. But it was the kindness of my mother that was unlooked for and hardest to bear. After that one night when she came close to striking me, she forgave me completely, seeing how I was undone. And on the terrible nights afterwards when I woke from nightmares of Hamnet's pale face floating below the waters and his dead hands grasping me, she would reach her arms toward me and whisper, "Child, child," and beg me to sleep in the bed beside her. But I would not. I huddled in a ball on my mattress, and when I finally did sleep, I slept alone.

When warm weather came after the next planting season, I let my uncle Edmund go alone to see the traveling players in the town square. In the evenings Aunt Joan spun in the parlor and told merry tales of town courtships, and my mother and Uncle Gilbert and Susanna laughed, but I looked out the window and did not care. And years passed. But nothing assuaged my guilt.

I avoided the woods, and that narrow bend in the Avon.

I would gladly have blocked the whole river from my view, but I could not; it wound through the town like a snake as it ran on, always different and the same. In time I accepted the river's presence again, and I sometimes sat on its banks to read in the place where we'd once skipped stones.

I lacked playfellows. Having Hamnet, I had nurtured no other alliances. Without him, I would watch through the window as Susanna played hoodman blind or penny prick with my girl cousins and the neighborhood children. Only rarely would I join them. It is not that they prevented me, but that I did not know how. The games Hamnet and I had played had less to do with contest than with telling mad stories and then acting them out. Playing with dolls, as some girls did, was, I suppose, a kind of storytelling, a story that you were a mother and that the doll was your child and sometimes the child was sick and so forth. But it seemed an excellent dull story compared with that of the fairy king and queen.

Thrilling stories were the ones my father knew, or invented. And I read them, those plays of his, that were now printed and sold in the bookstalls in Stratford High Street. I read to lose myself in their high adventure, and I thought no more of the shadowy man who had conceived them, bending ardently over a tabletop in our parlor or a desk in a London room. I didn't want to think of that man, or to be that father's daughter. I only longed to drown myself in the words of the magical beings who had sprung from his pen. Mischievous Puck, and brawling Kate, and bad King Richard, and sweet Romeo and Juliet—they were his real children, after all.

So I read. From my aunt Joan's small store of books I

culled romances, tales of sea adventure and tragic partings and miraculous reunions and resurrections of the dead. My mother would look peeved when she passed me with my nose in a book in the garden, and more than once she sharply ordered me to put the thing down and look to the weeding. She said that even my mad father had laughed, watching me through the window, when she'd told him I read *those* foolish tales. I would obey her, and go to tend garden and house with my print-clouded eyes. But as soon as I was free I would go back to my stories.

My father was less and less to be found in Stratford. Now he rarely left London, where he penned his plays and performed in the public playhouses in the company of his fellows. And he only wrote to us erratically. As for myself, I never wrote a word urging him to come home. That wish had served me ill.

It was getting harder for my mother to find cause to complain of his absence, since from it we profited so extravagantly. Our state in Stratford was steadily improving because of his growing fame, and the townsfolk had gone from smirking at the shame of it to admiring his playhouse success, since that success had brought the one thing Stratford in its strongbox-heart respected: money.

Now the Shakespeare men spoke proudly to their friends of the investments my canny father had made possible, and of the land he had bought and the properties, including, most gloriously, the largest house in town. Called New Place, it was a twelve-roomed wonder to which my mother and sister and I were transported a year after I was untwinned. Here I could read and walk in an immense garden filled with peach and mulberry and apple trees and a hundred kinds of flowers, all of which my mother tended with the help of Gilbert and a gardener. Even Gilbert gave my father grudging praise for the place's beauty, provoking my father's wide-eyed surprise.

Of course, well might my uncle have praised him for the purchase, since to Gilbert fell much of the benefit. He visited our house more often now than when he'd lived right next door. Relaxing on our settle against the plush velvet cushions, he would drink his ales, his Dragon's Milk and his Huffcap and his Father Whoreson, strong brews that reduced him to melancholy and sometimes to sleep, while my mother's housemaid skinned the conies he had snared in the forest. My mother liked his presence. I did not care.

It was clear enough to us that my father meant the house as a bribe, or a penance, or a gift to repay us for his absence. My mother seemed willing to accept it and its furniture in place of him, or even in preference. Susanna loved New Place, because it put her in high standing among the girls of the town, and among the boys as well. At fifteen she was starting to dart saucy looks as she passed the Oxford lads talking in the street, home on holiday. She was all demure under her new French bonnet.

Only I was not contented in New Place, and I was sure Hamnet would have hated it. It was too close to the heart of town and too far from the river, at least from the quiet part of the river where we had liked to sit alone. And since Susanna, my mother, and I were now a mile from the rest of the Shakespeare clan who had crowded into the double house on Henley

Street, I found it difficult to pass unseen through rooms. There was too much space, and there were too few people. I could no longer go where I wanted, see what I wanted, or do what I wanted.

WHEN I was almost thirteen I was glad to accept an aunt's offer to lodge me in her household in Coventry. Susanna shed few tears at my departure, but my mother gave me a warm embrace and told me to write often. By this time she could read a little, since my uncle Gilbert was teaching her.

My aunt in Coventry was a bustling and frantic soul who let me wander the town more freely than was customary for young ladies, as long as I performed my daily duties. These included tutoring two female cousins aged eight and nine in reading and sewing, only one of which I did well. As I droned through the lessons I looked out my aunt's windows at the busy world outside. Sometimes I saw the town's roaring boys pass by, laughing and sparring. These loitered in the streets, to the constant disapproval of the town's grave councilmen. The youths mock-punched each other and drank from ale-bottles and practiced their swording, and all in all enjoyed a much livelier time of it than my aunt or my cousin—or me.

And they went to the plays.

Like my mother, my aunt disapproved of plays, but unlike my mother she did not mind me watching the London players when they visited. And so I began again to go. It would have shocked my aunt had she actually seen what I saw in the town square: men spattering their makeshift stages with pig's blood, then feigning their dyings most gloriously and horribly and long-windedly. I would stand with the roaring boys and a few bold girls in the forward area where we were let to watch, and because I was uncommon tall for my age I could see very well, and could even see the greasy paint dripping on the players' collars on the hot summer days.

At such a performance, I saw one of my father's plays, one that he had never read to us. In the playing of it, I could see why he had not, since in it a tongue is cut out, hands are chopped off, and a lady is raped by two men. And yet I was gleeful to see the carnage and the horror, not least because I saw that the young "lady" was in fact the same boy who had winked at me from under a flaxen wig on a Stratford scaffold some years before. His screams were something overdone, I thought, and sounded like something no real woman would ever have let fly from her mouth. But then, being overdone, they were in keeping with everything else about that play, which did not seem born of my father's usual tranquil good humor, but rather to be the product of a nightmare.

On that day in Coventry I saw players of whom I had heard my father speak, famous players, players from his own company. But I did not see my father. In those days my father had already begun to play less and less. As my mother told me, he spent his time writing and money-managing in London and, finally, with building an amazing new playhouse just south of the city, scarring his own hands to lay the stage planks. There was work enough in London, always something to busy him there, and now it was not only the town of Stratford but the open road he avoided when he could.

So it was that two years passed during which I did not see him at all. I visited Stratford often enough, and he himself went there at least once a year, but we never found ourselves under the gabled roof of New Place at the same time. And I was not very sorry, because I had long ago given over the hope that he would take me to London under his wing. As I grew to be a young woman, the distance between us and the time that had passed since I'd sat on his lap as he wrote had made me feel shy, and like a stranger to him.

I was fourteen years of age when I came across the papers.

I was over-tall, flat-chested, big-handed, and clunk-footed, and I walked with my shoulders slumped so as to seem as low as the other lasses in Stratford. I had been smitten that spring with my monthly women's course, and with its coming had vanished all the easy grace with which as a child I had scaled hedgerows and run to the river and climbed ash trees in the Arden Forest.

Now I never knew how to sit or stand or walk. My hair was lank and yellow, and I was always pushing it from my face and behind my two over-large ears. I had my mother's cornflower-blue eyes, and this, I was told by an aunt who meant—I think—to be kind, was my *one fair quality*. She instructed me to make the most of it. I had not the least notion what or how she meant. When I walked in the lane I kept those same eyes hidden, and my head low, for fear that I might catch someone else's bold eye and prompt a remark that, tongue-tied, I would not know how to answer.

Such was my miserable maidenly state when, visiting New Place at Easter, I discovered a discarded scroll which my father, just visiting at Lent, had scribbled on and left behind. It had been sloppily stuffed in a letter-hole of the fine cherrywood desk that he now used when he was home from London. As I dusted the reddish wood with the rag my mother had firmly placed in my hand, I saw on the half-unfurled scroll the word "Doubtless" written in my father's hand and scratched out and next to it the phrase *"Perchance* he is not drowned." I stopped still as a statue and then, as though dreaming, I slowly grasped the paper and drew it out for my overlooking.

It was a play. Or a piece of one, or rather the draft of a piece of one. I sank on the floor with my rag on my lap and the scroll in my hand. At first I did not read what I saw written thereon. Better to say that my eyes devoured it whole, like food whose taste was not entirely sweet and even something bitter, but that satisfied a long hunger.

> *And what should I do in Illyria?*
> *My brother he is in Elysium.*
> *Perchance he is not drowned.*

And then a response to the young woman who had thus spoken:

> *It is per chance that you yourself were saved.*

On I read. I saw cross-hatched passages and written-over lines and words I could barely decipher, so sloppily had they been set down. But I kept on, turning the scroll sideways and upside down until I had seen enough absolutely to know without any mistake that my father had taken my grief for Hamnet and turned it into poetry. And he was no doubt handing it on a clean scroll to some pimple-faced London youth who would indecently feign my sorrow. My grief would be laid bare on the stage, so that all might enjoy it for a penny in the yard or sixpence for a roofed seat in the galleries.

And not just one spot-faced fellow would play me, but two! For as I read I discovered there to be two grieving sisters and two dead brothers in this play, one maiden's twin drowned in the deep and the other brother felled by sickness, his memory now floating in the briny tears shed for him by his mournful sister, Olivia. Viola and Olivia. My father had doubled my own sorrow and my own self, and then chopped me into pieces of verse. *Why?*

For money.

When I finished the long scroll I ripped it in two and then wept until my face was slubbered and the papers in my hands were sodden wads. I wiped my nose on them and then added them to the sack of trash I would later carry to the dust heap. When I rose to my feet I spotted another scrap of paper in the desk-hole. It was of the same ink as that paper which I had just contemptuously snotted, and I grabbed the scrap, meaning to stop my nose against it too, but for curiosity I could not forbear first to read what it said. On it my father had written some abbreviated words intermixed with some Latin, all of which I made out to say the following: "Argument: Sebastian & Viola parted at sea, maid washes up on shore of Illyria. Garbs self as boy for no good reason (protection? entertainment?), falls in love, wordplay with Duke Orsino and Lady Olivia, *etc.* Catastrophe: Sebastian not drowned! Joy and amazement! Both twins stand facing each other before *omnes.* All present excepting Malvolio. *One face, one voice, one habit, and two children.* (Wearing same clothes an absurdity; all the better.)"

Here *"two children"* had been crossed out, and above it was written *"two persons."*

Then he had written, *"A cherry cleft in two is not more twin (said by Orsino?)."*

He had then crossed out "cherry" and over it written "apple." And underneath all of that he had written, "Olivia also saved through"—and then a word beginning with "l" which I could not read, so fast had it been scribbled.

So. It was worse yet.

My father found the facts of the matter too harsh to appeal to the paying London mob. What matter the bald truth? No matter that my brother was as dead as a doorpost and that I, Judith Shakespeare, had killed him, as everyone in Stratford knew and pretended not to; killed him with my fancies and my spells and my fairy games. My father was going to raise him from the dead on stage. All must be a comedy, a monstrous lie to please the public, no doubt to end in a gleeful morris dance.

My anger was huge.

It carried me uncloaked out the door, down the street, and to the edge of town to the licensed dust pit without me feeling the bite of the uncommonly cold May wind or even the ground underneath my feet. There, along with the rest of our household garbage, I threw the crumpled and sodden pulp of the play-draft, mingling the ruined pages with dead cats' bones and broken bottles and rank vegetables and some matter worse than that, from the smell of it.

Then I went to the riverbank and sat.

My first wild, enraged fantasy, as I strode down the street, had been of myself standing on my father's stage and exposing the lie in front of all watchers. I would steal to London and lurk in the shadows until the play's end, when I would run onto the boards and announce, "The magnificent playwright's son is *truly* dead! The drowned *do not* return, whatever happy magic all of you think you do here!" I would raise my hands to heaven and tell the gawking yardlings that it was those very hands that had killed my brother, or had failed to save him, which was the same thing.

I fancied myself like the Sunday sinners whom I sometimes saw in Holy Trinity Church. Dressed in white cassocks, announcing that they had done horrible things, beaten servants or robbed collection boxes or lain with a husband's brother, confessing so that they could be forgiven and take Communion with the rest. I had never done such a thing in the bare sanctuary, had never been asked to do it. But on the stage I would. My father's new theater, the great and glorious Globe, would be my church and my shrift.

This was wild dreaming, of course. But as I sat on the flattest, warmest rock I could find on the riverbank and watched the anglers cast line upstream, my anger at my father—how long had it lain dormant within me?—began to cool and harden. I passed from dreaming to thinking, and from thinking to planning.

Why should I *not* steal to London and shame him?

I had opportunity to do it, and wit enough to devise a way. Stratford was a pond, and naught could be hidden there. But London was an ocean. Could I arrive at a way to come there, I might slip like a drop into its sea of citizens. By the time my flight was discovered in Stratford or Coventry I would be well hidden indeed. Oh, my mother and grandparents and aunts would be angry, but I'd bear what punishment came after. I'd not think of it now. All I could think of, all I wanted to think of as I gazed at the sheen of the Avon, was my own anger, and its justice. I would steal off. I would find a way.

What way?

I considered.

I was, as I have said, more than common tall for fourteen, and therefore used to being mistaken for an older lass of eighteen or twenty. Those mistakings of others had been wont to plunge me into furious blushing and wordlessness, but why, after all, should I blush? Why should I not *profit* from my gangliness? I had some little savings from the spending allowances given me by my aunt and my mother. I could use my height to persuade a coachman that I was old enough to purchase passage, and use the money to do it.

And yet it was perilous. Though Hamnet and I had always laughed at my mother's frightening tales about London, I had never forgotten them. Perhaps there was something to her warnings. Perhaps a maid alone risked waylaying and ravishing;

perhaps the risk was greater for a lass who, like me, looked older than a young girl. Yet I *must* go. I knotted my fists in frustration. If only I were Edmund! If only I were . . .

And suddenly I knew.

I sat and schemed until darkness began to fall. Then I rose, and began to walk. I went to the churchyard, where I stood still and looked at my brother's grave. Night came, and I walked home, more slowly than I'd come forth.

At New Place I answered my mother's sharp questions with mild and ill-considered replies. I'd been looking for strawberries (*In May?* she asked); I'd been talking with anglers (*With those ill-bred louts by the river? Alone? Did they give you any fish?*). Susanna looked at me curiously as my mother stormed. But the reproofs glanced off me, so absorbed was I in plotting, and at length, as was usual with her, my mother repented of the harshness of her tongue and kissed me and told me that there might be something left for me to eat.

Susanna looked at me keenly as I ate the lukewarm rabbit stew, made from Gilbert's conies, that lay covered for me on the board. Susanna was two years my elder, but shorter than me. None, however, mistook her maturity, since she was as buxom as my mother had been at her age, which we knew from our mother's own testimony. Unlike me she was bold and direct in her stares and walked straight and proud without slumping, inviting attention, not shunning it. I envied her her free gait and wondered where she had learned it.

She seated herself on the bench across from me. "And who talked to you by the river?" she asked. "Were any of the Hall boys angling?"

"Yes," I said through a mouthful of bread. "They all were. All shaking their calves to hook the eyes of any idiot maid passing by on the footpath."

Susanna's eyes narrowed. "Stop thy jesting, Judy," she said. "Did any of them ask after me?"

"John Hall said he wondered whether your stomacher was stuffed with a cushion on top. I told him it was."

Susanna made a sound of disgust and left me to my reveries, which was what I wanted.

I was going to London.

As I lay abed I plotted the how of it. I would find work in some shop near the bankside, some grocery or some alehouse, and scout the lie of the land. I would polish my disguise and spy out the playhouses and see what they did there. I would visit my father's new theater, now almost complete and near ready to open. I would lurk and study, and when I was perfect in my performance—when I no longer feared betraying myself by some nervous, girlish gesture—I would find some way to enter my father's band of actors.

And then I would work my way into his frothy new play about drowned brothers who came back to life and weeping sisters who were saved by some illegible word. I would make that play tragic, indeed.

Of course, my father must not find me out first. I was sure he would not, if I took care. I had grown like a bean sprout these past two years; I was not the girl of twelve I'd been when he'd last laid his eyes on me.

And of course, I would not be a girl at all.

It would have been easiest, I thought at first, to wear Hamnet's very clothes. But it took me only a moment to realize that the few garments of Hamnet that my mother still stored in her trunk would not have fit him at fourteen, and would not fit me.

It did not matter. I'd find me other wear. With my hair cut short and a jerkin and some borrowed breeches and hose, with my big hands and feet, I thought I could well pass for a lad and avoid my father's recognition, if I made sure to avoid his eye. And that I could do, in the busy playhouse he'd described to us, a place where boys and men and stagehands and sewing women ran helter-skelter and all was a flurry of sawdust and noise.

Furthermore, it was not for nothing that I had listened throughout my childhood to my father talk about what was right and wrong and good and bad about boys in the playhouse. I knew what he and his partners looked for as they sought their apprentices: no loud mouths, a ready hand to do odd jobs, early risers, and above all the skill to con a script on short notice and to say just what was there, no more, no less. To all of this instruction I had devoutly listened at my father's feet, and I had never forgotten any of it.

I smiled to myself, and reached out my hand, as though I could once more touch Hamnet's across the straw mattress. *You are as good as a London play, Judy*, I heard him whisper in the dark.

.   .   .

It took me five days to collect the clothes I would need. Besides my own garments I required those that a young man might wear. At first I could think of no other place to get men's garb than my father's own store. It was kept in a trunk in my parents' chamber, next to their big bed, the one with the oaken headboard that was carved with the scene from the Garden of Eden where Eve offered Adam the apple. I had liked to trace it with my fingers when Hamnet and I bounced on their bed.

It was a small matter to enter their room with a broom in my hand and a helpful expression, give a few swipes to the floor, and then stop and look through my father's trunk. Some trunk-hose and shirts and breeches lay folded there, and looked nondescript enough, but I soon thought better of this intended theft—borrowing, I should say—because of the chance that my father, who to my observation remembered everything he ever saw, would remember these. If indeed my plan met with any success and I managed to gain entry to his fabulous and God-be-praised new miracle playhouse, I had to find clothes my father had never seen.

After pondering the matter, I decided that the best thing to do was to buy them in Coventry.

Therefore I let my mother know, a full two weeks before my expected departure date, that my aunt was anxious for me to return by late May to help prepare for her eldest son's wedding feast. This bold-faced lie required convincing my mother that her nephew in Coventry had made plans to marry and that her own sister had not told her of it. It caused an explosion of huffiness on her part, but, as I had hazarded, it also made her very certain not to send any message with me to my aunt at all, instead of her usual three pages of news, painstakingly written down by Aunt Joan.

My mother would send no letter to my aunt so as to display proudly her sense of injury, an attitude which she would sustain, I calculated, for a good three weeks at the least. Then she would turn about-face and ask Joan to send to my aunt and inquire whether she might bring something to her dear nephew's wedding in June?

Thus I plotted, and so it fell out.

On a morning five days after I'd read my father's draft, I slipped back into his writing room to make one final borrowing from a drawer in his desk, and then left, accompanied by my uncle Gilbert, for the Swan Tavern. There I boarded a coach bound for Coventry. It was a miserable roofed cart whose wheels were caked with road-mud even before we started. I sat by the rector's assistant, who read Saint Augustine as we bumped along. Across from us were a gouty-legged wool-trading confederate of my grandfather's and his queasy, pregnant wife, bound for a wedding themselves. (A real one.) All of these fine folk knew me. Happily none of them knew my Coventry aunt.

It took a half-day to get there, and all the time I felt impatient that we traveled northward, on a route so retrograde to my desire. If it had not been for my fellow travelers and their innocent expectation that I, young Judith Shakespeare, would alight with them in Coventry, I would surely have fled from the coach along the way in Warwick. We stopped there to buy refreshment and relieve ourselves and so on, and I had the opportunity. I could have spent a half crown for breeches and shirt, and been on my way southward with the next carrier. But of course I could not try it, and so I spent that stop dozing against a carriage wheel and watching the rector's assistant disappear into the trees. He reappeared in half a minute's time and I envied how easy it was for him to take a piss, as mine uncle Gilbert would have put it.

When we did get to Coventry, I bid a hypocritically fond farewell to my companions and refused their offer to accompany me to the house of my aunt, since it seemed that, for some reason, no relative had come to the coach-stop to meet me. I found myself perfect in politeness, and marveled that for the first time in years I felt no awkwardness at all addressing a youth, as I looked that young pastor-to-be in the eye and said, "Her house is near to here, and I know the way well." I already felt that I was pretending, so I could just as well pretend to be a brave person, one who could look a young man in the eye without flinching. Or something of the sort.

My aunt, in fact, lived on the opposite side of the town. I melted into the market square, and bought me some youth's clothing that was cheap, and bundled it into my slim traveling bag. I bought a pair of wool breeches, a flat cap, a linen shirt, netherstockings, and a thin jerkin. I thought that my own buckled shoes would do well enough, and I hazarded that the weather would stay warm and thus saved some pence on a man's doublet. And then I went to the Unicorn Inn and with all the boldness I could muster I inquired of the host whether any among his customers was a coachman bound for London. I was doubly lucky there. The host was too busy even to raise an eyebrow at a maid traveling alone, and he pointed me toward an affable driver who would be leaving within the hour. That friendly fellow looked me up and down and pronounced me thin enough to be squeezed in. So from him I bought passage to London, now nearly twenty miles farther away than it had been that morn.

We would take an eastern route, away from Stratford. I boarded the cart and sat on a hard seat, packed among three jolly travelers who did not know me at all.

Chapter Six

"What—be—thy—name, young mistress?" asked the portly man who faced me. The carriage was jolting through potholes on the road north of Oxford, and with each word his voice bounced. His question seemed prompted by boredom rather than suspicion; we had been sitting and dozing and bouncing almost two full hours.

"Sophronia Frisby, sir," I said shyly.

His eyes popped wide under his high-crowned hat. "Kin to the Frisbys of Manchester?"

"So distantly, that I could name none of them for you."

That was enough to start him on a long description of the wondrous Frisbys of Manchester, who had made their fortune selling cats to stint a plague of rats, a tale so fantastic and Dick-Whittington-like that I began to wonder if he was as great a liar as myself. Still, the story was pleasant to hear and it kept him occupied with himself and his own knowledge of the world, instead of with me and my fortunes. He disembarked in Oxford, where, he said, he was a purveyor of wines, on which poor students spent far too much of their slim funds when they should have been buying books.

I looked and marveled at the tall towers of the city's colleges as we rattled through Oxford Town, and suddenly recalled something I had overheard my mother say once, with pity and a shade of remorse, about my father and his ruined hopes of going to university some eighteen years before.

Susanna, I thought. *Of course! Susanna came, and he could not leave. He had to marry instead.*

I felt a pang for both my parents. To be forced to marry by circumstance! It would never happen to me, that I vowed. I looked suspiciously from under my modest cloth cap at a sniffling young man who had boarded the coach outside Brasenose College and was now squinting to read his Pliny by the dim light that came through the open slit of a window. Sensing my malevolent stare, he glanced up and met my eyes, then returned his own nervously to his text. I looked out the window, sighing, thinking that such a one was not likely to try my innocent virginity. In the south of London there were men rough enough to seize any young girl at all, though, to do their will and leave her ravaged. That unbidden thought made my blood grow suddenly cold. In stories young women died of shame after losing their virtue. I certainly could not afford such a foolish type of death before I'd achieved my purpose. Instinctively I clutched the bag that held my boy's garb. My protection.

I could not put it on in the coach; could not do so even were I the only occupant. The driver could not be so stupid that he would not note that a girl had gone in and a boy had come out. But I determined that as soon as I alighted in London, indeed before I sought work or lodging or even food, I would find a place to effect my metamorphosis.

I dozed as the carriage jolted along.

In my dream I was on a stage, dressed in breeches and a youth's cap, embracing my brother. Yet it was not my brother I embraced, but my sister, myself, who looked at me with tears of joy in her eyes, and it was I who was Hamnet, my brother. Then the wagon wheel plunged into a deep rut and the coach lurched to one side and stalled, and my eyes came unwillingly open. It was chilly, and dark, and for a moment I knew not where I was, until the young student's snoring as he slept on his book reminded me. I felt water come to my eyes, tears of rage and disappointment that I had been thus roughly awakened from my dream. I peeked through the window slit.

The driver and another man were standing in the road looking balefully at the wheel. "Need three fellows to push it," I heard the driver say. Behind him I could just discern, by weak moonlight, the shapes of mean housetops and, behind them, the high mast of a ship that gently rocked. I caught my breath.

We were in London.

The young student muttered in his sleep and shifted position. I grasped my bag, opened the coach's far door, and jumped to the rutted road. I rounded the coach, where I met with the driver, coming to wake the student and require his help in pushing.

"Pardon, sir," I asked politely. "What part of London would this be?"

"We are in Gracechurch Street, mistress," he said. "If you'll sit tight by us, we'll soon have our carriage right and will deliver you safely to the Moon and Star in Bishopsgate."

"Oh, but 'tis best I take leave of you here, sir," I said. "As it happens we are not two streets from my cousin's house. I know the way well."

"But you must not walk alone," he said.

" 'Tis no distance!" I said firmly.

The drowsy student had pulled himself to the door of the coach, and the driver looked up at him. "Have we three?" called the other man, the helpful citizen on the carriage's left side.

As I had calculated, the driver was more concerned with the righting of his coach than with my safeguarding, and he bid me good-bye, saying, "Have a care, mistress." I walked quickly into the shadows. At my back I heard him say, in dubious voice as he regarded the skinny scholar, "We have perhaps two and a half men. But we shall try it."

It was quiet in this part of London, or at least was quiet at this hour. What most pleased me was that it was dark. In an alley I changed my garb as quickly as I could, shivering and fearing every second that a drunken knave would round the corner and pounce on my ungainly nakedness. Swiftly I was transformed, and lacked only a glass to assure myself of my new identity.

I wore the wool breeches, netherstocks, linen shirt, and jerkin. My bosom, such as it was, did not worry me; my chest was too flat to need binding. I had tied my hair and piled it underneath the flat cap. I might have sold my girl's clothes, but knew not where to do it, and feared the suspicion such an act might arouse. So I bunched the kirtle and smock together and sank them in a stinking pool of ditchwater. Then, drying my hands on my breeches, I made my way back to the street.

From where I stood London looked much like Hell. Through the narrow spaces between houses I could just glimpse the river. A fog rose from the water and made all things murky, but bankside bonfires burned dimly through the swirl. Indeed, as I spotted lights flickering on the far edge of the great Thames, my heart pounded faster. I noted the tremendous width of it. The Avon was a trickle to this. Here a vast number of craft bobbed and glided, prows and sails coming ghostly out of the mist and disappearing again, as the boats moved or the fog drifted. I could hear the creak of boards and ropes, borne on the night breeze. Far down the bankside huddled the shrouded shapes of boatmen by their wherries, five men to a single lantern, waiting for custom even at this dark hour—the dim moon told me 'twas between two and three—to ferry them to the other side.

I felt fear tug at my heart. I knew nothing of this great city but my father's tales of the bankside, half of which had probably been false, and none of which had included counsel on finding a warm bed for mere pennies. I was alone. I missed my mother. In this huge place I knew no one, save one man—and to him I could not go. I was cold, and the air smelled dank and fishy foul. And I had not the faintest notion where I was.

Hamnet, I prayed silently. *What do we do now?*

And the answer came to me.

The river.

Of course. I would go to the river. I could find myself that way. I remembered my father speaking of the grey Tower that loomed by the Thames' north bank, and the great bridge to the west. I would wait till the sun rose, and then I would see the way to cross.

I touched my purse, and was heartened by the weight of the coins inside. I would use them with care. I would save a boatman's penny; I would walk the length of London Bridge.

I heard voices, men singing, coming down the bankside. *And let me the cannikin clink, clink, clink, and let me the cannikin clink!* the revelers chanted. My instinct was to run, but I stopped myself. I was a boy, a tall boy, not a girl. What had I to fear from two or three drunken fellows?

With measured pace, I began to walk toward the river. The singers passed me on the way. One of them tapped my shoulder. "Boy."

I turned, my heart in my mouth. With as low a voice as I could summon into my throat, I said, "My masters?"

"Which way is Saint Dunstan's Hill? We're bound for an alehouse there."

"Saint Dunstan's is above us," I said, though I had no earthly idea.

The men laughed. "Were it not, 'twould be in the water," said a second one. "But *where* above us?"

"Marry, pray to Saint Dunstan and no doubt he'll direct you," I said, and walked quickly off.

A burst of laughter came from the three throats behind me, and the first man said, "Well answered, lad! Come for a tankard!" But I only waved and kept walking, not wanting to press my disguise's safety so far, until I had better mastered the way of it.

I walked past silent shops and houses, making my way by the mist-shrouded moon. My heart beat quick with the thrill of it all and I could not keep the corners of my mouth down. *Why*, I wondered, *why did I not simply say, "I know not"? Would not that have been the safest reply?* But the words had jumped out of my mouth as though my boy's disguise had a life of its own; as though I was now not a boy but a particular boy, a rather rascally and witty and bold one. I did not know what boy this might be.

I reached the water. I turned and walked westward, toward the bridge, as I guessed, though I could see little in the fog. I thought the closer I got to my crossing point the better. If I found it, I thought, I might cross tonight. But when I got to the bridge I saw that its gate was closed and that I would indeed need to wait until morning. Guards diced in groups of two or three at the base of the bridge, their swords grazing the earth, next to burning braziers. Some of them had food, joints of mutton or hunks of bread that they dipped in stew. Although it was almost summer, the night was damp, and I longed to warm my hands by the fires and beg a meal, and was even tempted to boy it again, jesting with these guards as I had with the three singing men, but I mastered the temptation. Those men had not looked at me closely. And these guards were not drunk.

So I made my way down to a bush by the bank, some quarter-mile up from London Bridge. I had a half a loaf of bread and some Cheshire cheese that I'd bought in Oxford. I contented myself with that, and though I thirsted, I was not mad enough to drink from the river. I wrapped myself in my cloak, and something fitfully, I slept.

I woke to the sound of gulls squawking and a woman crying, "Oysters!"

I sat up. By the sun it was not yet six, but the fog had cleared and the gates had been raised over the bridge-mouths and traffic was busy crossing the river. The bridge itself barely looked like a bridge, so packed was it with houses and shops. I could see all manner of folk streaming under its northern gate: coopers carrying their basket-mending gear, carters with wheelbarrows, gowned men bearing books, and strong women like the one selling shellfish just above me, yoked with buckets of provender that hung below either shoulder.

All was cheerier in the sunlight than it had been in the night's blinding fog, but the swarms of people frightened me a little. I fought my dread, reminding myself that the London crowds were what I had sought. It would be easy enough for me, a nondescript rumpled lad, to lose myself among them.

As I rose and walked toward the bridge I said a guilty and hopeful prayer, asking God to speed me in my enterprise and to forgive me for it at the same time. I was aware that this prayer was something contradictory, and on the whole the praying of it made me think that I might be better off relying on my own wits than on God's for the present. When I was almost to the bridge I glanced south, and saw something that drove any thought of God straight out of my mind, stopped me in my tracks, and made my knees near-buckle in horror.

I knew what it was; everyone knew the stories of what headed the pikes of the Great South Gate on London Bridge. In my busy concern to pass muster as a boy and find a place to sleep, I had forgotten entirely that to go under that gate I would need to witness the half-rotted heads of the realm's traitors, or of those whom the queen thought traitors. I knew, in fact, that I had a relative on my father's side whose head was stuck up there, but for once I got the better of my curiosity; I did not stop to look for his skull. I looked straight ahead and walked as briskly as I could under the northern gate and over the wooden throughway. At the bridge's other end I looked down, trying to whistle, and soon I was past it, and hungry again, my mouth watering at the smells of cooked cod and sausage that women were offering for sale on the southern bank. There I stopped and bought a penny's worth of bread and fish and a skin of milk, all of which I swallowed as undaintily and boylike as I could. I wished I had more, but I would buy no more food, I vowed, until I found work.

It could not be playhouse work yet. I dared not approach players without more time spent being a boy. I wanted a place to get money and practice, a place bustling and busy enough that folk lacked time to watch each other closely. Now I surveyed the swinging tavern-signs that lined the bankside streets. "Father Whoreson's Ale," boasted a placard in one window. I thought of Uncle Gilbert, and of the time years before when, blear-eyed after a night of grog-pounding, he had mistaken me for my brother. *A place where folk are too drunk to see*, I thought.

I walked about for an hour or more, surveying the doorways of this stew or that alehouse. I pondered the lay of the streets as I chewed what was left of my bread, and I studied the looks and gestures of the boys I passed. Sometimes I felt bold, but each time I approached a door, meaning to enter a place and ask for hire, I turned cold and shrank back. Finally I stopped and sat down at the edge of a church graveyard. I had drifted streets away from the waterside, and had eaten all my food. It occurred to me that mine was a mad enterprise, and I thought again of my mother. Then I started to cry. I ground my fists into my eyes, pressing back the tears. I tried to swallow past the knot in my throat. A passing lad looked curiously at me, and I looked away, to the side.

It was then that I saw it.

It stood a half-mile west of me, by the river, higher by half than any of the houses. Had the streets by the bridge been wider, the houses farther apart, I would have noted it right away. Now I blinked and stared. Its circle of walls was as white as ash, and its half-finished roof shone like gold in the sun. Then my eye caught the other playhouses. First one, then another, high-walled and thatch-topped and glistening like the towers of Troy, with banners flying. But my gaze was drawn back to the highest one, the newest of them all.

My father's Globe. It could be no other, it so exactly matched the description my father had given in his letters.

I forgot to be frightened, or sick for home, or anything. The playhouse was so glorious that for a moment I forgot I hated it.

But then I remembered.

I rose quickly, wiping my face with my sleeve. The street before me was empty. I pointed across the housetops to the Globe's roof with an extravagant gesture, thinking of the foolish play that my father meant to stage on that theater's boards: that mockery of my grief that he might even now be rehearsing, on its scaffold, or on another. "Thou shalt fail!" I said, as firmly as I could. I sounded squeaky and girl-like. I cleared my throat, and repeated myself in deeper voice, this time shaking my other fist for good measure.

This playlet made me feel entirely well.

Have at it, then! I'd be bold. I tightened my cap over my unruly hair, and walked riverward. I reached the bankside once more, and this time walked its edge. In a short time I noted a merry-looking house with a bright red hat painted on its outside, the one facing the water. "The Cardinal's Cap," read its swinging sign. At this early hour the place's customers were few, but its yard was full of men and boys coming and going, bearing crates of wine and foodstuffs and bags of malt, and sweeping and cleaning and such. I navigated the yard with narrowed eyes, thinking that here was as good a place as any to offer myself for some simple labor. I touched my cap and assured myself that my hair was well stored underneath it. Then I put my hands in my pockets and walked up to a stout man who was rolling a barrel of something toward a side door.

"Good morrow, my master," I said to him.

"Huh," he grunted. "Away with you. I've no pennies to spare."

"I'd not beg pennies, but earn pennies. Or groats, for that matter. Hast thou work for an able youth?"

The man balanced his barrel and looked at me keenly. I raised my eyebrows at him hopefully, and he laughed. "I'm not the innkeeper," he said, wiping sweat off his chin with his sleeve. He yelled, "Abraham!"

A flaxen-haired man wearing an apron came into the courtyard, rubbing his hands. "What would ye?" he asked.

"The lad craves employment."

Abraham the innkeeper turned his gaze on me. He frowned at the cap that still rode on my head, but of course I couldn't doff it to him. "And what can ye do, sirrah rudesby?" he asked.

"Lift, carry, and whatever you will teach me, sir."

"Hmm. From the midlands, I'd say, from the sound of ye." He squinted at me banefully. "Thou hast not thy letters, I'd guess."

I pointed above to the swinging sign. "*The Cardinal's Cap. Abraham Cowley, proprietor*," I read dutifully.

"Well!" he said with surprise. "Well, well. A lad with his letters might come in handy. The last one I paid could not tell the difference between a label that said 'malt' and one that said 'millet.' Wreaked havoc with the ale. And what be *thy* label, young wizard of the midlands?"

I had a good one ready. "Hieronymus Chupple is my name."

"And a fine one it is. Follow me."

He led me into the dark inner rooms of the house. He showed me the kitchen maids and the barrels of ale and the common rooms for guests and the posts in the yard to hold the horses of the commoner patrons and the stables to stall the horses of the rich. It did not take any great wit to see that the patrons of this establishment were more often common than rich. He showed me a storeroom behind the kitchen where I might sleep, and gestured vaguely upward to some "private rooms" upstairs where some activities went on that he did not speak full clearly about.

He was businesslike, but kindly enough, and my interview with him went a long way toward calming my fear that I would be taken for the girl that I was. Where folk expected a lad, folk saw a lad. Master Cowley's eyes were sharp enough—indeed, I once saw him spy another lad lift two farthings out of the till from across a crowded room of revelers. Still, I could judge by speaking with him that morning that people saw what they wanted to see, and that their own ideas went three-fourths of the way toward painting the world in front of them.

Indeed, my father had once told me something like it.

It heartened me beyond measure to have found work so quickly and so close to the playhouses, though it struck a certain fear into me as well. My father was very near. For all my disdain for his pomps and works, I felt an odd longing to see him. Yet I dreaded his seeing me. He might be at the playhouse now, scribbling on prompt-books or counseling actors or checking his costume for the afternoon's performance. Or he might be abed in his lodgings, hard by the Globe. In a few hours' time he might even be on his way to a glass of hard cider at the Cardinal's Cap.

I hastened inside and completed my water-and-barrel-carrying as fast as could be, imagining that boy's muscles sprang bigger from my sore arms with every step I took. Whenever the busy staff's eyes were turned elsewhere I nervously pulled my cap down over my face and pushed up the strands of hair that kept falling out from under its brim. At noon, given leave to rest and eat in the storeroom behind the kitchen, I pulled from a sack a pair of kitchen shears I had borrowed from a hook in the scullery. I straightaway hacked off my offending long and stringy locks, until my crop of hair was as stiff and short as I could make it. I threw the hair into a dustbin and covered it with orange peels, feeling lighter in body and in mind.

As I turned from the bin I caught the eye of a young boy who glanced at me sidelong from not three feet away. I jumped in fright before I saw that the boy was my own reflection in the glass of a window. And then I could not forbear staring at the image for a full minute's time, in mingled sadness and joy.

For it—for I—was Hamnet indeed.

Chapter Seven

BUT only on the face of it.

The ghost that peered back at me from the window-glass was Hamnet as he would have looked, had he lived alongside me to reach gangly fourteen. Of that I had no doubt. But gentle Hamnet would never have behaved as I did in my boy's clothes.

To my own surprise, swaggering back and forth between kitchen and common rooms, I discovered that I had within my mind a thousand tricks of the bragging Jacks. Jesting with the scullery maids and the customers, singing a bawdy catch from time to time, I tried out bold attitudes and brave utterances that I'd seen and heard the roaring boys of Coventry exchange, and the Stratford youths who'd jostled for a view of my sister, passing with nose high by the Stratford Market Cross.

"What's this dried piece of fish, then?" asked a gallant fellow in a plumed hat, as he poked at a slab of overdone smelt on his trencher.

"So asked thy mistress when thy trunks slipped off," I said, pouring him an extra half-tankard as his fellows roared.

"Where's the bellows?" I heard the cook's maid say another time. "Young Hieronymus has the tool; I'll never blow this fire up."

"Young Hieronymus' tool will blow thy belly up," I was quick to respond, goosing her with the bellows from behind, to her considerable shrieking.

Indeed, this lewd jesting talk went well in the Cardinal's Cap, a place where the ale and food were good, but the patrons something degenerate. That is not to say that only thieves and ill-clad citizens consorted there. The customers were in the main well dressed, and on one night a table of silk-clad lords drank and jested loudly in a corner. But the place indulged a taste for bawdy talk, and sometimes more than talk.

On the second night of my employ I saw that same cook's maid I had goosed—no maid after all—being hustled upstairs by a black-bearded man who was already unbuttoning his breeches on the way, and she came back down no more than twenty minutes later counting her coin and smiling broadly. The sight of that chilled me, and I determined more fiercely to keep my own sex hidden. Whatever I did to earn my coins, it wouldn't be what she had done. I'd beg first, or I'd steal.

And I'd work, of course. And I did work. So quick was I in my work that I had some free time to wander Southwark in the days, and even to cross the bridge again on pilgrimages to the city's northern Liberties. At times, I confess, when custom was slow, I sneaked away. I walked the crowded, cobbly streets and gawked at the sights and marveled at the sounds. I heard the howls of chained beasts as I passed by the bear-pits, and also the howls of the men and women and children who watched the poor animals' combat. I could not bring myself to look, nor could I afford to waste a penny that way.

My pennies went elsewhere. Some of them went to another set of clothes and a little more went to food. But most of them went to the playhouses. I knew I had to study the actors, and study them quickly. For I was bent on coming to the Globe. So three afternoons a week, on earned or stolen time, I stood in different playhouse yards. I could find the Southwark playhouses easily enough, and when I was in them I dared to ask boys how to reach other places I'd heard my father speak of, the Curtain and the Bel Savage and the Cross Keys Inn. I watched how each boy pointed north or west, swinging an arm widely, shoving a hand in a pocket as he gestured. I mimicked those youths, and found their gestures unaccountably easy. In two days I did them without thinking.

As I waited for the revels to begin, I would scan the crowds. Despite my ill will toward my father, I could not help but marvel at how well he had described the folk there, the oyster wenches and the wool-capped apprentices and the goggle-eyed maids; the plumed ladies peeping from the lords' rooms, and the stylish fops who had paid extra money for seats on the very balcony, where they laughed too loud and made extravagant gestures and flaunted their cloth-of-gold capes as though they themselves were the play, and the players an afterthought. I learned to shun the middles of the yards after I saw—and smelled—a dead cat hurled from the galleries come down square on the head of an ill-fated fellow standing next to me.

Following the crowds to the playhouses, I learned what I needed to know of London's streets. And inside the theater yards, I learned how to eat for free. During a play at the Curtain, I saw an apple-vendor cut the purse of an unsuspecting farmer as he passed the good country fellow while hawking his wares. After that, I saw no harm in bobbing apples from that same vendor, who turned up at all the theaters.

Some playhouses had serene names that belied the wildness within. The Swan, of all things! And the Rose, which stank worse than the privy behind the Cardinal's Cap! But there was also the Globe.

In my mind I'd sneered at the Globe, my father's company's great creation, since I'd heard of its building some months ago. The Globe, indeed. Another of my father's many investments; his urgent reasons to be in London rather than in Stratford. Ten days before, I'd mocked its brave white frame and its shining, half-built roof.

But when I finally saw its interior I could not sneer or do anything but stare like an idiot.

It was not scheduled to open for another fortnight. But near the end of my first week in London, I felt brave and boylike enough to approach it. It was a hive of activity. I managed to lose myself in a crowd of thatch-carriers and bench-layers, many of whom, I took from their conversation, were the very players who would perform there. From the outside, as I walked among them, I could see that the Globe was indeed wider and taller than the Rose or the Swan.

With an industrious air I seized a board from a stack. I held it so it half-shielded my face, and followed two chatting workmen through an entranceway into the theater. Once in I lagged behind, dropped the board, and stood, all agog and staring.

My eyes traveled the circular walls and came to rest on the sprawling stage. It was two-thirds covered by an ornate wooden balcony, whose under-roof was etched with all the symbols of the Zodiac, fretted in gold and backed with dark blue. Below it, between two parallel doors that gave the players access to the stage, jutted a third entrance, a middle opening that gave into a recessed space, now hidden by embroidered curtains. Around the thrust scaffold, the empty yard of the playhouse was strewn with sawdust and soft ash. Beyond the yard stretched, upward and up, the planked galleries, smelling of freshly sanded wood.

Behind the two pillars that stretched up from the stage to support the overhanging balcony, I could see a dark-headed man painting the faces of Roman gods on the rear wall that separated the stage from the tiring-rooms. But I hardly noted the paintings, so taken was I with the stage pillars themselves. For these were made of live wood. From a distance I had not seen that the green branches hanging over the Globe were actually part of the theater. The stage had been built around two huge ash trees, as large as the largest in Stratford, ashes that sprouted leaves under the house's thatched roof and waved their tallest branches from ten feet above the thatch.

After I had seen the Globe, I thought little of the Rose and the Swan; and less of the Curtain and the Cross Keys and Bel Savage, north of the Thames.

AMONG those playhouses and inns, my father's company, I knew, had shuttled for years. In those lesser places I now watched the men perform during my afternoons' stolen liberty. As my father told me he had done when he first came to London, I crowded as close to the yard-fronts as I could get and still view the action on stage. The best distance was some six feet back, since at each of the playhouses the stage itself was a foot above my head and those pressed to its rim saw mostly the players' lower legs and feet. But from a few feet away, as I stood elbows out to fend off the press of people, I could see and hear everything: the bombast of a noted tragic player that I'd heard my father mock; the merriment of a clown I'd heard him praise.

I saw plays my father had written, plays I knew well. I heard plays whose lines I could have recited side by side with the players. Under my breath, from the yard, I sometimes did so, fuming if a man or boy did the emphasis ill or marred all with a distracting gesture. I began to wonder how my father bore with their folly, although even my envious self had to acknowledge, most sourly, that in the main, these were the best actors I had ever seen.

On my third afternoon in London, my father himself did the scaffold some grace. At the Curtain, my heart gave a jolt and nearly jumped from my throat when I realized that the reedy-voiced greybeard who stood before me on stage, railing against his daughter Hermia's disobedience, was in fact my own sire in a powdered wig. Instinctively I stepped back, and trod on the toe of a grocer's wife who had been breathing down my neck. She gave such a cry that I then stood in more danger of my father's discovering me than if I had stayed frozen in place. Yet I need not have worried. My father did not pause in his speech, but went on with his harsh condemnations of his terrible and willful daughter, words that made me sweat indeed, for reasons the grocer's wife could not have guessed at. I could see that my father, like his fellow players, was so used to the outbursts of the crowd that he was in no way distracted by any of it.

Not that he and the other players did not give answer to the crowd's japes when they saw fit. On that same afternoon, when a rude roaring boy loudly yelled, "Egeus to the mines, for defying his daughter!" my father whirled and called back, "And the bear-pit for you, sir! Demetrius has bought her!" to the applause and laughter of everyone, including me. I laughed even harder at the wit of the boy who was playing Egeus' daughter, Hermia.

This boy was something short, shorter than me, I guessed; but he made up for his lack of height with a highly energetic bustle about the stage, giving a slight thrusting of his false bosom and a subtle sway of his hips. It was not so pronounced as to be clownish but evident enough to cause ripples of merriment in the watchers every time he walked to and fro. He provoked whistles and lewd comments from the youths in the yard. After one young man yelled out a very frank proposition indeed to this gentle Hermia, Hermia simply turned toward the youth and, dropping her false womanliness for the moment, full-out grabbed her crotch, which when so grabbed could most plainly be seen to be the crotch of a he!

At that moment I recognized him. He was the saucy lad who'd winked at me six years before in the Stratford town square, and whom I'd seen again in Coventry the summer before, the raped Lavinia in my father's nightmarish *Titus Andronicus*.

I thought him altogether marvelous.

I wanted to be him.

So I watched and listened. I watched rollicking comedies and tearful tragedies and studied, studied, studied, conning each gesture and expression and tone of the players.

Thus, though I looked, as I knew, like Hamnet, I began to feel, in an odd way, like my father. As the days went by and I bustled through my work at the Cardinal's Cap and crept out, if I could, to see a play, I thought of the tales he'd once told of his first London months: how he'd done piecework on other men's scripts and stood for hours setting copy at a friend's printing shop and then worn out his boots trudging to playhouses. He'd watched from the yards, raging inside, craning his neck for a better view, burning to be part of what he saw on the scaffold before him. Now I struggled to hold fast to my own cold wrath for this man I hadn't seen for two years, and whose face I could barely remember. Yet, try though I did to stop it, that rage was melting into another thing: sympathy, or awe, or some feeling I couldn't name. I thought of him as he must have been years before, doing what I was doing now, hiding in a crowd of milling, yelling folk and watching and listening, watching and listening. And hoping. Nay, not hoping. My father was not one to launch his soul in so slim a vessel as hope. Not hoping. *Vowing*.

Vowing that one day, he, too, would find his place on the stage.

OF course, I did not have the months and years that my father had had at his disposal to expend in an education in the ways of the playhouse. I had to gain some entry into his company quick. In this short time in London I had lost my rage, and my desire to destroy his work had all but vanished. But something else had taken the place of those things. My ambition now was simpler, and more familiar. As when Hamnet and I were children, I wanted to be in his play. I thought there was nothing I would not do to speak his lines on the scaffold of the Globe. Yet if I was to do it at all, it had to be before my mother wrote to him and he summoned forth the thirdboroughs of London to cull the streets of the city for his rogue daughter.

I might not have spoken to him in two years, but he'd guess well enough where I was.

And thus it was that on the afternoon my father's theater was to open, I was standing cap in hand by the entrance to the Globe's freshly painted tiring-house, waiting for some noteworthy playing personage—anyone but my father—to arrive for the day's rehearsals. I had performed my morning's floor-sweepings and offal-tossing at the Cardinal's Cap, and I hoped very hard that I had performed them for the last time. I had also new-chopped my hair, so fearful was I that my father would spot and recognize me. My hands itched to jam my cap back on my head and shove it low, but I knew enough to understand that I'd never get the meanest sort of employment here without showing proper respect.

So I stood, cap in hand, and soon enough a tall and handsome and darkly bearded man stepped from a wherry on the bankside and began to walk up the hill toward the playhouse. I straightened nervously. I knew right away who he was. Within the last week I had seen him painting the Roman gods on the Globe's wall, and I had also seen him twice on the corner of the Curtain's stage, his body twisted, declaiming with a voice so viciously velvet that I and every other quaking citizen in the yard were ready to hold two fingers up to ward off his evil eye and swear that he was indeed wicked King Richard the Third.

But today he looked pleasant enough.

I gave a small bow as he approached. "Master Burbage, sir?"

"Is it work you want, boy?" he asked, looking keenly at me, and making me instantly glad that I more resembled my mother than my father, at least in my coloring. "Can you pound nails?" he said.

"It is and I can," I said. "But I'd rather be a player, sir."

He laughed. "A lot of you say the same. But the Lord

Chamberlain's Men has boys enough. And it's not as easy as you think, lad."

"I do not think 'tis easy. Sir."

"You're from the country."

I looked down, then up again. "We have our plays in the country, too, sir."

"Boy, we've odd jobs enough to do around here." He pointed to the flag flying above the Globe's thatched roof. "We open this afternoon, you know."

I nodded.

He smiled, and moved toward the tiring-house. "We'll be happy to pay thee pennies for fetching and carrying and what-not if you're as quick as you seem, and you can see the play for free. Would you like that?"

"It depends what it is."

He stopped and frowned at me. "Have you ever heard it said that beggars cannot be choosers?"

"Oft, Master Burbage. But I am no beggar. I offer work."

"The play's *Julius Caesar,* by William Shakespeare. You've heard of him, I think."

"I'm no fool though I am from the country. I've heard of Julius Caesar."

"I meant . . ." Richard Burbage paused and shook his finger at me. "You may be a bit *too* quick for my liking, lad. What's your name?"

"Castor Popworthy."

"Well, I don't believe that, but all's one. No doubt you have a twin named Pollux Popworthy, and you stepped out of a Greek storybook."

I kept my face expressionless. "I know nothing of Greek,

sir," I said. "But Castor is my name, and I'd serve you well in small parts. I'm willing to listen and learn."

"Do you know that this is the best company in London? We appear before the queen."

"And like the queen, I have long admired your playing."

He laughed again. "I suppose you think yourself Her Majesty's peer. My point is that we are all of us well trained, every man-jack, and down to the merest boy. Our lads start with us when they're seven or eight, not thirteen, as I take you to be. And what's more, a quickness of wit does not of necessity make for a quickness in line-learning, or for a capable presence on the stage. You have no experience playing a part."

"Are you sure of that, sir?"

"Enough of your sauciness, sirrah," he said, turning back to the door. "Pennies for sweeping, and the play gratis, from the yard."

I watched him mount the steps to the tiring-house, and then I spoke again, quickly. "We have our plays in the country, sir!" I began to recite.

> At Pentecost,
> When all our pageants of delight were played,
> Our youth got me to play the woman's part.
> And I was trimmed in Madam Julia's gown,
> Which servèd me as fit, by all men's judgments,
> As if the garment had been made for me.

He had turned and was now staring at me. I approached him, looked at him squarely, and continued. *"Therefore,"* I said, placing my cap on my head, *"I know she is about my height. And at that time I made her weep agood. For I did play a lamentable part! Madam, 'twas Ariadne passioning, for Theseus' perjury and unjust flight; which I so lively acted with my tears, that my poor mistress, movèd there withal, wept bitterly; and would I might be dead—if I in thought felt not her very—"*

"Who are you?" he said suddenly, and grabbed my shoulder so quick that I jumped. "Be you one of Henslowe's boys from the Rose? Sent to spy on our playhouse? To mar our first performance?"

I shook my head in bewilderment, and I think it was clear to him that I did not know who Henslowe was. "I'm not from the Rose," I said. "I—like plays. That one I read—"

"Read? But that one is not printed." He frowned. "Unless some knave hath stolen—"

"Nay," I said hastily, fearing to launch a panic. "I meant to say, I read from a hawker's bill that that play was Master Shakespeare's work. I have heard it on stage many times, and parts of it stuck in my brain. It had a brave title, *The Two Gentle—*"

"I know the title, young scallywag," he said, still gripping my shoulder. He was looking keenly at my face, and I felt the sweat start to drip down my back. Then, releasing me so abruptly that I stumbled, he said, "I suppose you could pass for a female."

I was a touch stewed by that.

"Nathan Field plays for us, you know," he said. "Our Hermia for *A Midsummer Night's Dream.* And Sander Cooke. You'll not get many parts while they're still piping with boys' voices."

"I would be honored to play any part, Master Burbage." It was one of the few true things I'd said to him, but I worried that it sounded false, like flattery.

He smiled. " 'Any part.' No, you want to be Juliet. Or Portia. Well, you won't be. But you're good enough to be Lucius this afternoon, which is my good fortune, because it happens that young Robert Gough has broken his leg. Come on."

"Lucius?" I asked, scurrying after him. I was amazed at my luck.

"A small part. You bring on a lamp and have some small speech with Brutus. If you can carry it well enough in this morning's rehearsal, we'll put you on."

"Brutus?" I repeated, something stupidly.

"Yes, Brutus! Me! Thou art my slave." He extracted a scroll from his jerkin and rapped my head with it. "So do exactly as I say."

And so I went to work as a player.

As I traded lines with the others that day in rehearsal, I forgot my fear of everything—except my fear of being unmasked by my father. My heart pounded the first time he and I stood on the scaffold together, even though we were separated by some twenty feet. I told myself that if he noted a resemblance between me and the smock-clad daughter he'd last seen reading romances in his leafy New Place garden—well, he would never make much of it. My being in Southwark dressed as a boy was a fact so outlandish that even he would not dream it could be, unless in a fanciful romp on the stage.

I told myself this, but my heart still threatened to jump from my chest whenever I saw him glance my way, and I took care always to pull my hat down low. The riskiest time came when we shared a scene. Luckily I did not have to speak, and could stand on the far side of the stage from him until the moment came when I could race off. At times I saw his grey eyes briefly linger on me. His look was enigmatic and sad. Then, suddenly, he would turn to an actor and say, "Next time stress 'glove'!" or " 'Obedient' has three syllables there," as though his mind had been on his poetry all along. He puzzled me as much as ever he had.

I know now that he too saw Hamnet in me. So plain a thing should not have escaped me, but of course, I could not see my own face. In the tiring-house mirror I could, but when I stared in that I was far too busy caking myself with powder to think of my brother.

My father's sadness touched me, though I saw it from a distance, and though my fear that he'd catch and beat me defeated my total sympathy. I feared him, but in his playhouse I could not summon the red tide of wrath that had brought me to London: the rage that had fired my heart when I first read his hateful play. I still could not fathom why he'd written it, but the matter troubled me less as other things stole my attention. Around me actors hammered and chattered and stretched and laughed and muttered poetry. I smelled sawdust and powder, and the air trembled with music. The drummer drummed and the flutist tuned his pipe on the balcony. This new world dwarfed my old one. I wasn't a fool. I knew my stay would be brief. But now, awash in the thrill of the playhouse, I cared only to avoid capture as long as I could.

As it turned out, I need not have worried so much. My first day in the playhouse, my father could not have minded me less. He spent the morning arguing with a garishly dressed fellow whom I discovered to be the famous clown Will Kempe. Master Kempe was to play a minor part that afternoon, and my father was warning him not to gesture so wildly or scream so loudly while falling dead in the Roman street. Kempe was protesting that he had not much training in falling dead on a Roman street, and that he should have been given a different part, one that included dancing. My father told him it was too late for that or for any other of his nonsense. No happy resolution to their combat seemed likely.

As for me, I was showing Master Burbage what a very slavish Roman slave I could be.

We rested after rehearsal, and I sat by the river, saying my few lines over and over in my head. I saw my father traipsing up the bankside path toward the tiring-house, muttering to himself, and looking, with uncombed hair and unfastened doublet, as though he'd escaped from Bedlam, which, I had been told at the Cardinal's Cap, was only two streets to the west. He gave me an odd look—I then remembered that I had taken off my cap—but nothing came of it. Another player approached him, and I quickly slipped back inside the playhouse. Then I shoved my cap firmly on my head, and waited nervously until our performance began.

.   .   .

I could not, of course, wear my cap during the play. What slave would wear a cap in his master's presence? My costume was greasepaint and the plain clothes I was already wearing. But the lines I was given to say, few though they were, served better than any costume to make me feel that I was indeed a person of ancient Rome, though a passing lowly one.

"Called you, my lord?"

"I will, my lord."

"I know not, sir."

"I will, sir!"

"Sir, 'tis your brother Cassius at the door, who doth desire to see you."

I was wondrous beyond wonders! I was Juliet and Kate and Portia and Hermia and Helena, all packaged in one. Nay, more! I was Richard the Third and Henry the Fifth and Julius Caesar himself! And when the crowd clapped at the play's end, I stood and bowed with my new fellows in the players' half-circle, finally viewing the oyster wenches from the right end of the house.

As the watchers hooted and clapped and roared, I was sure in my heart that most of their noise was for me.

Chapter Eight

AFTER the performance, I was bursting with postplay pride and a sense of fellowship. But when the rest of the boys went off to play camp-ball in the garbage-strewn yard, I was left to entertain myself. Some of them had been apprenticed for nearly a year without being given speaking parts. When they saw me exchanging lines with Richard Burbage, their chief player and one of the most famous actors in London, they decided not to admit me to their casual fraternity.

This was well, I told myself. I needed a wash at the pump, and that might be hard to manage in front of their eyes. Only now did I start to think on the perils of scrubbing myself and changing my clothes before the boys and the men. There were my new sleeping arrangements to consider. As part of my keep, I would share a garret room with two other boys in the nearby house of Master Henry Condell. I knew of Condell; he was one of the profit-sharers in my father's company, and my father had spoken well of him at home. I was grateful for the lodging, but I shuddered at the thought of rubbing elbows with boy bedfellows. I would have to face the wall as much as I could. At other times, it would be best to hang apart.

I knew this. And yet I felt an emptiness as I watched the boys exchanging shoves and shouts and good-humored insults.

I had no one to talk to, no one to share a laugh with about how Cassius had slipped on the pig's blood and nearly landed on his noble Republican arse. Or to glory with over the audience's reverent silence during Mark Antony's eulogy by Brutus' dead body.

Some of the men had simply wiped off their greasepaint, tossed the rag at a boy, and gone home to their wives and their suppers. It had been another working day to them. The company sharers, my father among them, were more animated. But they talked not about my playing or indeed anyone's playing so much as about the strengths and failings of the new scaffold and how well the sound had carried and why in sweet Jesus' name Will Kempe had gone and spoiled the new tragedy by sneaking back on stage and dancing a jig at the end of it! I got a pat on the shoulder and a "Well done, Castor!" from Richard Burbage, and then he was off to an ordinary to have supper.

I, of course, was not invited along.

And so I sat by myself on the stair leading down from the tiring-house, munching the bread and cheese and cold fowl that had been left for the boys, and gazing at the river. I watched the wherries rowing back and forth, and thought of the Avon and its swans and ducks, and the lads who fished in the shallows. After a time I grew a touch melancholy, despite the fact that thus far my plans had succeeded astonishingly well. I thought of my mother, and how she would feel when my aunt finally wrote her from Coventry asking where I was and it dawned on her that I had run away. I pictured her in our family pew at Holy Trinity Church, weeping and praying for my safety. I looked at the spire of Saint Saviour's Church, stark against the evening sky above the Southwark housetops, and I wondered whether God was taking note of my activities. I looked at the moon, and thought about the goddess Hecate. I took another bite of my supper. Hecate, *indeed*.

Then I heard a door shut behind me and turned quickly, my mouth full of cheese.

There, at the top of the stair, stood the boy Nathan Field, squinting at me.

I had never before seen him without his greasepaint and one or another false head of hair. His scrubbed skin was fair and smooth, except for the sparsest of moustaches above his lip. He kept his thick brown hair choppy and short, as did all the lads, the better to fit their wigs on their heads. He wore a plain pair of brown woolen trousers, leather boots, and a white linen shirt, and over his shoulder he carried a sack bulging with what seemed to be nails.

His eyes were uncommonly green.

"*Cas*tor *Pop*worthy," he said. His voice was something between boyhood and manhood. That very afternoon I had much heard it, speaking the lines of Portia, Brutus' wife. But there was nothing of Portia's somber, tragic cast to him now. He sounded amused.

"*Cas*tor *Pop*worthy," he repeated. "Marry, that's a good one. What master are *you* running from?"

I wiped my lips with my handkerchief and brushed the crumbs from my lap, while he gazed at me attentively, unsettling me. "What's that to thee?" I said indifferently.

"Nothing." He slung his bag onto his other shoulder and descended the stairs, passing me on the way. At the bottom he turned. "The lads think Master Burbage owed thee some favor to put you on as Lucius."

I turned bright red; I could feel my skin glow. "And what think you?" I said, as gruffly as I could.

"I think they don't know Dick Burbage. There is nothing in his mind but acting. Ever."

"And so?"

"He saw you as Lucius. Heard you as Lucius. And that is what I told the lads."

I bobbed my chin, still unsettled by his stare, but pleased. "Well, that should endear me to them most mightily," I said.

"Why should you care who holds you dear?" he asked. "Think of thyself. That's what I do. And speaking of that, hear me well." He bent toward my face. "And you try to play a part that's marked for me, I'll kick your stones till they clatter in the street."

At that I laughed out loud.

I quickly covered my mouth, as he drew back and looked

at me narrowly. "I—will remember that," I said, struggling to look grave. "Fear me not, Nathan Field."

"Fear *you*! What reason have I to fear *you*?"

"No reason," I said. Then I spit on the ground in a way I had seen boys do. "I'faith, I would be friends with you," I said. On an impulse I stretched out my hand. Field stared at it for a moment, then took it and pressed it. As he did so I felt a warm current run all the way through my body, from my fingers to my toes. It shocked me. I cannot say I liked it. I was glad when he dropped my hand.

"Till tomorrow, then. There'll be drama enough here tomorrow without you and me coming to blows."

"What mean you?"

"Nothing."

"Where are you bound with a sackful of nails?"

He raised his brows. "A thousand questions, and none of them your business."

"Do you think me a spy? Look ye, I can guess your purpose."

"Marry, can you?"

"Those were left over from the building, and you're going to sell them to an ironmonger." He frowned at me, and I hastened to fill the silence. "Go your ways. I'll not blab, and you'll give me half of what you get."

He frowned more fiercely. "A third."

"Half."

"Well," he said after a moment. "Half, then, Castor. And we'll spend it on ale at the Cardinal's Cap."

"The Knavish Loon has better ale," I said quickly.

"The Loon, then. Farewell." He disappeared along the path into the trees.

I sat by myself on the stair until the moon rose full over the river. I did not think of Stratford anymore.

After a time I made my way to Master Condell's house and bed.

FORTUNE favored me that night. My bedmates were snoring and I was able to take off my loose shirt in darkness and slip on the nightgown Mistress Condell had lent me without being heard, let alone seen. In the morning I rose first, and dressed and ate quickly. I was anxious to return to the Globe.

Yet the day was something rainy, and the flag did not fly. The Lord Chamberlain's Men would not play. I was directed back to Master Condell's house, where I spent the day scrubbing Mistress Condell's leaded glass windows and practicing my whistle. I wished I were at the playhouse—wished, though I could scarce admit it, that I could speak once more with Nathan Field.

The next day was rainy again, yet I felt an anxious excitement. I did not clearly know what I felt—fear, or soaring ambition, or the vestiges of rage at my father—but I knew the cause of my heart's quickening pace. Today the company was scheduled to begin rehearsals for a new play. I knew what the new play was.

A comedy. A light bauble of a play, wherein lovers jested

and married, and siblings were parted and then happily re-joined. It was called *Twelfth Night*.

I had already been given my part in this play, in a rolled-up scroll that contained only cues and my own brief speeches. I was to play a servant again, and as I'd unfurled the paper and eaten the part with my eyes I'd tried to plan how I would use my father's words to serve my own ends, and those of Hamnet's ghost. Will Kempe had danced and ruined my father's tragedy. As the servant Fabian, I might weep, or do some sad thing, and alter my father's comedy.

I say "alter," and not "ruin," because my purpose had changed from what it was when I'd first boarded a coach in Stratford. I knew now that I honored playing as much as I honored my brother. In some small measure, I had already tasted the wine of desire shared by a brotherhood of actors on stage—desire to please and transport those who'd paid to watch us. I could not betray that promise.

But something I had to do, or fail myself utterly. If Hamnet's death had been the ground of this play, then grief must be shown in it. Somehow I had to speak melancholy into my father's comedy.

Nothing easy, in a farce named for a holiday.

Yet when I arrived at the Globe at eight of the clock all was strangely somber. The mood was nothing comic. I under-stood the cause of the sharers' grim looks when I overheard some of the players talking. It seemed that Will Kempe, the great clown, had been dismissed from the company, not for his clowning—inapt, I knew, to *Julius Caesar*—but over some business of a stolen prompt-book.

One of my father's plays had turned up some time ago in the possession of a rival company, and now someone had informed him that Kempe had been the thief and profiteer.

And the company gave thieves no quarter.

The sharers had booted him from their gorgeous new playhouse the day before, and Kempe, according to one of the boys—who covertly made the sign against the evil eye as he whispered it to me—had cursed my father's company. I thought a clown's curse a foolish enough thing, but the players were all mightily superstitious, and passing fearful of what might happen to them now.

I was more fearful of what might happen to me if it was discovered that I had been Nathan Field's accessory in the hawking of stolen nails. I thought of Nathan's sly grin that very morning as he'd tossed a silver coin at me as I entered. I had blushed then, and I blushed again recalling my ill-gotten gain and his white flash of teeth. But a bag of nails was only a bag of nails, I told myself.

A prompt-book was—a play.

I sat on the stage with the other players, my hat pulled low, all of us rattling our scrolls and studying our parts. Once more I struggled to recall what had driven me to London: to summon my sad anger over my father's sale of the Shakespeares' grief.

But it was not easy to do.

Instead, I listened to the players' murmurs as they brought

their lines to life. I found myself practicing ways to respond, in proper time and measure. I knit my brow over new questions: how to speak my father's verse trippingly, and whether "Here comes my *noble* gull-catcher" sounded better than "*Here* comes my noble gull-catcher." Or perhaps better yet was "Here comes my noble *gull*-catcher." Then I became so absorbed in covertly listening to my father's direction of Sander Cooke, who would play the lady Olivia, that I almost forgot who I was, let alone what I'd come for.

"*Good my mouse of virtue, answer me,*" my father said to young Master Cooke, a pale youth who looked like a sprouting weed.

"*Well, sir, for want of other idleness, I'll answer you,*" said the boy. To my surprise, his voice was warm and rich with teasing humor. He sounded like Susanna practicing her wit against one of the Hall lads, and I had to blink to reassure myself that this boy was a boy indeed.

"That's wrong, but no matter," said my father. He rubbed his forehead and frowned at his scroll.

Pulling my cap even lower, I turned slightly. Then, for the first time since I'd lied my way into my father's playhouse, I truly looked at him.

I saw that the forehead he'd rubbed looked larger than it had when I'd last seen him in Stratford, which is to say it had less hair behind it. But apart from that change he looked uncommonly well, heavier and ruddier and stronger than I'd ever known him to be. No doubt this was from porting thatch and pounding boards for the Globe.

"Here," he said, scratching through a line on Sander

Cooke's scroll. "We'll be rid of that. Answer me now, '*Good madonna, why mourn'st thou?*'"

"*Good fool, for my brother's death.*"

"*I think his soul is in Hell, madonna.*"

"*I know his soul is in Heaven, fool.*"

"*The more fool, madonna, to mourn for your brother's soul, being in Heaven.*" My father rapped Sander Cooke on the head with his scroll. "*Take away the fool, gentlemen.*"

"Master Shakespeare, you should not have rapped me on the head."

"You are right. The man who I hope will play this part would never do such a thing. Olivia's fool is not rudely comic; he is only witty."

"You did not write the part for Master Kempe, then."

My father looked at the boy sharply, and said, "Leave that theme alone, boy. Now—a touch of anger in *I know his soul is in Heaven, fool*. Do you understand why?"

"Must I understand why?"

"For me you must."

Richard Burbage approached my father. "Waste no more time with this, Will," he said, in a mildly weary tone that suggested he had said this or something like it many times before. "We need him memorizing, not probing his every motive."

"Do you *understand why?*" my father repeated, ignoring Burbage.

I listened with suspended breath.

"Marry, I suppose it's because I'm worried that the fool is right and my brother may be in Hell."

"You are wiser than I took you for," said my father, but he said it kindly. "That is a terrible thought, is it not? Why do you harbor it?"

"Well," said Cooke. "He died young. Who knows whether he died cursing God for his poor luck? And was sent to the devil for it?"

"Yes, you might wonder that, Olivia," my father said. "Although it's not at all likely that God would punish a poor lad so, you are just the sort of melancholy and self-absorbed young lady who would fear it. You go about by yourself, head all crammed with frightening fancies, perpetually mourning, as though you truly thought yourself the best judge of how you should behave. Care's an enemy to life. Why don't you stop it?" My father's voice rose, as did the scroll, which once more threatened the boy's head. "Stop it!"

Laughing, Cooke threw up his hands. "Pray do not hit me again, Master Shakespeare," he said. "Remember, my fool is my servant! He is not my father."

"True enough," said my father in a milder tone, lowering his hand. "And as I said, our *new* clown will address you with most unmerited politeness." He handed Cooke the scroll. "Study."

My father crossed the stage, passing me by inches, and jumped to the yard, which some of the boys were raking and smoothing. He crossed to the galleries and joined Richard Burbage and another man in conversation.

I sat with my eyes glued to my own scroll, but it was some minutes before I could return my thoughts to what was written there.

· · ·

WE rehearsed *Twelfth Night* every day, even when the weather cleared and the flag flew again above the high thatched roof and we had to give a play in the afternoon. On those days we played for two hours, supped, then met on the stage and practiced our comedy until the moon was high and candles and torches lit our faces.

True to my father's hopeful promise, we were joined within the week by a mournful and musical man named Robert Armin, who would be Will Kempe's replacement, the company's new clown, or *fool*, as he preferred to be worded. I know not how better to describe him than to say he was humorous and sad at once, and barely needed a word of instruction to say jesting Feste's lines with a melancholy merriment that sent my father into ecstasies. And he sang. He brought his own music and played the sweetest, most wistful pipe and tabor I had ever heard, bringing tears to more eyes than mine in the hearing of it.

It was thus, as I listened and watched in the playhouse each day, that I started to see that this play was sad enough without my tampering. That is not, of course, to say that it was not at the same time merry. But it was sad. It was happy and sad. I can say it no better.

· · ·

I practiced my role until I was perfect, and even something bored with it, since of course I craved a larger part. I envied Sander Cooke and Nathan Field, who would capture the audience's eyes and ears for most of the play, Cooke in a velvet gown as Olivia, Field in a boy's servant-livery as Viola in boy's disguise. It was a happy new idea of my father's to have his boys play girls dressed as boys, and Field had done it before more than once. I could see he now thought himself perfect in the trick.

He would swagger on stage with his hands in his breeches-pockets and then make all of us laugh—even I, who was green with jealousy—by grabbing his crotch and shaking it.

"Marry, give over," my father said, the first time Field did this. "You are a girl."

"Posing as a boy," Field said. I noticed that he did not add "sir" or "master" to his comment, as the other boys did when addressing the men. "I know how to act like a boy."

"I do not want you to act like a boy. I want you to act like a girl acting like a boy."

"Well, would she not do this?" Field asked, shaking his crotch in my father's direction. "Sir?"

Burbage threw down a planing tool at this, and started in Field's direction, but my father's mild voice stopped him.

"Never mind, Dick. No, Nate; she would not. And I do not have to tell you why, because you know. Now, stop thy foolery or thou'lt find thyself out in the street with Kempe."

Nate Field suddenly sobered and even looked fleetingly guilty, though at what I could hardly imagine, since he seemed to enjoy interrupting rehearsals with ribald jests. In fact, when he next came through the door as Viola, seeming all serious and chastened, he turned to show a colossal cucumber jutting from his breeches. Even Burbage laughed. But the men forgave Field his rudeness for one reason only.

There was no boy in London as good as he was.

I admitted this to myself when I heard him say the lines I so desperately wanted to say. As Viola in boy's disguise, pining for the love of the Duke Orsino, describing to him a "sister" whom she cannot admit is herself, Nathan nearly brought me to tears.

"She never told her love," he said, somber and low-voiced, avoiding the eye of Burbage, who was gowned as Orsino.

> *But let concealment, like a worm i' the bud,*
> *Feed on her damask cheek. She pined in thought,*
> *And with a green and yellow melancholy*
> *She sat like Patience on a monument,*
> *Smiling at grief.*

Yes, I thought as I peered at him. I was half-concealed by the curtain before the recessed space where I stood, at the back of the stage. *Yes.* The studied gestures, the servant's posture, the perfect, measured iambic. He was better than Cooke, and Cooke was good.

And yet, still—there seemed to me to be something mannered in his acted servitude; something a jot conventional in his demure posture as he sat at Orsino's feet, head tilted, feigning to be a girl feigning to be a boy. Across the yard, in the galleries, I saw my watching father shift position and frown slightly—or I thought I saw him frown; in the twilight and from that distance it was hard to tell—and I wondered if he thought as I did.

"*Was not this love indeed?*" Nate Field continued. It seemed to me that he looked right at me then, as I stood in my hiding place. At once I forgot any thought of his deficiencies. I blushed. I felt the sudden welling of all the griefs and joys and longings of my life. When Nate's eyes met mine as he said my father's line, I felt that all was understood.

But that—his look—may have been only my fancy. For a moment later he was gazing at the floorboards, nodding seriously, as from the yard my father directed his speaking.

He was thinking of nothing but the play.

Chapter Nine

"Why waste thy time with talk of drowning and guilt and so on?" I heard Richard Burbage say a week later. His voice came through the open door of the tiring-room.

I was standing in my breeches, trying to change my shirt while keeping my back to the men stocking costumes in a trunk. This was not easy to do without placing myself directly in front of the room's large mirror and thus giving up the game entirely to anyone who happened to glance over. But after two weeks at the Globe I had much practice, from guarding myself morn, noon, and night in the Condells' upper chamber and these places behind the stage where men jostled with boys for space to change costume.

I was getting passing good at it.

"We've a bare two days to be perfect in this comedy, and thy philosophizing takes *time*," Burbage continued.

" 'Tis not 'philosophizing,' " came my father's voice, a little sharply. "As I have told thee before, if the player knows who he is meant to be, it is easier for him to remember the lines. And what is more, thou hast *seen* this to be true, time and time again, not just in others but in thyself, Dick Burbage, or may I call thee Richard Three, or Henry Five. . . ."

The door to the outer world slammed and the voices faded.

Quickly I thrust my head through my boy's shirt, awkwardly keeping my upper arms pressed to my chest, and darted from the room. The outer passage was deserted. Barefoot, I stepped lightly to the trap in the passageway and yanked its wooden handle. The door came up with a flurry of sawdust, and I slipped down the ladder into the blackness of the cellarage, the place the players called Hell.

It was inky black at the bottom, and smelled of dust. The first time I had lowered myself here, I'd been near scared out of my small-clothes. Even now I breathed faster, but I willed myself not to shake. I took a flint-box and candle from my pocket, struck a light, and looked about. The guts of the Globe lay around me. My eyes raked old stools and gilt thrones and clothes racks, and came to rest on a middle-sized trunk with an iron lock that stood a few feet from the livelier trunk of a stage tree.

I breathed easier. It had been moved a few paces to the left, but it was still there.

Several times in the past week I had seen my father slip down the ladder of the passageway trap or one of the other traps that gave from the stage, bearing prompt-books. I knew that the stage Hell was where he stored them, and on my second day here I had rightly guessed exactly where. Now I threaded my way past the flotsam and jetsam of the cellarage and knelt before the locked box.

There were only two keys to this trunk. The first my father carried with him; I had twice seen him pocket it on his return upladder from Hell to the daylight world. There was no getting the first. The second he kept in a drawer in Stratford, or I should say he *had* kept it there.

Now it was in my hand.

I twisted the key in the lock. It turned, and I lifted the trunk's heavy lid.

Before me, neatly piled, lay the prompt-books of some twenty plays. Only one of them concerned me. From the top of the pile I plucked *Twelfth Night* and stuffed it in my waistband. Then I went to the other ladder, the one that led to one of the two stage-traps. I blew out the candle, climbed up, and opened the trap, thanking Hecate—or God—for its oiled hinges.

Then I listened.

The only sound was the thrum of my heart in my ears. After three minutes I was sure that the playhouse was deserted. It was ten of the clock, and the boys and men would have gone to a tavern or to bed to rest themselves for the next day's playing of one play and practice of another. So I hopped onto the stage, relit my candle, sat on the floor, and hunched over the script.

I had been studying the play every night of the past seven, sitting for hours until my back ached, sometimes not reaching Henry Condell's house until well past one in the morning. At that hour I had to shinny up a tree and dive through a window to reach the room where I slept with the other young players, and in the mornings I was red-eyed at breakfast.

I don't think I fooled Condell or his wife or any of the others in the house into thinking I had been sleeping peacefully through the night. But, as in so many other ways since I had come to London, luck was with me in that house. Mistress Condell was so busy minding her five children and cooking breakfast and mending clothes for ten—including the Chamberlain's Men's boys—that she could not be bothered to complain because a boy wandered Southwark late, as long as he broke no furniture or made no noise coming in. And I didn't. My bedmates seemed to think I was spending my time kissing a wench in the trees by the Thames, and since this fantasy improved their opinion of me, I did not try to correct it.

By now I was line-perfect in the part of the play I cared most about, which was the part of Viola, loving Orsino while mourning her brother Sebastian, the twin she thought drowned. Viola did not let her grief stop her from occasional merriment, and indeed from other passions. Quite specifically, she did not let her grief bar her from falling in love. And although I had never before contemplated falling in love, the spirit of the play in rehearsal had affected me. I wondered whether, given the chance and the right fellow, I might actually try it.

On the stage, I mean.

This night, as I had hoped, I no longer needed the book, for after a quick glance, I knew I had the lines now in my head. So I did not need to sit cramped and hunched on the floor any longer. Instead, I could rise to my feet and say Viola's part; nay, more, I could *act* Viola's part, giving it life with brave or subtle gestures. With my candle I lit the torch that stood in the holder on the wall. Then I commenced walking and strutting over that great expanse of scaffolding, shrugging, kicking an imaginary stone with my foot, and speaking the lines that my father had written and that I had come to adore.

I was in the midst of the scene where Viola tries to avoid a duel with Sir Andrew Aguecheek. I'd in fact just said in my most fearful tones, *"A little thing would make me tell them how much I lack of a man!"* when I heard a sharp sound come from my right and echo from the walls, and then another, and another.

Slowly, mockingly, someone was clapping.

At the first clap I had jumped like a hare and knocked myself onto my rear end. Now I got to my feet and looked to my right. There, leaning against the post of one of the open stage doors, stood Nathan Field.

I was horribly embarrassed, but I made myself speak calmly. "Thank you," I said coolly, and crouched to retrieve the prompt-book, which I'd trampled. I stood up again, and spoke quickly. "You need not fear me stealing thy part. It was only play."

"Oh, I do not fear it," he said. He picked up something from the floor next to him and dropped it into his shoulder bag. Then he walked onto the stage. "I do not fear it," he repeated. "You do not even know how to play it."

I was stung. "Oh?" I said. "And you think *you* do? Gesturing like a—a—a windmill?" I snorted. "When a maid is scared she does not shoot her arms skyward as though she would presently perform a handstand."

He gave me an odd look. "Ah, so you say. And what *does* she do?"

"Turns pale," I said. "Bites her lip." I bit my lip.

He reached out his hand. "Give me that. You sound like—"

I snatched the prompt-book back and retreated three paces, then stopped. I wanted to jump off the stage and escape through the yard, but I knew I had to return the play to my father's trunk. Had I locked it? I flicked my eyes to the trap door.

Nathan Field still stood before me with his hand outstretched, his gaze fixed on me. "Give me the prompt-book," he said, his voice low and threatening.

"Never, thou spitting windmill," I said, and sprinted for the stage-trap.

I was fast, but he was faster. My hand was grasping the trap's handle when he grabbed me around the waist and pulled me from it. I turned and kicked him away, fell, picked myself up, and ran through the open stage door. But he was right behind me, and as I came into the passage outside the tiring-rooms he grabbed me again about the waist and pulled me into the room where I had left my tall candle burning in a holder on the wall. I elbowed him, aiming for his groin but getting only his stomach, and we tumbled about the room, toppling tin crowns and wig-stands and pots of snowy powder which flew up in a rush and near-blinded us. Finally he pinned me on the floor and with one hand reached for the crotch of my now-torn breeches and squeezed me hard. Then he kissed me.

I had never been kissed on the mouth in my life.

In the midst of that desperate combat, I did not at first

know what he was doing. I imagined he was trying to stop me from breathing. By the time the truth of it became clear to my whirling brain I had already bitten him hard on the lip, and he had sat up like a jack-in-the-box, saying, "Hell take thee, bitch!" I crawled backward until I hit the room's far wall and then we both sat panting, staring at one another in the flickering candlelight.

I think I was the first to laugh. Indeed, I think I was the only one to laugh.

Nathan squinted at me.

"Hast a smear of greasepaint on thy cheek," I said.

He wiped it with a sleeve. "Thou also." Again he stared at me. "Where be the prompt-book?"

"I am sitting on it," I said, guessing, rightly as it turned out, that the sharp thing jutting into my left thigh was the prompt-book's corner. "Reach for it and thou wilt be kicked most mightily." I grinned. "Kicked till thy stones clatter in the street."

He stayed put. "How didst thou pry open the trunk?" he asked, sounding like a fellow who'd tried it and failed.

"How didst thou know me for a maid?" I replied.

"Ah, I knew you at the first," he said contemptuously. "I knew it when I saw you eating on the stoop that day. There's not a boy in Southwark who dabs his lips with a napkin as thou didst, Mistress Dainty." He frowned. "There's not a girl in Southwark who does either, come to note it. But then there was your laugh."

I looked down, suddenly shy. "What *of* my laugh?" I muttered.

"Boys do not laugh that way," he said, and that was his

sole comment on the matter. "In any case, now I have you. Tell me your name."

" 'Tis Castor."

"Tell me your woman's name."

"Well enough, and you like not Castor, you may call me Viola."

"Oh, thou *wouldst* like that, wouldst thou not, for all thy talk of not stealing a part. Very well. Mistress *Viola*."

"I thank thee, Mistress Viola."

He looked suddenly angry. "Call me not that. I am not on the stage now."

"No, you are not," I said. "You are behind it." I glanced toward the door, wondering just what he had meant by "I have you," and doubting that I could jump to my feet and run out without him attacking me again.

"Well, thou shalt have to pay me now," he said with determination.

"I have nothing to pay you with." I glanced at him nervously.

"I think you do," he replied evenly. "You are some hare-brained maid from a wealthy squire's family, run to London for an adventure. You read and you speak well, for all your country voice. You have money, or you know someone who does. But money's not what I want from you."

"What do you want?"

"I want to know how you opened the trunk, and I want that play."

"I am passing good at picking locks; there's your answer. And you'll not get the prompt-book. It goes back to the trunk.

If you take it from me I'll tell the masters where it's gone, and then you'll be gone yourself, like Will Kempe."

I narrowed my eyes, suddenly suspicious.

"Why are you here at midnight, Nathan Field?"

He didn't answer that. "You will tell no one anything about me," he said. "Because if you do I will tell them about you."

At that I had nothing to say.

"Give me the prompt-book," he said, again holding out his hand.

"No."

He could, of course, have forced it from me. Instead he relaxed his position and leaned back against the wall facing me, one leg flat on the ground and the other bent, an arm resting on his knee. He tapped his cap with a finger. "Then keep it," he said. "Or return it to the trunk. I do not need it."

"Then why were you so hot for it?"

"That is not your business."

I shrugged. "Well enough. I care not. I only want to go to bed."

"Good. You'll have to, now."

"What?" I said, turning hot.

"Since you'll not give me the prompt-book, you can give me your maidenhead. Else I will expose you to the masters."

I stared at him in disbelief, stunned by the choice he'd just laid before me. I should not have been so surprised; I should have known from the kiss what he aimed at, or one of the things he aimed at. I knew that I had the power to thwart him by telling who I really was.

But I did not.

"Fie!" I simply said. "I do not think you would be so base."

In fact I *did* think it, but pretended to think him nobler than he was. This was the type of thing that the virgins in my father's plays did when caught in similar situations. But Nathan had read those plays too—in fact he'd *played* some of those threatened virgins himself. Now he responded as a stage villain would have. "I would be so base indeed." Then he wiggled his eyebrows fearfully.

I almost laughed, as he meant me to. But I didn't. My plight wasn't comic.

He thought it was, though, and smiled pleasantly. "Do you think a man who's lately done what I've done would stint at ravishing a skinny maid like thee?"

Skinny. "You're not a man," I said furiously. "And I don't know what you've lately done, past steal a bag of nails."

"And you won't know."

"I don't want to know. I only want to—"

"Go to bed, I know. Fair enough. And since I'm not a man—as you say—you need not fear I'll get you with child. My voice cracks only when I sing. For that, I don't sing. When it cracks all the time, then I'm a full man, and then you may fear my weapon's potency."

That was among the most foolish things I'd ever heard, but the truth of it was I did not know much about the subject. He might have been telling the truth. I parried. "It's little of a weapon, if it lacks potency."

He smirked. "It will be a formidable weapon in time. You had best enjoy it while it's blunted by my tender youth. And it's not little."

"Then 'tis too big." I could not believe the bawdy matter that was rolling off my tongue. I credited it to my ale-pouring stint at the Cardinal's Cap. "What's big would maim a simple virgin like myself," I explained.

"Virgin I think you are. But you are not simple." He gave me a shrewd look, then smiled again, as if to sweeten me. " 'Tis not so big."

"Players will say anything, will they not?"

"Anything to the purpose, and my purpose is you."

"How old art thou?"

"Sixteen last May Day."

The bells of Saint Saviour's rang one. I started nervously. "I cannot stay here for any more of this pleasant chat," I said. "The Condells are lax, but they will not abide me dancing in at breakfast."

"It would not take that long, but you're safe for the present," Nathan said, rising and extending his hand. I grasped it, and felt the same warm rush of blood I'd felt when he'd taken my hand on the outside stair nearly two weeks before. It angered me, even more than his mocking smile angered me. Still, firmly grasping *Twelfth Night*'s script in my other hand, I let him pull me up.

Even barefoot, I stood an inch taller than he, which made me feel awkward, but did not seem to pall him in the slightest. "I've an appointment in Eastcheap," he said. "So our interlude must wait till tomorrow night. Meet me here. I came through a loose window; I know not how you got in, but you will find a way. At ten of the clock."

I shook my head. "It is mad."

"Why mad? It is reasonable." His eyes were green and merry. I wanted to slap him.

"*You* are mad," I said. "It seems passing foolish for me to make an appointment to be raped."

"Then only be on the stage at ten, saying your lines—pardon, *my* lines—as you did tonight. I'll jump on you from behind the arras when the moment suits me. Maybe you'll find surprise more seemly."

"And if you do not find me here?"

"Then you know what follows," he said. "We play *Twelfth Night* the day after. We, but not you. You'll have been sent home to your dam, who will beat you black and blue."

This sounded uncannily like he knew my mother, but I told myself that the image was common enough. Perhaps he had a strict mother, too, although it was hard to imagine Nathan Field having any mother at all.

"I play Fabian," I argued weakly. "They will need Fabian."

"They will need Fabian, but he will not be you. John Rice knows the lines." He named the ruder of my two roommates. "He will play the part."

I frowned angrily. "He will not."

"Then I will see you here tomorrow night."

At that Nathan walked from the tiring-room. I heard him go back out to the stage and pick up his bag. Then I heard the scrape of a window and the thud of his boots on the soft ground outside.

And then I was alone, my candle sputtering and my heart hammering and my feet still altogether shoeless.

Chapter Ten

I did not put much store by virginity. I knew my mother was
no virgin when she married my father, and from a jesting
remark I'd once heard her make to Aunt Joan, I was not sure
she hadn't given herself up quite a while before then. I didn't
see why I should be any purer than she was, and as long as
no one knew of it, there might be no harm in the loss. As I
lay awake in bed, amidst snores and rude smells, what frightened me were two other things.

First was the thought that, for all Nathan's mad-brained
argument, he would indeed get me with child. And that I had
vowed could not happen. Second and worse was a fear harder
to name. The best I can do to describe it is to say that I did
not want him to hurt me. I was passing tired of loss.

.   .   .

THE next day was fair, and we played *Caesar* again. I was angry at myself for quivering during the short scene when I had to speak with Nathan, all bewigged and painted and bedecked in the robes of a Roman matron. Shaking did not harm my performance; a quivering hand was not amiss in a Roman slave taking orders from his mistress, especially when that mistress was bigger than he was, and Nathan did stand taller than me in his two-inch chopines. But I didn't like that Nathan saw my tremors and guessed the cause, as I knew he had from the sly look in his eye.

I also thought him something over-imperious. He was, after all, playing Portia, not Caesar. *"I prithee, boy, run to the Senate House,"* he charged me strictly. Then he grabbed my shoulders, as he never had before, and shook me so my head bobbed. *"Stay not to answer me, but get thee gone,"* he snapped, still holding me tight. *"Why dost thou stay?"*

I looked at him murderously.

Indeed, I would have liked to be gone, but I knew I must play the play, and he knew it. He had me. I gave my line, and he railed at me some more, clearly glad that his part gave him license to torment me. *"I have a man's mind, but a woman's might,"* he complained, a hand to his forehead, then winked at me so quickly that I almost thought I'd dreamed it. I'faith, I thought he was still overacting, and I judged I would tell him so later.

I could hurt his player's pride if I could wound him no other way.

Then entered the Soothsayer, which happened to be my father in tattered robes and powdery hair. I kept my head down as I always did at this tricky pass, during which I happily had to say nothing. Between my father on the right hand and Nate Field on the left I was in the hottest spot where ever I'd stood. After a minute I saw from the corner of my eye that Nathan was again trying to hook my glance and get off another wink, as he cried, *"Ay me, how* weak *a thing the heart of woman is!"*

I wouldn't give him the pleasure.

Finally, the scene ended and I was able to scurry off the stage.

Nathan followed hard at my heels, and pinched my bottom when no one was looking. "Go kill thyself for true, Portia," I hissed, before noticing my father hobbling behind him. For a heart-stopping moment I thought I was discovered, but my father only raised his walking stick and mildly swatted Nathan's calf. "Cease quarreling, boys," he said, and was gone again to the stage door for his next entrance.

My part was done, and my nerves were frayed, and I could have run from the tiring-house down to the river and sat and watched the boats to calm myself, except that our masters knew what better use to make of their boys' time. So I was sent to stock greasepaint in one of the tiring-rooms.

Nathan sat at the far end of the room and doffed his wig and swigged some ale, jesting loudly. But the room was crowded and we shared no more speech, which was well for me, because I was consumed with a mingle of rage and shyness and was truly out of words to say to him.

Still, I was pleased with "Go kill thyself for true, Portia," and said it over to myself three or four times.

THAT night we rehearsed for the last time for the morrow's first performance of *Twelfth Night*. Watching Nathan as Viola, I could have sworn that his gestures and voice were less extravagant, and I saw my father nodding approvingly from where he sat on the stage's far corner, thumbing the prompt-book. Then he turned a page and frowned. I heard him ask one of the men, "Who stepped on this book, now?" and I quickly looked away.

Nathan had finished his scene, and he leaned against the far stage wall, his arms folded. I glanced at him covertly, trying to memorize his young-man's posture—arms folded, feet planted widely. I felt a sudden despair over ever properly playing a boy. It was a wonder that I'd succeeded as far as I had—a streak of luck, a trick of low-pulled caps and hanging in shadows and stage paint and talking from five feet away, helped along by the expectations of the innkeepers and tavern wenches and players whose company I'd shared. Nathan had seen right away through my disguise, once he'd viewed me closely. I began to worry that the others knew as well, and to backward-interpret some smiles as knowing smirks. Perhaps John Rice would try to ambush me too, and steal my honor.

Or expose me in order to get me thrown from the company, and steal my play-part.

I took a deep breath. My performance must come to an end one day, I told myself, but I would not let it happen before I'd trod the boards before an audience in *Twelfth Night*. I squared my skinny shoulders and looked boldly up, hoping to give Nathan a ferocious masculine scowl, and saw disappointedly that he was Viola again, back in the center of the stage and not regarding me at all.

WHEN the rehearsal ended my father was not satisfied, and thought a thousand things wrong. But the other sharers persuaded him that all would be well, that all was always well. "All is *not* always well, and well you know it!" I heard my father saying as Dick Burbage hustled him from the house.

By half past nine I found myself alone in the dark theater as I'd been in nights past, this time hiding in a wicker trunk in the smaller tiring-room. I had resolved to do it.

When all had been silent for a good ten minutes I lifted the trunk lid and jumped out, struck my flint, and washed myself exceedingly well in a bucket of water that stood hard by. I stared at myself in the mirror, pinching my cheeks and smoothing my butchered locks. Then I slipped through the middle opening and onto the stage.

I began to say Viola's first lines, the few she utters in women's garb before she dives into her boy's disguise. I stood on the coast of Illyria, mourning my brother's drowning, then wondering if perhaps, beyond hope, he was not truly dead, but saved, rescued, redeemed. Perhaps I would see him again! The thought seemed to fill me with golden light.

But as my practicing progressed—vain practicing, since I would never say these lines before any paying audience—I began to grow worried, and my voice faltered. Saint Saviour's bells had rung ten, and Nathan was not there.

I should have been relieved, but instead I felt anxious and sad.

It was not possible that he had forgotten our bargain. It must be, I thought, that he had spoken in cruel jest. That meant that I was not safe, that he was heartless enough to destroy my playing hopes with a word to Richard Burbage or one of the other masters, on the morrow, before the play began.

The bells rang half past the hour. I snuffed the torch, and now abandoned the part I'd been speaking and sat against one of the ash trees, hearing its leafy branches rustle high above the stage's thatched roof. Above me shone the stars and a crescent moon. He would not come. And why should he? Not only could I not properly play a boy, I could not properly play a girl. I was big and odd and blunt-featured and awkward and not fair enough even to be ravished, let alone loved.

"Viola?"

I started, then scrambled to my feet. I heard the rasp of flint, then saw the light of the candle he held aloft in his hand. I stood under the tree, breathing hard.

"Surprised, my lad?" he said. "I'faith, I feared *you* would slight our bargain."

I folded my arms and leaned back against the tree, trying to imitate his posture of that afternoon. "*I am honest*," I said.

He laughed. "I would not call it that. But 'tis good—you keep your word." He came toward me jauntily, wearing scuffed boots and woolen breeches and a fine cambric shirt that I was sure he had taken from the tiring-room. "*Come, thou day in night*," he said, grabbing my hand none too tenderly.

"You are no Romeo," I said, as he hurried me into the tiring-house.

"Romeo!" he laughed. "Nay. I am Juliet. That was her line."

WHEN it was over he sat up nakedly and lit a candle, while I curled in a ball and hid my eyes.

"There," he said, tossing a cloak on me. "I know you are trying to be modest."

I waited for him to take to his heels now that our business was done, half-expecting him to tell me he had an appointment at the Knavish Loon, where we never had shared the ale he'd promised. But he only sat and looked at me. He seemed to want to say something and, for once, not to know what.

Finally he came out with it. "You know Master Shakespeare's plays."

I burrowed into the cloak. "I have read them since I was a little girl," I said in a muffled voice.

After a moment he said, "He is a very great poet, but he does more harm than good in the playhouse, do you not think?"

I did think it, though my reasons were not all in all the same as his, and I felt something offended at the comment.

"What mean you?" I asked, looking at him squarely.

He rose and pulled on his breeches. "I mean he's a meddling tyrant who should give over the plays and then leave us alone. I tire of being told what to think while I play. I think what I think. He does not own the players, or even the plays; he only owns a piece of them." He sat down again on the floor. "What think you, sweet Viola?"

I was silent, less from shock or anger than from the surprise of his sharing these thoughts with me as though I were his equal. As though I were a fellow player. I said, " 'Meddling tyrant' is something strong. I think you should suffer him and then think what you think and play as you play. You'd not be who you are without him, you know. 'Tis not every London company has a William Shakespeare."

He nodded, his face thoughtful and open. "That's true enough. Yet he's not the only playwright in London. There's another, Ben Jonson, who's hot on his heels and some say as good."

I had heard of this man, even seen him in the Cardinal's Cap one night. He was a giant of a fellow with a loud, blustering voice and a table-pounding manner, as different from my gentle father as any man could be. I frowned. "He can't be as good," I said.

"He writes for an all-boys' company."

"Then play for *him*."

Nathan laughed. "What future for me there? Dost thou think I'll boy it much longer? I'm ripe for man's parts."

I felt I could not argue with this.

"And when I'm *full* ripe for those parts I'll be in straits, for all my fame. I'll have Burbage and Edward Alleyn of the Rose and a score of others to vie for parts with."

"You still lack a man's voice," I said.

"I lack it as long as I can. All of us do. Mark," he said, leaning to the side. He loosened a floorboard and reached into a hollow below it. Then he withdrew a tin, which he opened. Inside lay some dried, sweet-smelling herbs.

"Rue," I said.

"Aye. I know not what else it's good for, but we powder and boil and drink it before every play."

" 'We'?"

"The boys. Or the older ones, at any rate; me and Sander and John Rice. It keeps the voice sweet; staves off the mannish crack. For a few hours." He grimaced. "Shouldst drink it too, if you want to keep playing the part of Castor Poopworthy."

"*Pop*worthy."

"Why not call thyself John Smith? I'faith, I think you *want* to be caught."

I rested my head on my elbow. "Tell me. When your boy's voice goes, will you play no more for the Lord Chamberlain's Men?"

"They'd keep me. They're bound to me. But I would not play at center stage."

"Ah. And that's what matters."

He nodded. "It does," he said simply. "It matters to me. To keep doing it I'll need to start my own company, and I will."

I laughed. "Then you'll have to find a patron, and he'll lend you nothing but his name. You'll have to pay playwrights and buy costumes and rent playhouses. You've not got such money. No player does."

He looked at me straight, the hardness returning to his face. "I'm going to get it," he said.

"From where?"

"Mayhap you'll give it to me for keeping your secret."

I rose to my elbows. "Where would *I* get it?"

"Are you saying your family is poor?"

"I said nothing of that kind. I'm of better parentage than you are."

"Are you sure of that?" He gave a short, hard laugh.

I frowned. "What is your family, then?"

"Thinkst thou I'm the bastard son of some whore at the Cardinal's Cap?"

"Well, thou'rt a player."

"So art thou."

"You have me."

"I had you. I might have you again tomorrow night."

"Stop thy bawdy talk," I said. "I've paid your price. Your knavish ways show me you've no fine family to boast of."

At that he laughed loud and long. "Visit Saint Margaret's Church by the Guildhall any Sunday and you will find my fine father there, preaching against the stink and plague and sin of the playhouses. He's the pastor John Field, a passing famous

Puritan, you should know. His house was too godly for me before I was six. I ran to Southwark. So you see, I know something about running away."

I was amazed. "Why did he not pull you from the theaters?"

"He wants naught to do with me, nor I with him. I'faith, he won't even touch the money I earn, that's his by right, since ' 'tis tainted with playhouse sin.' I think he's jealous. I bring in bigger crowds than he does."

"So you're a player to spite him," I said slowly.

That angered him. "I'm a player for I'm a player," he said. "An actor." His voice cracked slightly on "actor," and I could see that embarrassed him, which made him angrier. "I'm the best player of women's parts you will see on the stages of London."

"I'll not argue," I said, wanting to tease him. "You are. But that does not mean you are good at it. You overplay."

He looked full angry now. "You know nothing," he said. "I've played a hundred parts. You come in from the country and think you can better the rest of us. You are just like—"

"I only think I can better *you*." I'faith, he irked me! "*I* know what it is to feel a maid's grief, and to lose—to lose—something. You only know how to go about winking and stealing and then get on a stage and *pretend* to feel grief and fear and—" I pulled the cloak closer around me. "And shame."

"Yes, I know how to do that!" He jumped to his feet. " 'Tis called acting!" He put on his shirt and pulled on his boots, then kicked my boys' clothes toward me. At the tiring-room door he turned and smirked. "I'll keep thy secret," he said. "I've nothing to fear from thee. A girl like thee knows how to lose something, yes—her maidenhead. Marry, I thank you for it! But girls can't act."

He shouldn't have said that.

I waited only long enough to hear the window scrape open and the thud of his boots on the ground below. Then I was up and dressed and scooping the tin box from under the loose board he'd shown me. I replaced the board carefully, and then I was out in the passage and following him through the window. I didn't know which way he had gone, but I knew my own course. I hurried down the bank to the river and into the stinking privies that stood at the Thames' edge, for the ease of the playgoers swarming from the Rose and the Swan and the Globe after afternoon performances. Holding my nose, I shook the box's contents down into the depths of one foul hole.

"Sweeten *that*, rue," I said to the falling herbs. Then I threw the box in after them, and limped, something sore, off to bed.

Chapter Eleven

The next day I had to walk hobbling to the washbasin.

This brought great guffaws from John Rice and a ribald jest about whether the wench I'd put to the squeak was as sore as I. I muttered that I hoped so but doubted it, at which he laughed some more and clapped me on the back so hard that I splashed my chest with cold water. 'Twas the friendliest gesture he'd made toward me since I got the part of Fabian, leaving him to be Second Sailor. Indeed, it gave me hope that we'd one day be friends, and clink tankards in the Knavish Loon after a day's performance. He'd lie to me about the lasses he'd laid low, and I'd lie to him about the virgins who'd died of love for me, and then we'd sing catches together and stagger out to collapse in muddy Maid Lane. There we'd be run over by a cart-horse, fulfilling my mother's dire prediction for the evil youth of London Town.

With this fantasy I entertained myself as I quickly finished my porridge among the noisy Condell clan, and then rose and walked to the playhouse. I was happy to find that with walking my soreness diminished and finally subsided to a distant pain. Otherwise I would have had to invent a cause for Fabian to limp and tell it to the audience, and I knew what my father thought of players who improvised their lines.

Besides soreness, something else plagued me, concerning the thing I had done. I placed no great value on my virginity, that was certain. But it occurred to me, as I walked down the bankside path, that I had allowed someone else to price my maidenhead for me, and had then agreed to the price.

For all my pride, I had sold my body like the whores at the Cardinal's Cap. They were paid with coin, while I was paid with a secret kept.

And a chance to be in the new play today.

It was worth it.

WORD of sweet Master Shakespeare's new comedy had already spread through London. When I came into the playhouse I sat quietly inside the recessed middle space, murmured my lines to myself, and avoided everyone's eye, as always. Then I began to listen to all the hubbub around me, while pretending to polish a shoe.

I'truth, I was more nervous than ever I'd been for the performing of *Julius Caesar,* even on that first afternoon, when all had seemed like a dream. An hour before the trumpet for the play's beginning, there were already folk jostling outside the Globe's doors, hoping for a fine gallery seat or the best place in the yard when the house opened. They had cheered for every man or boy who entered the tiring-house, including me. I had not been able to keep from bowing to them, and now I chided myself for my lack of dignity.

Chaos reigned before and behind me. Players' wives were stitching costumes and curtains, and boys were fighting for the mirror in the tiring-rooms, and Burbage, forever pounding or painting or sanding, was hammering a loose plank on the scaffold and muttering that there were never enough nails. I closed my eyes and sat still, saying every line in the play in my head, and marking my cues with my mind.

My memory is my best proof that I am my father's daughter.

Then Nathan entered, breeched and wigless and sheathing a sword as he debated with one of the masters. I could feel my pulse quicken and the blood come to my cheeks, but I would not directly look at him. I feared what he would say to me. I think I feared most of all that he would say nothing. And so I looked down, repeating Fabian's first line over and over to myself.

But I could hear Nathan. The master, John Lowin, was advising him how to bring off the dueling scene, the foolish fight between Viola and Sir Andrew. "Marry, don't draw on *I beseech you, what manner of man is he?*" Lowin scolded. "Throw your hands in the air. You are disguised as a boy, but you're not a boy, and you do not want to have this swordfight. You be quaking in your boots!"

"*I know* I be quaking," Field said, with his customary defiance. "But a girl who is scared does not spin her arms in the air like a windmill! I am Viola, and however scared I be, I don't flee from a challenge. I hide my fear. I bite my lip. I do what's expected of me, though I shake in the doing of it." I heard the sound of a sword being pulled from a scabbard. "So I draw. *So*." His last *So* shrilled through the theater, a mannish crack, an echoing squeak.

I looked up and saw Nathan standing frozen with his sword high. I saw that the whole house was staring just as I was.

My father, pale as a sheet, stood before the half-curtained inner stage. "No," he whispered. His was the only voice in the playhouse, and I heard it well. So did Nate, who turned to him in a sort of despair, looking more like a boy to me than he ever had.

"No!" my father said loudly, striding toward Nathan, hurling the play's prompt-book to the stage. "No!"

Dick Burbage ran to separate the two, fearing I don't know what violence, since both of them looked half-crazed. He sat my father down under one of the ash trees, and left him there staring up at the painted Zodiac and numbly repeating his "No! No! No!" Then Burbage ran Nathan through a few of the play's lines. Nathan's voice cracked on every one, until it became clear to Master Burbage and to everyone else that Nathan could not play the woman's part. His boying-girling days were over.

"Thou'rt a man, lad," Master Burbage said kindly, clapping him on the shoulder. Nathan looked completely and utterly miserable. "Thou'lt soon have a beard in. 'Tis not thy fault. It comes to us all."

"To half of us, my dearest," called his wife, who was repairing Robert Armin's cap and bells.

Ignoring her, Burbage knelt to talk to my father, who was now gazing Hellward, his head in his hands. I heard him say something about Nathan being sixteen and past old enough, and that it was nature's course. Then my father stopped him short by saying that was all to the good, but it didn't give us a Viola, did it, and that Will Kempe's curse seemed to be working. Then some other actors joined them and the voices all drowned one another.

I looked at Nathan, who had turned expressionless. He took off his sword belt and gently laid it on the floorboards, then walked off the stage.

I blinked back tears. I was furious at Nathan Field, but at that moment I pitied him too. I think that is why I wanted very much to run after him. And I might have done it, and risked his turning from me in anger or disgust. But there was something else I wanted more.

I stood and walked from the middle space onto the stage proper. For the first time since I'd been hired at the Globe, I went directly toward my father.

But at the last moment I quailed and veered toward Burbage instead.

"Master Burbage," I whispered, tugging his elbow.

He turned from the group. "Not now, Castor. We've a problem to solve."

"Please," I said. "Please you, sir. I know the lines."

At that my father looked up. On instinct I looked down, feigning shyness, and heard him sigh. I could almost hear his thought. *So fainthearted a lad could not carry this role.* But I could not dare to look him in the face.

My father spoke, his voice rough with worry. "You know Viola's lines, sirrah?"

I nodded, but kept looking at the floor. There was silence for a moment, and then he said wearily, "I'm sorry, boy. No." He rose, and told the others, "We'll give them another play."

A chorus of voices protested that the audience had come for a comedy; that they didn't want *Julius Caesar* or a history again, and *Twelfth Night* must go on. My father shook his head and went into the tiring-house.

I went quickly over to John Rice, who had listened to all of the conversation and was looking perplexed and disgruntled. "You know Fabian's lines, do you not?" I asked him.

"I *do*, friend," he said.

"Then come." The two of us went back to the group of masters huddled by the stage post, the group which now included Condell and Robert Armin and every one of the sharers, save my father. "Tell them," I muttered, prodding Rice.

"Masters, I can say Fabian's lines in my sleep."

"That is just what we fear, young Rice," Robert Armin said with a sad smile.

"Nay, I can speak them well enough, but Fabian's a small matter."

"Not as small a matter as you think," said Armin.

"But not as big a matter as Viola, and I *can* speak Viola,

whatever my—Master Shakespeare—may say," I broke in. "He's not heard me try it."

The men looked at each other, and then they looked at the boisterous crowd that was already beginning to spill into the yard, hooting and grinning and pennies-paid-up for a merry afternoon. Dick Burbage gave a nod. "Do it, then."

And I did. I turned to tall, thin Master John Saint Clair, cocked my head to the side, and pitched into Viola's first speech: *"There is a fair behavior in thee, Captain, and though that nature with a beauteous wall doth oft close in pollution, yet of thee I will believe thou hast a mind that suits with this, thy fair and outward character."*

I reached the end and looked expectantly at Saint Clair, who looked at Burbage, who looked at Lowin, who looked back at Saint Clair, who looked back at me and then said his captain's lines. That was exactly what I'd been hoping for him to do.

THEY made me be Viola to Dick Burbage's Orsino, and to Lowin's Sir Toby Belch. Then Sander Cooke strode over, be-wigged and bare-chested, and they all laughed to see such an indecent Olivia, but I ran through a mocking dialogue with him, too. In eighteen minutes' time they were all satisfied, which was a good thing, because the flag was up and the crowd was in and if the play did not start soon we'd all be pelted with rotten eggs.

"Wait here," Burbage told me. "Nay, wait not. Get thy

face painted quick, and put on women's weeds." And he went to seek my father.

I rushed into the small tiring-room. Nathan was there on a stool with his shirt off, consoling himself with a stoup of ale. He glared greenly at me as I reached for the paint pot and began to slather my face. "Come not near me," he said.

"Marry, then move aside. You do not own this tiring-room."

"I should have known not to trust a woman."

"*Hsst!*" I whispered, dabbing furiously.

"You stole my rue."

"I have no inkling what you may mean," I said, smiling sweetly at his face in the glass.

"You lying wench. Delilah."

At that I laughed outright. "I know my Bible, and you have it wrong. Delilah cut Samson's hair to rob his strength, but I cut my *own* hair, and it's only made me stronger."

I could see his face go red in the mirror. "You wanted to ruin me," he said, leaning toward me angrily. "I could have done the part with the herbs, but I couldn't find them."

"Your girl-playing days were numbered before you met me. You told me as much. Blame not me for your sorrows."

"Poxy *bitch!*"

"I be not poxy," I countered, as I outlined my eyes with kohl. "And if I am, 'tis you who has poxed me." That thought shook me a bit; it was a fear I hadn't thought on. But I could ill afford to dwell on it now.

"Would that I *had,*" he said. "But I'll do you one worse. I'll betray you, as you did me. I'll rip your shirt off in front of the masters. I'll show them what you are. I could do it right now."

"But you won't."

"Why won't I?"

I turned and faced him squarely. "Because you are an actor, and you know that the play must be played."

I had him with that. I knew enough of Nathan Field to know that the world could career off to Hell for all he cared, but the playhouse was a sacred thing, and he'd never destroy a play. He might steal one, but he'd not ruin one.

Robert Armin poked his head in the door, cap and bells jingling. "Orsino's started talking, Viola," he said. "*Music be the food of love,* and so on."

I doused Viola's gown and wig in a pail, dragged the gown over my head, and jammed on my wig. "Enough chat," I told Nathan. "I've a part to play." He looked as though he would cheerfully murder me.

I left the room swaggering boylike, whistling whilst I dripped.

HAD I not been so new to the trade I would have known about the boy with the bucket by the stage door, waiting there to splash me so I could enter as wet as a half-drowned Viola should. But I didn't know, and so I got surprised, and came on twice-soaked and looking, I'm sure, like a water rat. It gave the groundlings a reason to laugh heartily, which they'd been waiting to do anyway, thwarted as they were by Orsino's first speech, which is something melancholy. I gave the yardlings their guffaw, but it was not long before, drippy though I was, I had them in my hand feeling the sadness of my brother's sea-wreck and the dim hope that he might not be drowned after all. I could feel what they felt. I could see it in the eyes of the goodwives and the blacksmiths' apprentices and the farmers-in-London-for-the-day, and in the expressions of the rich fops who sat on the balcony, forgetting for once to toss their plumed hats so that all might look at them. No, they were looking at me. They were all looking at me.

And they were listening.

That was the wondrous part. Can anyone imagine being given the rapt ear of a thousand folk at once, when 'tis so rare in this life, when it comes time to speak your woes, to gain the listening of even one? And best of all, it was not only looking and listening the audience yielded me.

It was love.

I cannot claim the success was my doing. That credit belongs to another Shakespeare. I would have stood like a babbling ninny and had eggs thrown at my head had I not been given a gift. Words. My father's words.

They rolled off my tongue. There was measure and rhythm in all of it, so that when one fellow spoke and stopped another would *know* when to start—nay, would *be* started, as though carried on a wave. With Feste, with Olivia, with Orsino, my tongue went trippingly forward, and all went back and forth and high and higher as the wit bounced and climbed. We carried the audience with us, until I thought they might rise through the open roof and float off through the blue Southwark sky, and that I would float with them.

Such was his magic. Such was real magic.

In the time between my scenes I mopped my brow and hunched on a stool within the inner stage, watching the play proceed. Nathan was gone from the tiring-house, which bothered me, since I'd wanted him to see—nay, *hear*—that I could do what he'd said a girl couldn't. Yet my heart could not crack over it, so happy was I to be smiled at and patted on the shoulder by my fellows, who were more than middling pleased with my performance and thought me a hero of sorts.

I made a few mistakes. When, in my boy's disguise, I confided in Duke Orsino, something made me stumble on the line *My father had a daughter lov'd a man*, so that it came out something like *My father had a daughter was a man*. Burbage, as Orsino, raised an eyebrow, and from the corner of my eye I saw Henry Condell wince as he sat behind the curtain that hid the middle space, finger poised above the prompt-book. And when I came on to fight Sir Andrew my sword belt came loose and I tripped over the scabbard, falling right on my chin, which really hurt, and made me for a moment glad that Nathan was not there to see me fub the scene I'd mocked *his* acting in.

Yet the audience only laughed the more at both these botches, and I saw that clowning could sometimes be the sole remedy for a player's stumble. Nathan was right: there were things I didn't know.

I had full hit my stride as swaggering Viola, bantering with the jester Robert Armin. I had just said, *"I warrant thou art a merry fellow, and car'st for nothing!"* and Armin had replied, *"Not so, sir, I do care for something; but in my conscience, sir, I do not care for you!"* when behind Armin's belled head I saw my father.

He had taken over the prompt-book from Henry Condell, but he was not sitting on Condell's stool. Instead he had risen to his feet in the curtained middle space. The book was on the floor. His arms were folded and he was looking at me very closely indeed. His face did not look sad or melancholy or enigmatic or anything else of the kind.

It looked purple.

My mind went white. There was a long moment of silence, and I felt the sweat-beads popping on my forehead. Armin looked at me expectantly, then raised his eyebrows. He saw I was all at sea, and he began to sing a snatch of doggerel that somehow pulled out his jest, to give me time to remember, but I could think of nothing. I sweated, and my face-paint began to run down into my eyes, and it stung. I wanted to die. I wanted to sink through the trap into Hell.

And then I heard my father's whisper, low and measured. He said: *"Art not thou the lady Olivia's fool?"*

And I said it, and Armin answered, and I was saved, restored, redeemed from the shipwreck. We went on, and I was as good as I had been. For the rest of the play I would not look at anyone but my fellow players and the audience, or think of anything but the lines. By the play's end I had almost forgotten my father's purple face and what it was going to mean.

The last scene near undid me, because in it my brother was restored. Of course, my second malodorous roommate looked little like Hamnet and less like me, even as we stood hand in hand clad in identical sarcenet doublets and velvet trunks. But that mattered neither to the audience nor me. We were all moved. Again it was words that did it.

> *How have you made division of yourself?*
> *An apple, cleft in two, is not more twin*
> *Than these two creatures.*

We stared at each other, the boy and I, and then I made my last mistake, which haply no one noted. I could not forbear mouthing along with my twin the lines that only he was meant to say:

> *Were you a woman,*
> *I should my tears let fall upon your cheek,*
> *And say, "Thrice welcome, drownèd Viola!"*

A small error it was, which nothing hindered the audience from roaring for me and the rest of the players as we stood in our half-circle at play's end.

Then the spell was over.

I turned away from the crowd, clapped my cap back on my head, and slipped off the stage.

My father saw me, but my luck held in one thing. He had been waiting at the other stage exit, and that gave me a few precious seconds to walk apace through the tiring-house, fling wide the door to the outside, and tumble to the ground.

And then I was up and running.

Chapter Twelve

ALL the grace and power I'd owned as a child came back to my bones and sinews as I raced from the tiring-house down the green toward the river, past the trees and the boats and the stinking privies. I was a deer, a wild and full-hearted hart, bounding through the bracken and ash trees of the sacred Arden Forest. But it wasn't enough. My father was faster, and he caught me.

He spun me by the elbow at the muddy riverbank.

My cap fell to the ground. There was nothing to do but face him, and I did.

He shook me until I thought my head would bounce from my shoulders. He threatened to beat me to a bloody pulp, to break my legs, to throw me in the river and let the fish chew my bones. He cursed me with every curse I'd ever heard and some I am sure he invented, and those were the most fearsome of all. By the time he had tired of shaking and cursing, a small crowd had gathered and was watching us with great interest. No one tried to intervene. No doubt they thought me a cut-purse, and my punishment well deserved.

My father let me go and I staggered back, then forward, then against him. I grabbed him about the waist and hung there, and for the first time since I'd read Viola's part on our dusty Stratford floor, I cried.

Then my da waved the watchers away and sat me on the grass in his lap and rocked me. He rested his chin on the top of my head and made a strange sound. I recognized it from the long-ago time when I'd hid, rocking myself on the floor of the kitchen storeroom, just after Hamnet drowned and my father came home. My grandfather had held him and both of them had wept together. Like me, my father was crying.

At last I myself was done weeping.

My nose was running and I wiped it on his doublet. He wiped the smear with a rag, saying, "You are nothing ladylike, but I see it has been your aim not to be." Then he gave me the rag and told me to stop my own nose; that he wouldn't do that for me. He held my chin in his hand and looked at me hard. "You have grown like a dandelion and are almost a woman," he said.

I knew there was one person in Southwark who thought I already *was* a woman, but I would not speak of that. I said, "So I look like a weed. I thank you."

"You look like a terrible horror with your face a mess of snot and tears and greasepaint," he said. He shook his head. "I cannot credit it that I did not know you."

"It has been two years, Da," I said.

"It has not!" he cried. "How could it be!"

I stared at him. "Yes, it has. Even more. I last saw you at Lent in the first year I went to Coventry."

He looked at me in perplexity, rubbing his forehead. I could see that the anger had gone from him. He would not break my legs. This gladdened me.

"Well, come, my headstrong," he said after a moment, pulling me to my feet.

"Where will you take me?"

"I should take you yonder, to the Clink. Or would you prefer Bedlam? Another good place for you." He gestured vaguely westward, to the dark buildings beyond the trees. "No. We go to a tavern, to leave a letter. You yourself may guess who the letter is for."

I did not need to guess. "She will beat me," I said as we walked. "She will do all those things you threatened to do."

"Good," he said. "I can think of no lass who better deserves it. How long have you been gone from Stratford? Or is it Coventry?"

"Three weeks," I said, shamefacedly.

"JesuMary*Joseph*! And I knew nothing of it!"

"Then perhaps no one knows, if no one wrote."

"They wrote me, Judith. I tossed the letters in a drawer to read later. I had no time, with the Globe's opening and the two new plays. How did you get here? Where had you money?"

"I had some of my own, enough to ride in a carriage from Coventry to London."

"Where your aunt thought you were in Stratford, while your mother thought you were in Coventry."

"Yes," I said, looking down at the ground. "And when I arrived I found employment."

"Where?"

"I worked in the Cardinal's Cap."

"You *what*?!?" He stopped and spun me to face him, and for a moment I feared that we would begin the shaking and cursing all over again. "You *worked* in the *Cardinal's Cap*? Doing *what*, pray tell?"

"Porting ale! As a lad! And then Master Burbage hired me for small parts."

"JesuMaryJoseph."

We started off again. We had entered a lane crowded with folk, mostly pedestrians. These were Londoners of all ages who had come to the bankside seeking entertainment, bear-baits or cockfights or plays. Among them walked players from the Globe and even the Rose whom I had come to know by sight if not by name. Some of them hailed my father or nodded. One man asked jovially, "Thy son, Master Shakespeare?" and my father shook his head, sadly, I thought. None of them seemed to find us a strange pair.

"Do you see? They all think me a boy," I whispered.

"They see what they think they see," my father said. "Now, stop thy mouth."

. . .

We climbed the stair to his rooms in a house at the end of a quiet court.

He sat me down and I looked about me.

I remembered that in picturing this room, I'd thought that if I ever saw it it would reveal infinite secrets about my father and his London life; it would show me what he found here and why he lived here. For long years I'd thought that there must be a woman in London, some dark and quiet and mysterious beauty who was everything my mother wasn't, or who wasn't everything she was, and that here where he dwelt I might find her traces. Her handkerchief or her gloves would sit on a chair; a sonnet praising her splendor would lie half-finished on a writing desk, or perhaps her Orient perfume would rise from the pillow where she'd laid her head.

My mother believed intensely that she had a London rival. I knew this, as I knew most of what did or didn't happen between my parents, because I listened to stray comments, merry or mocking or bitter, that passed between my mother and my uncle Gilbert or aunt Joan. She was so sure my father loved someone in London that the image of a mistress had grown as real to me as my own father's image in the past two years.

But the room revealed nothing I didn't know of him already. Walls bare save for a map of England, pinned above a broad writing desk. A strongbox, through which my father now was riffling. Papers on the writing desk, the same cheap, scribbled-on stuff that he tossed about at home. Books, books, and more books, piled on shelves and on the floor. The Gospels. Plutarch's *Parallel Lives*. The poems of Ovid. *The Canterbury Tales*. A half-burnt candle.

Through a doorway, I had a glimpse of a straw pallet, barely big enough for one. Clothes strewn about, but no women's garments that I could see. If there was a woman, they didn't meet here. And while her existence was possible, I suppose, I found I no longer needed to believe in her as the cause of his being in London. After all, I'd played at the Globe.

"Father, did you think I was good?" I asked.

"Adequate," he said, breaking the seal on a letter he'd plucked from the strongbox. "Not as good as Nate Field. Yet the folk had paid to see a play."

That stung me into quiet.

After a minute or two the silence unnerved me, so I spoke again. "What's this?" I picked up a thick volume that sat open on the floor by his desk, something dog-eared and missing its dedication page, which looked to have been torn out.

He glanced up, then down again. "Montaigne."

"What's he?"

"He writes the story of his life."

"Why?"

"To instruct others by the light of his own experiences and his meditations on them."

"Ah!" I said. "What a good idea!"

He looked up. "Judy, do not speak. Cease trying to distract me from your crime."

" 'Crime'!" I said. "That's something harsh, Da." I looked to see if there was any spark of merriment in his eyes at all, but he kept them bland and fixed seriously on the letter before him. He was, after all, an actor.

"Are you not happy to see me safe and sound?" I asked.

"As I said, I did not dream you were otherwise. Had I tended to my messages I would have had an inkling. Read you this." He tossed me the letter.

It was my mother's words, in my aunt Joan's hand.

The letter was full of the expected outcries. My mother was sure I had been kidnapped and raped, and had my father had a letter asking for ransom? I handed the letter back to him, avoiding his eye.

"You did not finish it. It says that when your aunt wrote from Coventry asking when you were returning there, your mother spent a night seeking you in Arden Forest."

"Why there?" I asked, startled.

"You used to hide amongst the trees there, did you not? Ah, now, Judy, all the family knew *that*. You and Hamnet. But she only got scratched with brambles for her trouble. Then 'twas discovered from a farmer that you *had* gone to Coventry; he had ridden with you in the coach. Since none could trace you any farther than that, it was thought that you met with foul doings in Coventry. That whole town was alerted and seeking for you."

I looked down, my face burning with shame. That was not the sort of fame I had craved for myself. "I am sorry, Father," I said.

"You may make your apologies to your mother and your aunt. And to everyone else in the family who's been mad with worry and grief. As for me, I was busy with my *plays*."

I looked up at him. He was frowning deeply, gazing out the window into the court below. At least he was no longer frowning at me. I heard children dancing ring-around-the-rosy below, singing with clear voices, falling in the dust and laughing.

After a moment he turned to me, looking careworn and sad. "So. Thy mother will hear of thy safety within these two days, and after that we'll have thee home."

I swallowed. Home, meaning Stratford. I had known it would come to that, of course. My life in the theater was done.

"Tell me now what in the name of holy God you thought you were *doing!*"

"I . . . wanted to speak in one of your plays, sir."

He gazed at me as though he would bore through my eyes and into my brain. "Well, you did speak in two of them. Did you get what you wanted, then?"

I bit my lip.

"Marry, do not look so scared, Judy. I want to know whether you got what you wanted."

"I got—I didn't get—didn't get—*him*." New tears sprang to my eyes. I wasn't even sure which "him" I meant, but my father knew, or thought he did.

"Judith." He came and knelt by my side and hugged me again, most tenderly. "So you read *Twelfth Night,* and you thought of Hamnet, and you wanted to play a part in my play, to honor him."

"Yes," I sobbed. There was more to it, of course. Or more had come into it. But I couldn't begin to explain. "I was dusting thy papers." I sniffled piteously. "I read a foul-paper scroll you left at New Place."

"Ah. That will explain it."

"And I wished to say the lines. I only wished to say the lines."

"Viola's lines?"

"I think so."

"That is odd." He laughed. "I thought of you more as Olivia. But all's one. Judy, someone will pirate the play, or more like the men will sell it to be printed. Whatever I say on the matter, it will be printed before two years are out. You could have read all the lines to yourself in Stratford, and said them anywhere."

"I wanted to say them on the stage."

"And you did, moon-mad. You did something past dreaming of. Are you happy?"

"No."

"Nor am I. It is one of the saddest plays I have ever written."

I looked at him, blinking and wiping my nose with the sodden rag. "Ah," I said. "I am so much worse than anyone thinks. He is *dead* because of me."

"Never say that, Judith," he said. "He is dead because he played a game with you and drowned by accident. You must stop thinking *you* did it. You are not as important as you think."

I felt words clawing to get out of me. "Yet I cast that spell and prayed that you would come home, and then you *did* come home, and so—"

"What, now?" He cupped my chin in his hand.

"Yes, I made a spell, as from—the fairies, and we played Oberon and Titania, and . . ."

"A spell to bring *me* home?"

I looked at his eyes, which had gone wide. "Did not our mother tell you that?"

"Nay." He rose and went to the window, looking down at the dancing children, or at nothing. "Nay," he said softly. "She spared me that much."

OVER the hours we talked he asked me why I would bother to believe in such a fool divinity as Hecate the moon goddess. When I told him the moon seemed powerful enough in *A Midsummer Night's Dream,* he asked me whether I was not well schooled enough to know the difference between real life and a play. I said that sometimes it was hard to tell any difference, and then he told me that in truth, I was right, but that a belief in Hecate wasn't useful in my case, and I should follow his track and only believe in what was useful, and only for as long as it was. I told him I didn't really think I believed in sprites or fairies or moon goddesses, but that they sometimes seemed closer than Christ or Mary or God himself, and he said, "Hush."

He fell now into spells of brooding silence, broken by muttering. "Her mother told me of her melancholy," I heard him murmur, as though I were not there. "Two years! I have taken too little care of this."

He kept me in my boys' clothes when he took me to sup at a citizens' ordinary in the next lane. All in all, he said, it was better to be a lad than a lass in those places. But he rushed me out as soon as I'd finished my barley stew and custard in a pastry coffin, and marched me back to the Globe's tiring-house, where he borrowed a maid's smock and kirtle and cap, and a woman's nightgown. He made me put on the kirtle and cap and smock in one of the tiring-rooms, while he stood guard untrustingly by the door. He meant not to protect me from being burst in on, I knew, but to protect himself from another mad escape on my part.

When I came out in my women's clothes he said, "There's my girl back again," and hugged me so I thought my bones would crack. I said, "Hold! Thou wouldst not crush a maid so frail." Then we both began to laugh, and could not stop laughing all the way back to Paradise Court, where he dwelt. I told him how close he'd come to spying me out on the day of the Globe's first opening, when our paths nearly crossed by the door as he walked along muttering to himself like a madman just fled Bedlam.

"I thought you looked at me strangely," I said.

"I thought you the ghost of Hamnet!"

That set me going again, and I thought how odd it was that the hearing of Hamnet's name should make me laugh, when for years it had made me want to drown myself in my own salt tears.

Chapter Thirteen

SAINT Saviour's bell had tolled midnight. My father and I were trading bloody tales of murder and revenge that we'd read in the ha'-penny broadsheets when a hard knock came on the door. My father called out that it was unlocked, a piece of information I thought it unwise to share at that hour, but as it turned out we had nothing to fear from the three fellows who tumbled in.

One was only a blear-eyed boy, some ten years of age, whom I'd seen before rough-and-tumbling it and making all manner of mischief on the Stratford streets. He came in on the heels of his father, a family friend come to London money-borrowing, to keep his wine business afloat. My father was to lend him ten pounds. The third fellow was a stripling youth with a small tuft of auburn beard, a belted sword, and a theatrical stare. He wore a dark woolen cape that looked too hot for June, but which billowed behind him impressively. He was my uncle Edmund Shakespeare, much impressed with himself and the message he had come to convey.

"Dire news, brother mine," he said, striding to the center of the room, gesturing widely as he talked. "Thy frantic wife hath sent me hither—" He stopped short, staring at me where I sat on the floor hugging my knees in my borrowed nightgown. "What is that?" he asked suspiciously.

"What do you think it be?" replied my father. "Greetings, good Edmund. Greetings, good Richard Quiney. And you, young Tom." I thought perhaps my father meant that young Tom was *not* good.

"I think it be Judith," my uncle said, looking, like a pricked pig's bladder, something deflated. "Marry, thou hast anticipated my dark endeavor. For I had come to report her defection!"

"Ha!" laughed my father, fetching cushions for the three to sit on. "There is little enough to eat here, and I am sorry for it, you Quineys, but not sorry for Ned, who has stuffed himself with words in advance of this visit. Let us have more of them, Ned! 'Tis good to hear thee."

Ned still stood in the middle of the room, looking baffled. "What has become of her hair?" he asked.

"Marry, will you not ask her? She's not a mute," said my father. "She is very far from being a mute."

"Judy?" Edmund said.

"You may tell my uncle what's become of my hair," I said to my father.

"She chopped it off in mourning."

"Nay, nay, sir!" I said, jumping up. "Will you not tell the truth of it?"

"Is that not the truth of it?"

I turned to Edmund. Behind him sat the Quineys, an expectant audience. I saw that Edmund had planned to be the main speaker, and was not happy to cede the part to me. But he was curious, too, so he listened. "I will tell you all, though you will little credit it," I said. "I have boyed it on the stage of my father's Globe!"

Edmund's jaw dropped, and a light flared briefly in his eyes. I could have sworn it was a light of jealousy.

My father raised his hands. "I did not know of it, Ned. Not until today. Be sure you tell *her* that."

I looked at him. "What mean you, that he should tell her that? Have you not written her yourself?"

"That's true, I have. But she will bear with reminding."

"Then *you* must remind her, Will," Edmund said, sinking to the floor with the Quineys. "For I'll not go back to Stratford."

The Quineys' gaze shifted to him, as did my father's, and I looked at Edmund a little angrily. He had diverted attention from me, and I had scarce begun my tale.

"What mean you by this?" asked my father. "Art thou come south to be a soldier? To frighten the Spanish with thy snappish sword, which please take off, and thy grand, gorgeous cape?"

"Nay, nay," Edmund said indifferently, picking at a rind of cheese which stood on a plate at his elbow. "I come to be a player."

"Ah, no, lad," said my father. "No. Jesus God, the whole house of Shakespeare is crashing down on me in London! Thou'lt have to go back, and take Jude with thee."

Edmund pulled out a knife and stabbed the cheese. "Nay."

IN the end I did tell my tale to Edmund and the Quineys. Probably the truest version, too, since it was fresh in my head. I could still hear the cheers of the audience ringing in my ears and run my hands through my stubbly hair, and feel like a Lord Chamberlain's boy indeed.

Edmund could not be persuaded to leave Southwark, despite my father's pleas. When two days later I left London in a coach with the Quineys, he was standing by my father's side waving good cheer, his big cape flapping in the breeze. My father had put him in charge of the tires at the Globe. Though caring for robes and hats and shoes was not what he had thought to do in the playhouse, he bore with it for the nonce, dreaming and plotting that he would one day stun the world as a player. I wished him the best, for he was a kindred spirit.

Two days of rain hindered playing, which was well for my father's company, who had lost two Violas—one grown into a man, and one simply vanished. They groaned and swore, and had to scurry to rehearse something else—a revival of a history, *Henry the Fifth*—until another boy could be trained. All this I heard from my father, for he kept me locked in the house, safe under the Quineys' eyes or his own, until the hour of our coach's leaving.

I would not say he trusted me overmuch.

So my last glimpse of Southwark was a grey and fleeting one. I boarded a carriage in front of an inn with my linen cap pulled down past my ears, this time not to hide my being a girl, but to hide my still seeming a boy.

My father gave me his copy of Montaigne's *Essais*, saying he could find another in the bookstalls of Paul's Yard. He added a few other books to my traveling bag, telling me to read them in Stratford, if not in the carriage. "No more romances," he said. "Your mind is better than the stuff you feed it with."

"I read your plays."

"Do not. 'Tis not by my will they're in print. They are only poor mirrorings of what I read, and what I see." He paused, reflecting. "And what I endure."

"Poor mirrorings! Da, come home with us now. We could speak more of plays." I knew what his answer would be, but I had to ask it.

"Nay, Judith." He shook his head, looking pained. "I'll come anon, later in the year. As it is you have cost me two days of writing."

"And a son." It slipped out.

His face darkened further. "Will you not have done with that?" he asked. "You feel shame at the wrong things."

"And what should I feel shame at, if not for Hamnet?"

"For this," he said. "For all this. Hamnet's death was an accident. But this you did by design."

I knew he did not mean my cutting my hair or dressing as a boy or porting ale at the Cardinal's Cap, or even displaying a breeched leg on the Southwark stage. I knew the shame he meant was the worry and grief I had caused my family.

And it *was* a shame, a face-burning shame. I hung my head.

Then he kissed the top of it. "All's well that ends well, Jude."

I thought that while that might be true, all had not ended yet. But I said only, "Pardon."

"God pardons all."

"But dost thou?"

"I told you, I was never offended, except for thy mother's sake."

"I am sorry."

"Tell *her* of thy sorrow."

On the journey home my heart was lighter than you might think, considering what awaited me—namely a furious mother with a hard hand, and a Puritanical town that held out no invitation to me to declaim poetry on any wide wooden stage. In the coach, the Quineys kept me merry by making me retell my story over and over, and ten-year-old Tom seemed to think me an outright goddess, to judge by his goggle-eyed stare.

When we stopped in Oxford the cramped coach became full to bursting, and lively with other conversations, and I looked out at the churches and colleges feeling as though it were a hundred years since I'd passed them before, and not a mere four weeks. Nay, not even four. I felt I had dreamed what I'd done. But I knew I hadn't. My memories of the Globe were clearer than any dream could be.

I was sorry to have been caught. Yet all in all I realized the thing could not have come out better, which is not to say that it came out well, only that things could have gone much worse. Surely Nathan Field was angry enough to have spilled my secret after the play was done. I could well believe he might have returned from whatever alehouse he was pouting in to pull the shirt from my back in the tiring-room, out of jealousy and rage and the thought that he had nothing more to lose with the Lord Chamberlain's Men. He might even have bragged that he'd had me! My father's discovering me had saved me from that. And now that I was gone into thin air, mayhap Nathan would hold his tongue.

Oh God, let Nathan hold his tongue, I prayed.

I had the fleeting thought that had I rested content with small parts like Lucius and Fabian, I might have gone on much longer as a boy. But then I remembered the hazards. There was Edmund, who would have told my father of my flight, and who had seen my face less than one month before, not two years in the past. With Edmund and my father hunting me down, my game would have been up in a trice.

And until I was caught, I might have had to lie with young Master Field every night to ensure his keeping my secret. That might not have been an utterly loathsome thing, but still, there was the danger of his getting me with child, if he hadn't already, or poxing me, if he hadn't done that, too. I shivered mightily at the thought of all the harms that son-of-a-preacher had exposed me to.

Delilah, indeed.

Would Nate Field talk? I hoped not. I thought not. I would not be there for him to hurt, so what gain? And besides, who would believe him?

My father would keep the secret. He had made it plain to me, and to Edmund and to the Quineys as well, that he'd no plan to share the news that young Castor Popworthy, player of many parts, had been his daughter. He advised us to hide it as well, although I could not bring myself to keep quiet. It was too good a story, and as for young Tom Quiney, we were not two days in Stratford before he'd told every boy in the town.

But in London, only my father and his brother Edmund knew. To the Lord Chamberlain's Men I became the skillful lad who vanished, who melted into the street parade, who turned Puritan and felt such shame to have once worn a lady's gown on the stage that he'd fled to be ship's boy on one of Sir Walter Raleigh's New World voyages. Sadly, the brave bark had met with a storm, all hands down, poor Castor lost, and those are pearls that were his eyes.

It was my father who spun that last tale. I know because when he bade me good-bye in Southwark he hinted at stories he would tell to cover my absence, or Castor's absence, as I should say. And that was like him. But then he said a thing more odd. That was:

"Judy, Judy. I believe you may be my daughter after all."

Chapter Fourteen

OUR carriage left us in late afternoon at the Bear Tavern, where some of the townsmen were idling up the pathway for a tankard or two before supper. It was full summer in Stratford now, the ash trees thick and green-leaved, and the swans drifting dreamlike on the Avon. As I stretched my cramped legs I looked from the river to the tavern. I had always looked upon the Bear as a haunt for local scofflaws, the type of folk who would rather be fined a sixpence than attend a Sunday service. As, in truth, would I, had I sixpence to spare. But as I glanced through its windows I could only think how tame and safe and regular the patrons looked, compared with the folk I'd met in Southwark.

Of course, that did not mean I thought Stratford itself was safe. I knew it was a place where the worst things in the world could happen.

Bearing that in mind, I squared my shoulders and let myself be escorted homeward by the Quineys, young Tom hopping madly all the way and saying, "Let me hear thee tell thy sister the story, Judith!"

"She knows it full well already. My father wrote to them." He kept up his chatter, but I paid him no more mind than I would a fly.

We passed the greengrocery owned by my godfather, Hamnet Sadler, he who had lent his name to my poor brother. "Good *evening*, Master Quiney, and young Tom, and Judith," Sadler said, as he fixed lettuces in a bin. "So you were visiting your father in London? Something of a mix-up, something of a confusion?"

"Something of that, Master Sadler," I said, not slowing my pace. "Good evening to thee, and thy wife."

New Place loomed. The Quineys walked with me to the gate of it. There Master Quiney said knowingly, "We'll leave you to your mother now, mistress." Then he pulled his disappointed son down the street to their supper.

My mother was sitting in a chair by the window, looking out at her garden. The sight of that garden warmed me even in my grim fright. I'd never fully noted its loveliness. Today I saw banks of flowering bushes and climbing roses, red and white and yellow; and pink carnations and purple columbine and marigolds and pansies. At the garden's bottom stood the trees of the arbor, plum and apple and pear, their branches pleached and interwoven and waving in the breeze. Among them grew a stray ash, its seed blown in on the wind.

"The lilies came in well this year," my mother said softly.

"You are a master gardener, Mama."

She turned slowly and looked, not at me, but behind me, at the still-open door. "He is not with you, then," she said after a moment. Her voice was heavy with old disappointments.

It occurred to me that I was not her sole preoccupation.

She looked at me then, and her face cleared a little. Indeed, she did not look half as careworn and haggard as I'd expected her to, considering the worries I'd brought her. Nor can I truly say she seemed sad. Something resigned, I would say of her expression that day. No doubt my father could have found a better word. But, of course, he wasn't there.

"Come, Judith," she said. Now she frowned. "Let me see thy hair."

I knelt by her chair and let her unlace my bonnet. She brushed the stiff bristles with her hand. "The townsfolk will think my children have lice."

"Susanna will not like that." The thought heartened me.

"Nor will I, my darling."

I felt my face crumple in a sob. "I did not mean to cause you worry, madam."

"Be not foolish, Judith. You knew you would worry me, and worry me near to death."

"Yes, but I did not mean to."

"You did not mean *not* to, which is as bad."

"Is it?" I asked, sniffling.

"For me, yes."

I sat and pondered that statement for a moment, and began to see her point. I laid my shorn head on her lap. "Please tell me if you are going to beat me, and with what kind of stick, and for how long a time," I said.

"What good would it do you to know that?"

"It would calm my imaginings."

"The truth might be worse than your imaginings."

"I do not think so."

My mother sighed impatiently, and put her hand under my chin. "Look up, Judith. Thou'rt not a child. Get thee a stool."

I did, and sat beside her.

"I will not beat you, girl. What you did was not mere waywardness. It was something nearer to madness, and it would be cruel to beat you for that."

"Oh, Mother, I am strange, but not mad," I said.

"Thou'rt like thy father, then."

"Aye, like him."

"Hmmm. And so you will steal back to London when you next get a chance, and find some way of living in the shadow of the theaters, and so I will have lost three of you to play-acting."

"Three?"

"Thy father, and Hamnet, and thee."

"Ah."

It was the woman in me, not the child, who, despite her impatience, came and sat on her lap then, though I hadn't done it for years. I kissed the top of her head, so grateful and full of pity for her that I could hardly speak. When I could I said, "Fear me not. I do not need to go back there."

"And why not? Warwickshire's dull enough for one who's been to London. Don't think I don't know it."

"Yes, London is wild and full of life. And I only saw a smidgen of the whole. But for a girl . . ."

I was quiet for a moment, thinking of the women I'd seen in London: the scullery maids and the ten-penny whores of the Cardinal's Cap, the coarsely clad sellers of oysters and hazelnuts on the bankside. And the players' wives. Red-faced Mistress Condell, racing about a table to serve mutton stew to a husband, five jostling children, and two loud, hungry youths, in addition to me. Dick Burbage's pretty wife, stitching costumes on the side of the stage, calling out witty jests that her husband ignored.

" 'Tis a wondrous place for man or boy," I told my mother. "But it affords little scope for a woman."

She nodded as though she had concluded that long ago. "Well," she said. "So you begin to admit that you are one."

"A woman?" I blushed. "I suppose I must be, perforce."

"Then be one where you can do it most freely."

I looked at her closely. "You have never been to London."

"Dost think I do not know that?" she said impatiently. "Now, off of my lap. Thou'rt too big."

I slid to the floor, where I sat sprawling and still a little pink at the thought of myself as a woman. My mother shook her head at me. "Thou'lt have to unlearn some habits now, daughter." I crossed my legs, and she scrutinized me. "What *did* you do in Southwark?" Her frown had returned.

I knew exactly what she meant, but I was not idiot enough to tell her.

"I cavorted on a stage, a girl playing a boy playing a girl playing a boy," I said. "I fooled everyone, until my father looked close at me."

She nodded, still looking sharply at me. I don't think she believed I was telling the whole truth, but at length she let it rest. "I hope I may not find out differently in months to come," she said.

I hoped so, too.

So I was greatly relieved when in two weeks' time I got evidence that I would not be giving birth to the bastard child of a player; nor had any signs of the pox appeared on my skin. As for my mother, I think it was four months before she stopped scrutinizing my belly as I made my way to and fro around the house and garden. She kept me in Stratford, and busy enough, though that was not wholly her choice. My Coventry aunt, who now knew of my flight and return—though not the interesting details—had decided she had trouble enough with her own brood, and could no longer risk housing me.

I was not, it seemed, a desirable model for the younger girls.

My sister, Susanna, spent even more time ignoring me now than she had done before. She seemed to think I was stark mad, and to be embarrassed by the stories of my wild doings in London which were soon enlivening the town. Those tales spread thanks not only to little saucer-eyed Tom Quiney, but to me. For when the bright-eyed Stratford maids and youths questioned me about my doings, I discovered I enjoyed the celebrity. I cast the tale wider and higher as the days and weeks went by, in marketplace conversations and in the yard of Holy Trinity Church, where I'd stand after Sunday service, surrounded by a gaggle of young folk.

When my mother wasn't looking I would tip up my hat to show my short locks, which were growing out thicker and healthier than ever they'd been before. I would tell how I'd scaled the iron bars of London Bridge's great gate at midnight, toppling three skulls from their pikes, and then raced to the river's northern bank, with the lord mayor's guardsmen in hot pursuit. I told how I'd worked in the Cardinal's Cap and one night had served ale to the queen's advisors, Sir Walter Raleigh and Sir Francis Bacon. And how the two of them had sat me down for a tankard and asked me whom I favored for the succession, nodding sagely as I said that King James of Scotland was surely the man. I described the Globe, and said that on my first afternoon in the playhouse a groundling had flung a dead cat at the clown Will Kempe's head, not liking his performance as Cinna the Poet in *Julius Caesar*. I claimed I had caught it by the tail just before it hit, and cast it sky-high to the balcony, where it bounced off the feathered cap of a perfumed lord and was seized by Sander Cooke, who was playing Calpurnia. Some of this was true, and some of it wasn't.

But all of it might have been.

Whether they believed them or not, everyone seemed to like my tales, and I found I had more friends in Stratford than ever I'd had—though of course I had not had very many before. I stopped stooping and walked with a straight posture, as I'd had to do on the stage, and gone was my trait of nervously pushing my hair behind my ears—at first because I no longer had hair to push, and later, when I did, because I had lost the habit. I looked folk in the eye now, smiling, or bold and belligerent if they seemed to have their noses up too high, although few in town would snub a Shakespeare nowadays.

All in all I queened it in Stratford. But it was not chiefly pride in my outlandish accomplishments that spurred me to behave so, even walking with my head uncovered into Trinity Church the first Sunday after my return, despite Susanna's shame. It was this: what I had lately done went so far beyond the pale limiting a good young woman's behavior that I could see nothing else to do but brazen it out. Else I must enter a nunnery, and though my hair was short enough for that, there were no nunneries in England anymore.

My mother made me work in the New Place garden, pulling weeds and lifting rocks and trimming branches, wearing thick gloves made by my grandfather in the Woolery. It was men's work, I complained, which only made her laugh. She did not, after all, mind so much what the townsfolk thought of me. Save for Aunt Joan, she was the only woman in the family who understood that if my choice was either to flaunt what I'd done or to creep about with my head down in shame, I should flaunt.

It seemed as though it were a wisdom she'd owned for some time.

Not long after my return, I was watching from a window above when a neighbor came and rapped on our door. I heard her in the parlor below telling my mother that I must stand in a white sheet in church and confess my wrongdoing. My mother said, "But what be her sin, Good Mistress Botts?" as though the suggestion came as a great surprise. Mistress Botts said, "Dishonor to father and mother, for one thing, Mistress Shakespeare," and my mother replied, "My husband and I may judge if we be dishonored."

"Well, then," our neighbor stammered, "she has dressed as a boy, and it says in Deuteronomy—"

At that my mother saw her to the door and slammed it behind her, snorting that all of Stratford would be white-sheeted in the sanctuary if the Bible were read with such a magnifying glass, and none left in the pews to cast shame on them.

So life in the parish turned out to be better than I'd expected when I rattled home in the carriage from London, the fear of my mother's wrath growing as each turn of the wheels brought me closer to her. Now I saw her more clearly than before, and she and I were friends. I spent much time with her and Aunt Joan and Gilbert, the three of whom still preferred each other's company to anyone else's, and with Gilbert I helped along my mother's slow progress in reading, which she meant to be an utter surprise to my father one day.

And I read, too. I visited the Stratford bookstalls whenever

I could, and there I found North's translation of Plutarch's *Parallel Lives* that I'd seen in my father's rooms; and even Plato's dialogues, put in Latin, which I'd also seen there. I worked in the garden, and I read in the garden, and I thought.

True to what I had told my mother, I did not long to return to busy London, or anyway not overmuch. Still, I cannot say I was altogether content in Stratford, despite the fact that my life was sunnier and contained more conversations and smiling faces than it had since I was very small. There were still times when I was cast low and haunted by sadness and questions and longings. Some of the longings were old ones, and some of them were newer, and some of them I could not even name. There were late-summer days when I spent whole afternoons by the bank of the river, hidden in the rushes, staring at the water, trying to dream myself into another time and place. At times I struggled to remember his face, and at other times to forget it.

My grandfather died, and my father came home.

He stood in the snow by the deep grave, bareheaded and balding, looking as miserable as ever I'd seen him. He was thinner than he'd been the year before, and not as hale; there were signs of sleeplessness below his eyes.

I knew from his letters that the Globe's successes continued. Since they had booted the clown Will Kempe and then lost their best boy—which was not, in their consideration, me, but Nathan Field—they had moved toward the staging of tragedies, which had fewer women's parts than did comedies, and which therefore required fewer boys. My father's last letter had also remarked, in a tone which I thought middling gleeful, that with tragedies they could hurt the business of their great rivals, the Admiral's Men, who had long specialized in death and bloodshed on the boards of the nearby Rose Theater.

Now at the churchyard, he looked to have taken on a tragic look reflecting the plays he was writing. Or perhaps it was not the plays at all that made his mouth sag, but the sight of the box in the pit that held the man who had cradled him in his infancy. Or maybe it was the older, smaller grave that bore our name, and stood hard by the new one.

After the pastor spoke, my father slowly walked my frail grandmother to the carriage which would take her home. She mounted with two of my uncles, and then he walked home with us.

"I am the middle one," he said as we left the churchyard. "Alone in the middle." He laughed shortly and sadly. "Left with the questions I never asked him."

"Grandfer?" I said hesitantly, not wanting to mention the other name.

"He. Would that he would come from the grave now, to give me more of his country thoughts! And to tell me what lies beyond."

"What should lie beyond?" my mother said. "May angels sing him to his rest."

"Aye, may they do so," my father said. "I hope."

"Don't fear on that score, Will," she said. "Thy father was a good Christian."

"Who had not seen the inside of a church in twenty years."

"That matters not," said Joan, who had chosen to come with us. "Our da was a good man, and no papist. He needed no confession to put him in a state of grace."

My father didn't answer, and my mother seemed to think they had comforted him, but I thought, stealing a glance at him, that he was comforting himself in the best way he knew how.

He was plotting a play.

We turned the corner into Henley Street. My father stopped in front of the old house, gazing at the Woolery, where years of his life had been spent, him cutting and stitching and stumbling about bearing piles of skins half as high as he was. He was blinking very quickly. My father owned the Woolery now, as well as the rest of the house, but I was sure he would give the running of it to Uncle Gilbert, who had worked there for years and who managed the apprentices.

Gilbert came out of the house, thick-waisted, blear-eyed, and sad. "There are neighbors within," he said. Susanna and Joan and my mother moved toward the door, talking, but my father stayed behind, still looking at the window of the glove shop. I glanced back at him.

"A coat of arms I bought him," I heard him tell Gilbert. "A motto. *Non sans droict.* I made him a gentleman. It was what he wanted."

"It was what you wanted," Gilbert said. "And now you're the gentleman. Master Shakespeare, of the Warwickshire gentry. The last in the line."

I thought it impossibly cruel.

.　　.　　.

THOUGH my father said nothing then, perhaps those words caused what happened between him and Gilbert later that day, in the snowy yard, by the woodpile, when most of the guests had gone home and the sun was setting.

I was in the kitchen. I heard some talk, with voices raised, and then the crack of bone on bone and the slam of the front door, and then I saw my father on his way up the stairs, his face set and angry. I looked out the window, and there was Gilbert sitting in the snow, his nose a red grog-blossom spouting blood. He had clapped a glove to it and was trying to laugh.

My father said little more to my mother that afternoon, and spent that evening with his own mother in Henley Street, while our family returned to New Place.

The next day my father was back for his clothes, and soon after, he left us, riding a rented nag south. I stood before New Place and watched him grow smaller and smaller until he and his horse were swallowed by road. I knew that he carried his grief with him like an ink he'd swallowed. It pooled inside him, and it would spill forth through his hands, in poetry that would drown the stage. I knew how it would go.

But my mother only thought him cold.

That night I went back to the Henley Street house, where I was born. I read to my grandmother from the Book of Lamentations. When she was asleep I went down the stairs and sat in my grandfather's workshop. I saw and smelled the scraps of cheveril and leather and the uncut animal skins. I touched the flat table and its cutting instruments. Then I closed my eyes and did not need to conjure Grandfer; he was just there, with his cackling laugh and his hunched-over shuffle and his smell of hard cider and pipeweed.

But when I opened my eyes he was gone.

"Your son would like to see you again, Grandfer," I whispered to the air. "So would I."

THROUGHOUT that winter and into the spring my mother kept me busy, training me in the ways of household management. For her this now included the buying and selling of land and corn and wool. Unlettered though she was, my mother had become as shrewd in business as my grandfather had been, and as my father, in his Londonish way, was as well. Sadly, I was not good at the accounts she taught me to keep, nor skillful at the cookery she loved so well.

At fifteen years of age, I had an unmistakable bosom, and even some noticeable hips. I was used to being looked at, first for being William Shakespeare's daughter, and next for being the wild maid who had run off to London and trod the stage boards as a boy. Lately, though, I sensed I was looked at by some just for being a fresh-faced girl. If none came close, I saw no harm in that, and kept at my reading and gardening. I was passing good at gardening.

.   .   .

ON Saturdays in April, Gilbert, our jack-of-all-trades, helped me in the garden, showing me how to graft flower shoots and tap fruit trees and mend their broken limbs. I asked him where he had learned it all, and he said, "About," which was what he always said when asked where he'd learned this or that.

"Thy father is good at writing about all of this," he said one day as we planted. "Of binding up apricocks and trimming the sprays. But he does not do it."

"And why should he, Uncle?" I answered with some heat.

"Why, indeed? He has me to plant his seed for him."

I finished the rows of peas, pushing them deep in the earth. Then I dusted my hands on my smock and stood up and went inside. I passed Susanna embroidering cushions and chattering with a friend in the parlor. I mounted the stairs to my mother's bedroom, where she was folding clothes and stowing them in a trunk.

"Madam," I said.

"Ah, 'tis a formal question." She smiled.

"Is Gilbert my father?"

She caught her breath. "No."

I sat on her wide, heavy bed and looked at the headboard. Adam and Eve in the Garden, carved into the heavy oak. The serpent between them on the tree.

She had stopped what she was doing, and now looked at me. "I thought you would ask me one day. Susanna did."

"Did she?" I asked, surprised. "She spoke not to me."

"You speak little enough to her."

I was silent at that. My mother resumed folding, still looking at me. "Is that what he thinks?"

"Uncle Gilbert?"

"Nay!" she laughed. "Thy father."

I stretched on her bed and stared at the thatch. "I know not what he thinks. I think he knows not what to think."

After a minute she stopped folding, and said, "Judith, thou art young for understanding. But I will tell thee this. Thy father hath reasons of his own to lodge in London. But by thinking himself wronged by me at home, he can stay there with a clearer conscience. His fancy is his fancy, and my life is my life."

I rose and went to the window. In the garden my bent uncle was throwing weeds into a basket. I thought of the times I'd visited Hamnet's grave, only to find a fresh lily or some columbine laid on it. My uncle's gift.

I turned to my mother. "And my uncle?" I asked. "Does he think it possible?"

Her lips grew tight. After a moment she said, "That is not a thing for you to ask me."

"You are my mother. I do not want to judge you. I only want to know why Gilbert hates him."

"It is not hate."

"What, then?"

"Daughter—" She sat with a folded shirt in her lap. "Can you see so much, and see no more? Thy father has everything. Wife, children, land, money, houses, and friends."

"Most of that he got with his wits."

"Yes, and even wit is a gift, is it not? Or a loan, I might say, since folk have been known to lose it in the end."

I was quiet. I had not thought of the matter that way. Then I said, defending, "Uncle Gilbert has the Woolery now."

"Yes, by his elder brother's sufferance. It stings Gilbert. So. If thine uncle can have one thing that thy father can't, or can make thy father think he doth, is he much to be blamed?"

"I know not, Ma." I walked to the door, but paused there, running my hand down the doorjamb. "I know not. It seems middling foolish, like boys at school. At any rate, I do not see what *you* gain from their rivalry."

She smiled. "Once it flattered my vanity. I am past that now. Now I'm not part of it at all. I think about this household, and my gossips, and you and Susanna. Sometimes a woman must make her life apart from what men do, or alongside it. Do you understand?"

"Since my brother died, I have never thought anything else," I said.

Chapter Fifteen

AND so there were family and books and friends and work. And festivals, though there were fewer of those each year, since the town did its best to stop them. The townsmen had long since chopped down the Maypoles, and now they punished disorderly Christmas-keeping with stocking in the market square. Public singing and dancing were forbidden.

Inside our houses at Christmastide, however, we were as merry as we cared to be, with plum pudding and holly sprig and boar's head on a spit and games and wassail and singing and gifts of apples and nutmegs and gloves. We now made Christmas without my father, since after the queen died his company became the King's Men, and he was always at one palace or another for the royal family's Christmas Revels.

It was much merrier there than in Stratford, he wrote, though he missed us.

When he visited in person during Lent, he spoke more freely, describing extravagant entertainments with myriad candles, and towering cakes stuffed with live singing blackbirds, and gowns made of cloth-of-gold. He told us that nobles throughout the land were as festive as monkeys from Christmas through Twelfth Night. They paid thousands of pounds for a fortnight of jollity, stuffing themselves with pheasant and goose, and goggling at the hired players, while the king taxed the towns for the money, and the Puritans in Parliament frowned more deeply each year. Gold flowed through King James's hands like water, he said.

And then he would plunk pieces of gold on my mother's table, and say, "Here, some of it ran to me."

Within a few weeks I would be standing in the yard or on Clopton Bridge, watching him and his horse grow smaller and smaller and finally disappear.

By the time I was eighteen I had suitors.

I was, after all, a catch, though an odd one. But I discouraged them all. I'd no interest in marriage. It seemed a peculiar institution, judging from how my parents managed it, and besides, if one has a twin, one can hardly think to knit one's soul with a third. I had lost my twin long ago, but there was a way in which I carried him inside of me, or so I felt. And so I was set in single life. I did well enough most of the time. It was not above ten evenings a year that I would close myself in my room to screech at the tops of my lungs. On those nights my mother would mount the stair and tap softly, and after a while she would go away.

In my twenty-second year I came home from a walk by the river and was putting my book down on a table by the front door when I noticed Susanna sitting by herself on the settle. She was not weaving or embroidering. She was only sitting still.

"What ails you?" I asked her. "The Hall lads are angling at the river; I thought you'd be strutting." I had only meant to tease, but I regretted my tone at once when she turned and I saw that she had been crying.

" 'Tis only Edmund," she said.

"Edmund?"

"Edmund. Our uncle, gone for a player in London."

"I know who Edmund is, Susan." I was feeling the grip of ice on my windpipe. "What of Edmund, then?"

"He's dead. That's what."

Then I saw the letter in my father's hand lying beside her, and I ran to read it.

It was true. Edmund was dead and buried in London. He had died in a day, with a fever caught when he'd played in cold weather on the open stage. He'd been ill when he started, but refused to come off, and by the next day he was gone.

That night I stayed home alone, while my mother and Susanna went to grieve with my grandmother. I sat in my mother's bedroom reading from the Book of Judith in the big

Bible my grandfather Hathaway had bequeathed to my parents. It lay open on a table. The Book of Judith was in the back of it, since the Protestants had cast her from the canon. Whysoever they did it, *my* guess was that it was because she wore festive garments and a tall-crowned hat when she went off by herself one fine night without anyone's by-your-leave to kill a drunken man whom she didn't much care for. The sodden sot was the Israelites' enemy, and a very nasty fellow. Even so, I guessed that the godly thought the less said the better of a woman of such startling imagination.

I liked to read of her, of course.

After I finished, I blew out the candle and opened the shutters and looked through the window at the full moon.

Then, as though it were someone else doing it, I found myself opening my father's trunk just as I'd done seven years before, at the start of my great London adventure. This time I went so far as to take out a serviceable pair of breeches and a shirt and a doublet and netherstocks. I went to my room and put on my boots and tied up my hair and put on a cap and picked up a coin-purse. Then I went downstairs, tiptoeing past the maid's and the cook's rooms, where I saw candles burning, and looked at myself in the glass in the parlor.

Then I was through the kitchen and out the door and to the stables and saddling a horse and onto the road, which was nearly empty at nine of the clock, and then I was crossing Clopton Bridge and headed for the neighboring town of Shottery.

I did not have a plan.

In my grief, I wanted only to do something out of the

ordinary. When I spied a low-looking inn at a crossroads where travelers stopped, and it seemed lively and crowded enough, I halted, and tied my horse, and walked inside, passing under a swinging sign that read, "The Phoenix."

THE place was so crowded with men and youths and bawdy lasses and serving wenches that I was not much looked at, but in an old gesture of nervousness I pulled down my cap just the same. I knew I was being reckless, but in an odd way I was feeling not only like myself but also like someone else, someone who could hold a glass's worth or two, and so I sat me down and ordered one, and then another.

Now, my family has never come to good fortune with the drinking of wine, which I think is why my father called drink a devil that would steal away your brains. I should not have dared that devil, but I did.

My memory of what happened after is something confused. I know that I began to talk, and that some young men at the table began to talk back to me, and that all in all it was a merry conversation, and one that went on for some time. It started when I joined an argument three London men were having about Guy Fawkes and the Catholic threat. This somehow turned into a bragging contest about the women we'd had in Italy.

At every fifth swallow I raised the cup to my uncle Edmund, until everyone was doing it, saying, "Another to my uncle Edmund!" or, "No, this to *my* uncle Edmund!" Then one of the fellows pulled off my cap and my hair fell over my shoulders and into my face, and the rest of them laughed, and one of them said, "Thou'rt a fine lass for a fellow, and well spoken, too, and what husband art thou fled from?"

Then two or more of them took my arms and pulled me out of the place.

I staggered a bit and laughed, because all in all I was having a merrier time than ever I'd had since I trod the boards in London, though my head had been cool then and now it was spinning like a top. One of the men unbuttoned my doublet, saying, "Let's see," and then I slumped back against the wall of the inn like a leaf of boiled spinach. I puked on the fellow and fell down. He tried to pick me up, but someone pulled him away and I heard a confusion of argument and some blows.

Then someone picked me up and threw me over his shoulder like a bag of oats, and I remember myself moaning, then a horrible time of bouncing as the fellow walked and walked for what seemed like hours, and then a knock on a door and the sound of its opening and my mother's voice saying, "What—*Judith!*"

Then she and Susanna in their nightgowns pulled me up the stairs and someone mopped my face and dumped me on a mattress and covered me up and then it was blessedly black.

THE next day I was sure I'd been poisoned, and indeed I had, though it was myself had done the poisoning. The blood in my arms and legs and chest felt polluted, and my head was as heavy and burning as molten lead. My stomach churned at the smell of bacon that was rising from the kitchen. The first thing I did was puke again in a bucket that someone had left me. Then I lay groaning and went back to sleep.

By evening I was better, and could hobble downstairs in my nightgown. Susanna only looked at me with disgust, but my mother looked at me with disgust and anger, too. And something else that I hoped was worry, because worry was likely to hurt less than the other two.

"Can you explain this?" she said. "This, in a week of grief?"

"No," I said miserably.

"I have never said that good name was everything, Judith. But good name is *something*. You care nothing for ours."

I felt worse now. "Is the whole town speaking of me again?" I asked. The first time I'd braved the talk, but on the whole I did not wish to bear it again, nor to see my family's shame.

"No, they are not, and 'tis our good fortune. The place you drank was a low place, full of travelers. None knew you were anything more than a mad adventuresome lass, and lucky you are that you escaped with no more harm than a sore head."

"And stomach," I said.

"Don't think I'll pity you, mistress."

"How do you know where I was, and what they thought?" I asked.

"Tom Quiney said it. He brought thee home. Thine uncle

went back today to seek the horse, when we saw it was gone from the stable. Gilbert missed time at the Woolery to do it."

"I am sorry for it," I said. Then I frowned. "Tom Quiney?"

"Yes."

I remembered a young boy a head shorter than me, listening to my tales of London in the carriage from the city to Stratford years ago. "How could he have carried me?" I said, rubbing my forehead. "I remember him small."

"He's bigger now. You'd do well to thank him, if you could do it with no one listening. He's apprenticed to his father now."

"The vintner?" I said, and winced at the word.

"The same."

My mother did not punish me, though she said that did I launch such a madcap scheme again, she'd have the thirdboroughs stall me in jail, and hang the shame.

I think she meant it, too.

At her request, two days after my drunken adventure, an apothecary came to see me, to look to the arm that I'd twisted when I fell against the wall of the inn. He was quiet and dark-bearded and thirtyish and well dressed.

He looked familiar to me.

Susanna curtsied to him with her eyes lowered, and asked

him if he would care for some wine. She did it, I'm sure, to peeve my stomach, which was still addled. Fortunately for me he politely refused her, though he seemed to think again as she left the room, swishing her sarcenet gown back and forth, and called out that he would like, by her leave, a small mug of cider, had she any in the kitchen. I looked carefully at the instruments and powders he was setting forth. "You are John Hall," I said. "Are you not? I remember thee and thy brothers, angling on the Avon."

"I've spent more time fishing the Cam of late," he said, now twisting my arm and making me yelp. "And it is Doctor Hall now."

"You will not say they gave *you* a Cambridge degree," I said. "Have you done anything more than set dogs' bones?"

He laughed. "Thy bone's not broken. Liniment and binding will make it right in a week." He uncapped a jar from a shelf of his traveling pharmacopoeia. What was inside smelled foul, and I wrinkled my nose. "What be that?"

"Powdered obsidian, linseed oil, and sheepgut."

"And who was your tutor in medicine?"

"Paracelsus is my master. Look ye, it may smell foul, but it draws out the pain. In France I used it on the chest of a fisherman who'd near-drowned off the coast by Calais. He'd choked down a gallon of brine, and his lungs were sore taxed." Doctor Hall was rubbing the stuff on my elbow and forearm all this while. He carefully recapped the jar, then bound my arm tight with a strip of linen. His fingers were dry and cool and sure, and his eyes a warm brown.

"Did he live?" I asked.

"The fisherman? Oh, yes. Coughed out a fish, then fried it for supper." He smiled for the first time, and I smiled with him.

Susanna came in silently with his mug of cider, and placed it by his elbow. He rose and nearly upset the mug in his bow to her. I steadied it. I noticed that she brought me no cider, but I forbore to mention it.

"Where dost thou practice thine art now?" I asked.

"Here. I am back in Stratford for good. I keep an apothecary's shop in the Old Town Road."

"And do folk truly come to you to have themselves rubbed with a sheep's intestines?"

"Marry, they flock to me."

"Ah, *vile* pun. Pun worthy of my father."

He laughed. "You are right." He closed up his cabinet of horrors. "Yes, Mistress Shakespeare, I have custom enough. My problem is too *much* work. I seek an assistant."

"Here I am."

He laughed again. I saw he had not touched the cider. "Marry, I'll drink this if you won't," I said, and drained the mug. "I've been passing thirsty these past two days."

"Don't drink spirits."

"I prithee; don't *say* spirits." I touched my stomach. "The word giveth me the quease."

He was taking a long time to gather up his shelves of curative poisons, standing handsomely by the settle.

"You think I jest," I said to him. "I do not. I would make a study of cures." As I spoke, my thoughts came clear and fast.

"I have a quick mind and my fingers are nimble enough when it comes to grafting flower shoots. I see no reason I could not help you, if you taught me to mix together your powdered jade and dried peacock dung and rotten finch's eggs and what have you."

I had no desire to marry—that I'd known for a long time—but I now realized I needed to do something with my hands and my brain besides weeding and folding and counting and cooking and reading. If I didn't I might go stark raving mad.

He looked at me, amused but skeptical. "Why should I work with a woman?"

"Because my family is rich and you need not pay me."

"Ah." He began to look interested.

I cocked an eyebrow at him. "And because I warrant my sister would come to visit me at your surgery."

He reddened. "Well," he said. "Well. If thy mother agrees, then . . ."

My arm healed in a week, which by my calculation was the time it would have taken to mend on its own, without the powdered obsidian and sheep's guts. When I could carry things easily I stopped at the vintner's. The bell rang as I entered, and a broad-shouldered youth in apron and brown worsted breeches turned from the shelves to see who had come in. His eyes went wide, and he climbed down his three-step ladder and came toward me, bowing awkwardly.

"Tom, two barrels of Canary are stocked with the French wines," I heard a voice call up from the cellar. "And I tasted the honeyed sack; it lacks sugar. You must order from—"

"Hold, sir," Tom Quiney called back. "We've a customer."

The boy's face was familiar enough, although, since I'd paid little mind to that face in the years since it had stared at me for two days in a carriage from London, its maturity surprised me. Tom now had a dusting of beard across his square jaw.

My cheeks were hot because of the reason I'd come. I would not have, except at my mother's insistence. My first impulse was to tell him that, but then I looked at his eyes—blue, candid, and admiring—and had not the heart to offend him. It was clear that he still saw me as the brave goddess who had sneaked onto the London stage. Though how he could sustain that high opinion I could ill imagine, after he'd seen me puke out half my guts behind the Phoenix inn, and then carried me groaning home like an unusually loud sack of corn. *Sack*. Ugh. I could not bear the word.

Tom Quiney broke the silence. "I was sorry to hear of thine uncle's death, Mistress Shakespeare."

"I thank thee," I said. I looked at the bottles stacked against the walls. Since I was here, I decided I should buy something, to give some color to my errand. "I will take two bottles of Rhenish."

A witty fellow would have answered, "Not for thee, I hope!" but Tom Quiney only nodded and bundled the bottles in a burlap sack.

"I wish to thank thee for thine—assistance of Tuesday evening," I said, looking at the wall.

"I was glad to be on hand to serve thee, Mistress Shakespeare."

"I'sooth, I am amazed that you *were* on hand at a place like that. A lad as young as you!"

He reddened, and muttered something about a game of dice.

"Well," I said. "I hope you won."

"In fact, I had to leave it importunely."

I looked down and counted the coin from my purse.

He leaned toward me and said, very seriously, "I thought you looked comely in breeches."

I had to laugh. His voice sounded as though it had cost him all his courage to come out with the compliment, odd praise though it was. And yet he'd been a bold and chattering boy! *So some youths grow as shy as maids,* I thought.

"I thank thee," I said, and took the sack he held out to me.

"Th'art much welcome."

"And I thank thee also for keeping thy mouth shut, because I'll make thee sorry if thou dost not." I had no idea how I would make him sorry, but no doubt that I would.

He looked abashed. "I'd no thought of causing thee shame, mistress!"

" 'Tis well. I need no partners in that enterprise. So do not think to spread this story all about the town as thou didst the other one."

"I am sorry," he stammered.

"Hast no need to be," I said, and reached for the door. "The first story was a good one, was it not?"

"Aye," he said. "Mistress Shakespeare—"

"What is it?" I stood in the half-open door.

"I might call on thee at New Place, if thou wouldst wish it."

I didn't wish it, but I tried to look courteous as I shook my head. "Nay, lad. 'Twould not be proper."

"But why? Our fathers are fast friends."

"That they may be, but you are too young for courting. And I could never consort with a fellow who drank at the Phoenix."

He looked hurt.

"That was by way of a jest," I explained.

"Oh!" He laughed. "Of course 'twas."

"I am going now, Tom. Good morrow." I shut the door.

Chapter Sixteen

In a little while, I had small time to waste being wooed by Tom Quiney or anyone else.

I spent my young womanhood in an apothecary's surgery, where I sometimes worked long after moonrise. John Hall, trained at Cambridge and on the Continent, and an apostle of the mystical Paracelsus, did not let me minister to his patients by myself. But he taught me to help him set bones and birth babies, and to gather and mix his medicines, which were so much like magical potions that it all made me feel like a witch.

And that was gratifying.

I tended the herbs that he kept in his garden, the rhubarb and senna and basil and rue, which I learned had many uses apart from keeping boy actors smoothy-voiced. I would gather the herbs and pound them with mortar and pestle, to mix them with the more exotic and costly ingredients in the doctor's pharmacopoeia. He kept a store of minerals and precious stones, and I grew expert at filing and weighing everything from onyx to pure gold, to add to poultices he used to draw down harmful vapors from a sick man's chest, or to mix with white wine and the powdered windpipe of a rooster as an elixir against plague.

Much depended, of course, on the fullness of the moon when such remedies were taken, and so I also helped him in his astronomical calculations.

On fair days I would walk through the fields near the edge of the Arden Forest, gathering maydew for skin ailments, and the wild mint and chamomile that fortified the milk of nursing mothers. Or I would pluck thyme and balsam to mix with the honey of bees, to administer for the ague. I remember a morn when I waded the river's shallows with a pail, wearing only my shift for ease of movement, and skimmed the water's sheeny surface for duckweed, while a large Avon swan watched all, looking as amused as a swan can look. The event stays with me, though I forget what we did with the duckweed.

To me, it was all a fascinating game. At times I had trouble suppressing my laughter when Doctor John Hall, *magister artium* of Cambridge, seriously lectured me on the healthful properties of the shell of the plover's egg once it had been treated with sulfur, or some such nonsense. Harebrained though he was, he was far from being a fool. He saw my skepticism, and at times was offended by it. More than once he came close to packing me back to New Place in the middle of the day, and we once had a fine quarrel when I refused to let him brush whalebone and mercury on my spaniel's paw to test those things' power over ulcers. We did not speak to one another for two days afterwards, until he broke the silence to tell me he'd be boiled in egg whites if I entered his surgery again.

I told him I'd ready the boilings; no doubt they'd be good for his piles.

But he was my brother-in-law by that time, and our quarrels were in the nature of family quarrels. He knew that a sister is not as easily shed as the odd idle townswoman who seeks matter for her wits to work on. Besides, I got very skilled at assisting him, and he came to depend on me. Though I never believed any of his cures could work, I hid my doubts from the patients, and was surprised to find that they *did* work more often than not. Which only proves that imagination is stronger than a good many illnesses.

All in all Doctor Hall did much good with his fanciful wizardry. And though a few of his patients got worse, so they might have done on their own and without him. His medicines never killed anyone.

At least, no one I knew of.

SUSANNA married John Hall the first year that I worked in his surgery. She was twenty-four and he was thirty-two. She left my mother and me in the great house at New Place, alone except for two servants, a gardener, and a friendly boarder who kept mostly to himself. A year after the wedding I stood with water and hot cloths and helped my sister's child come squallingly into the world. I placed her tiny, flailing, and slippery body in her mother's arms, and for a minute or two Susanna and I were the greatest friends in the parish.

"She shall be *Elizabeth*," Susanna said right away.

My sister was always a great royalist.

Later that day, while she lay like Queen Anne in her bed of state as she nursed the babe—my mother and John and I waiting on her hand and foot with pillows, and pullet's egg soup, and chamomile tea—she called me to her. "You must marry, Judith," she said. "Dost see how well thou art caring for me today? Thou wert born to be a mother thyself, though I never before did think it."

"I'll never marry," I told her.

"Fool," said Susanna, looking all sappy bliss at Elizabeth. "Mama, tell her she must."

"I will not," said my mother. "Why should she? Your great Queen Elizabeth did not."

Susanna had no answer to that, and I looked at my mother gratefully.

For I was tired of the dialogue. With my sister well wed, both sides of my family now thought themselves freely licensed to discuss my marriage prospects in front of me, and to propose solutions to the Judith problem. Even my father, who under-stood me better than anyone else, would not spare me. On his visits home he teased me, pointing openly to local swains as we walked the parish, and saying, "What's wrong with *that* fellow? Oh? Well, *him* then! His brother! Come, I'll get him for you."

He even threatened, as a jest, to take me back to London

and marry me to a player, a suggestion that made me first turn pale and then grow red as a beet.

"Ah, I have hit you there, Judy," he said. "Was it Dick Burbage you loved? Aye, and so do all the ladies, when he broods in his tight hose. Was it William Sly, shaking his foil? A proud Laertes?" My father would pinch me in the arm.

"Stop! Nay! You are all like women, with your lined eyes and powdered faces. I'll none of you."

"But Laertes, shaking his foil?"

"You forget I ne'er saw *Hamlet*."

"Then come to Coventry when next the King's Men are there. We will do it this summer. But I warn you, Burbage and Sly are both married, and too old for my Judy besides."

I jumped to the other subject. "I could not go to Coventry. Where would I stay? My aunt still hates me."

"Nay, I will speak to her. We will visit her together, and I will tell her she must come with you to the play, to see me as the Ghost."

"But it has been years since you traveled with the players in summer."

"I'll do it again, once. At least I'll go to Coventry. I will come here first, and then meet them there." He looked past me into the scullery, where my mother chopped onions and smiled distantly at our chatter. "Perhaps someone else will come with us."

·   ·   ·

As it happened, my father returned to London and grew so busy there that it was another year before we made the promised trip to Coventry.

And we did not go together.

My father came direct north from Oxford with the King's Men, who were all now rich enough to be a-horseback, and make quicker and easier journeys than in years past. My father had no time to stop in Stratford. One day he was playing Old Capulet before the wild university youths, who loved their *Romeo and Juliet.* The next he was crossing Warwickshire, and the day after that he was helping to set up the scaffold in the Coventry town square.

He had not, after all, visited my aunt, who had gone all godly and was not greatly proud to have a playwright in the family. But Aunt Joan had written her and said what a splendid reputation I had lately purchased in Stratford by helping good Doctor Hall. Since I had only once in the past four years been carted away from an alehouse in Shottery, and furthermore would not be in Coventry long enough to corrupt the youth, the Shakespeare family thought it not too bold a request that she give me a bed for the night.

Two pounds for my board accompanied the letter.

I am not Sir John Falstaff and never ate anything like two pounds' worth of food in a day. My aunt stood to make a clear profit and knew it. So she welcomed me to her door.

I went by myself to the play. It was *Hamlet,* as my father had promised. They played it on a plain scaffold, without the stage Hell and the traps and the spreading roof fretted with golden fire. And I saw that as magnificent as the Globe was, my father's art was not the playhouse, but something else again. Richard Burbage might have stood in the rye fields outside Coventry to speak his speech, and he would have been Hamlet still.

The Coventry townsfolk were nothing like as ribald and loud as the folk of Southwark. I would not have thought there would come a day when I'd miss the sight of a dead cat whizzing by my head. But as I perched on a barrel in the heat of the Coventry square, I thought I would give a groat for one, or for some youth to toss an egg at the boy playing Gertrude, just to test his quickness. Or for someone to cry out, "Hamlet's fat!"

As he was, a little; Burbage had aged, as my father had said.

I was tempted to yell it myself.

At the end of the play the applause was great, and I could see that the passed hat was filling, not only with pence but with sixpences and even a crown or two. I was surprised, then, to see a small group of frowning aldermen make their way to the side of the scaffold to address Master Burbage. I was not far from them, and I could hear their earnest plea that the players leave the town before sundown.

Master Burbage laughed. He was beginning to strip off his shirt, which was stained with pig's blood, but the bailiff's frown made him forbear. "Decorum, sir," the man said. "Women are present in the crowd."

Burbage bowed. "But I must refuse your request, my masters. We've an agreement with the city, and we've not yet been paid. And a comedy is planned for the morrow."

"You will be paid," the bailiff said. "But the council has voted again, and our agreement is that murder and incest are topics too raw for the children of a Christian township."

"Our children are as Christian as yours."

" 'Tis a wonder."

Burbage picked up a dropped foil, and the aldermen drew back. There were murmurs and gasps from the small crowd that still stood by the scaffold. But Burbage only laughed for a second time. "Marry, did you think I would fight you, good Puritans? But this is the *bated* foil." He wiped its wax tip. "I'll not argue the King's Men's case; there are audiences enough throughout England. We'll back to Oxford. *They* pay pounds, not farthings, to see murder and incest."

"I do not doubt it," said the bailiff, with a look of distaste. "Come to the town hall, and we'll see you paid."

Master Burbage's careless look turned sour as my father and some of the other players joined him by the scaffold, some of them picking up props, and all of them wiping their powdery faces with rags. Among them were many I'd known in my life as Castor Popworthy, and although it had been nearly ten years since I'd walked among them, and my hair was now long and dressed in a maid's fashion, and I wore a gingham gown, still, I hung back.

It was hard for me to believe that I would not be known by men so familiar to me—for they were all men, even Sander Cooke, now a bearded fellow of near six feet, dressed as Fortinbras, the Norwegian conqueror. There was, to be sure, a part of me that longed to be recognized and welcomed back into their company. But of course, that would not happen. All I could expect, if they discovered that the mysterious Castor had been a she, would be their embarrassment and shock.

"Marry, Will, here's another town too godly to stage an entertainment," Burbage said. "And we're the blessed King's Men!"

"I do not think royal patronage helps us here," my father said wryly. He seemed unperturbed, though it was his own play that had turned the selectmen against them.

"I would have thought *Hamlet* sufficiently Puritan," jested a sad-eyed fellow. It was Robert Armin, whose hair was now touched with grey.

Another actor struck a stance, one hand on a hip, the other palm up. "Deliver, good fool."

"Attend. Hamlet himself blasts drinking and dicing!"

The players laughed, and Armin bowed.

"They want no plays at all," my father said. "Fret not. Only get the money. And strike a deal. We'll leave on the morn if we can stay the night. I'm too old to bounce my bones on the road south without eight hours' rest."

> *Ridden from Cambridge on a rail,*
> *Set in the stocks by Coventry jail,*
> *To the New World I'll set sail,*
> *'Tis foul to be a King's Man!*

Armin sang, and the men laughed again.

MY father caught my eye as I hung shyly at the edge of the cart that bore their costumes. "Judith!" he called. I walked to the scaffold.

"My daughter," he said proudly. His fellows bowed and greeted me with interest but no signs of recognition. "My youngest."

I feared my father would renew his jests about my marrying a player in front of these men, but he was kinder than that. He saw my fear, or perhaps he himself was a little worried that Robert Armin or Sander Cooke might suddenly look strange and point at me and say, "Mark, now, you put me in mind of a marvelous lad who came to us once, on the bankside . . ."

At any rate, my father soon bowed to the men and excused us.

"So," he said, as we walked toward the home of my aunt. "She did not come to the play."

"My mother? No, nor to Coventry at all. She says she is busy with . . ." My voice trailed into nothing when I saw the disappointment on his face.

"Busy hobnobbing with Gilbert and Joan." He laughed shortly. "No good can come of those three witches." Then he smiled at me. " 'Tis no matter, Jude. I did not expect it."

In my scowling aunt's scullery he sponged the rest of the chalky powder from his face and shook the grey dust from his hair. It pained me to see how little of the grey came from stage powder, and how lined his face had become. "Aah," he finally said with relief, dousing his face with cool water, then mopping it with a towel. "Come, daughter. We'll not trouble thine aunt for a meal."

"Why not?" I whispered. "She hath two new pounds to buy it with."

"Time may unfold the meaning of that remark. But let's out. We'll walk the streets of this godly town."

He bought me supper at a very good inn, and asked me how I had liked the play.

"You had best ask me *whether* I liked the play," I said.

"A parser of words are you. I know you did."

"How?"

"I saw you from the scaffold. You were quaking with terror when I clanked out all ghostly in my armor."

"That was for fear you would trip."

He laughed. "It has happened before."

I put my chin in my hands and looked down at the table. "It is the greatest of plays, Da," I said. "The greatest of plays."

"I thank you. But the greatest of plays should not send you into a melancholy."

"Not even a tragedy?"

"No."

"It is only that . . ." I fought for the words that would not offend him or show that I guessed too much of his private thought. He had written *Hamlet* in the months after his father's funeral, after his violent argument with Gilbert in the yard of the house in Henley Street. It was clear as day to me that his grief for the loss of his father, and his anger at a wife's and a brother's betrayal, had crowded his brain until all flowered darkly forth in the play he had played today. And he himself had acted the ghostly father, craving remembrance, telling his story.

He played the ghost every time.

I looked up to see my father looking pensively through the window to the street. The sun was setting, and the bellman was crying the hour.

"You have a way to say what you feel," I said. "And to make people listen and feel it too. You have your poetry and your stage."

He was quiet.

"What do you say to that?" I asked after a moment. "What are you thinking?"

"That Sander Cooke came on too soon this afternoon. The bodies should lie on the stage a full three heartbeats before the drum sounds, and then three beats for the drum before he enters. *What warlike noise is this? Ta-ra-ra-rum!*" He banged his hands on the table. "*TA-RA-RA-RUM!*" He stopped, seeing my eyes. "Thy glare is bold and Hathaway blue. Ah, Judy. Come. Let us walk."

He paid the bill, and held my arm as we walked into the lane. The moon had come out. "See our goddess Hecate," he said.

" 'Tis three-quarters full, and 'tis near the equinox," I said sullenly.

"Do you study the moon, elf?"

"I have some skill in it. It has to do with thy son-in-law's potions."

"Ah, the mad Doctor Faustus. *To be eternized for some wondrous cure . . .*"

I said nothing.

"End thy pout, good daughter. I was listening to thee at supper." He stopped at the edge of the square where he'd played that afternoon. The townsmen had loosened the scaffold, and the players' horses and carts were gone to the inn where Burbage had persuaded the bailiff to let them stay till the next day's first light.

"Thirty-five years ago my father brought me here, and stood me on this very spot," my father said. "Do you know what I saw?"

"Plays."

"Plays! Bible plays. Herod storming and ranting, and Lot's wife and daughters, and the Massacre of the Innocents. Fireworks and blood and the Crucifixion!"

"Why will they not show those plays now?"

He smiled. "Too much murder and incest."

I looked at the empty scaffold, trying to imagine the scenes. My father walked to the stage's edge and hoisted himself upon it. "*Ooof!* This manner of thing was easier when I was twenty." He stood and struck a frightening pose. "Dost see me? I'm Cain with a rock for Abel!"

I shuddered. "Do not jest."

He jumped off the stage and came back to me. "Imagine it, Judith! A few tinkers and weavers and mercers playing

Moses and Pharaoh, and Herod's soldiers, and Joseph and the Virgin. When their funds were low they wore cookpots for helmets and wigs made of mops."

I giggled. "Then it *was* a jest."

"Nay, not so! It moved me. The man who wrote their lines was a master. A very great master. 'Twas his poetry that caught me, and not the fireworks. Not the blood."

"What was his name?"

"But that is the thing. He had no name."

"I know not what you mean."

"The Bible plays were great plays, but the writers and players never fixed their names to them. It was all for the glory of God, you see. For the people, and for God."

"Oh."

"Were I a better man, I'd do the same. I'd erase my name from everything I have written."

"You never would."

"I never would. But I struggle." He tapped his chest. "In here, I *struggle*."

I laughed. "You are a very . . . *player*."

"A player for our modern age, and not for the one that's past."

"I sense a moral in this for me. Must I hear it expounded?"

"You must. It is part of us, the will to be looked at and praised, but it does us little good. It is better to forget who you are than to puzzle over it all of the time, and pine for others' attention."

I shook my head in frustration. "You do not understand

me. When I said that *you* could put your heart on the stage for all to see and hear, I was not talking of fame. I meant only—" I balled my fists and shook them theatrically at the moon. "That you can *say* things. That you can make everyone hear you, and understand! Thy sorrow and thy . . . marry, everything! 'Tis naught to do with craving fame."

"Ah?" he said. "I think it has much to do with craving fame."

"It is only wanting to be heard, and you know nothing of what I mean."

"Judy." He grasped my shoulders. "I know you better than you think, and I must tell you roundly. You think sorrow is special, but it is not. There is one great grief, and all of us share it."

"What's that to do—"

"I am trying to explain it. My mother lost two babes before I was born, and another when the girl was only eight." He dropped his voice and spoke with quiet force. "An uncle I loved like a father was hunted down and killed by Elizabeth's men for no worse a crime than speaking his mind. And besides my own kin, I have lost more friends than I would tell you of, to plague or war or accident or the malice of the great, or to simple despair. Most died. One—" He swallowed hard. By the moon I could see the sudden bleakness of his face. "One purely vanished."

"What's all that to me?" I said fiercely. "You have your sorrows, and I have mine."

"We *all* live in loss, Judy. Your grandmother. Your mother.

Richard Burbage, and King James, and the boy who swept the scaffold today for tuppence. And me! Ope thine eyes; thou wilt see thou art not alone in it."

"But—"

"But me no buts, girl. *You* are special. *You* must have your sorrow applauded. You want to be marked by your grief, and famous for it." He tapped his chest. "I tell you, I know this, because I—"

"*Father!*" I heard my voice echo from the front of the town hall, and I lowered it in fear. "*Da!*" I whispered. "What you say has naught to do with me." My eyes brushed the empty scaffold before us. "Cain in the Bible play. 'Tis *I*, Father, not you. You were never—*responsible* for the *death* of a *brother!*"

"Was I *not*, Judy?" he hissed. "Was I *not*?"

For a moment I could not speak.

After some seconds my father bent to brush the scaffold-dust from his knees. "That boy did not earn his tuppence to-day," he said mildly. "I would not say so."

I watched him. "Your case is different," I finally said. "Edmund was different. He chose to be a player. He chose to join thy company, and to play when he was sick."

" 'Tis only different because you say it is." He straightened. "Come, now. Walk. Lights have been lit and the people look through their windows. A fine show we'll be, in a town that no longer likes plays."

But I wouldn't walk. "My case is different," I said, standing stubbornly still.

"My dear, I will tell you a thing." My father sighed. "I knew my son, Hamnet. You think you bewitched him with all your hocus-pocus and spell-casting games, but he believed in them no more than you. He loved the *game*."

"No, he believed in it. Because I encouraged him—"

"He did not. He was sorrowful for my absence. On my head be the guilt for that. Can you not imagine a child trying to uproot a sorrow by some desperate act of play? Marry, you of all folk *should* understand it."

I said nothing.

"And he loved to praise you, to be your audience. You liked that well, did you not? He's in a better place now, but you think it unfair that he can't watch you suffer."

"Stop it."

"The game you played was his as well as yours. I'll warrant it was *his* idea to go to the river that night—"

"*Stop it!*" I cried.

Then I ran.

I ran awkwardly, not gracefully, careening in the darkness in thin shoes that slipped on the cobblestones. My father could have caught me easily, but this time he let me go.

IN ten minutes I was in Gosford Street rapping on my aunt's oaken door. She opened it herself. "Mercy on us, child, what happened?" she asked. "Where is thy father?"

"Nothing," I said. "Nowhere." Then I sat myself down in a chair and shivered. She brought me hot cider and pressed me to talk. But all I would say was, "You are right about play-acting, Aunt, it is the devil. It is the devil!"

Chapter Seventeen

I did not see my father for another year, but it was only a matter of weeks before I had a letter from him. That same letter now lies in a box hidden deep in my trunk, where it keeps company with a pair of deerskin gloves my grandfather made me and three flat stones Hamnet and I once brought home from the Avon. Among other things, it said,

> There is a darkness in me, and sometimes it will out. There are times when I think I see all things truly, when all I see is my own black heart. Other times I am cursed with a thousand perspectives. What follows is that I am not the surest judge of the world, and perhaps my family, who should look most clear, are less plain to me than anything else. Folk are full of mystery, in the end.
>
> But believe me that even when I am wrong I speak to you

in love. You are my Olivia and my Viola in one, but most of all
you are my lion-heart Cordelia.

  Forgive me, my daughter.

I read those words ten times over before I folded the letter
and put it away.

I forgave him, of course.

But I knew he hadn't been wrong.

THREE years after that my father began to write us different
letters. These were frequent ones that insisted with urgency
that my mother come to London. He was not sick, and he did
not ask her to come to stay; but he knew that his days there
were nearing their end. He desperately wanted, I think, to
share with her something of his London life before it was over
forever.

I am sure he feared returning to Stratford to live out the
rest of his days with a woman who knew so little of who he
had been.

But my mother refused. "Let him come to me," she said.

"He *does* come to you," I said. "Every year, at least once.
And he has sent you his script of *The Winter's Tale*. He wrote
it for you. Does it not move you? Will you not see it acted?"

" 'Tis a piece of fluff."

" 'Tis a plea for your forgiveness for anything he's ever
done! How can you not see that his plays are the only way he
says anything?"

When I grew angry at her, she lost patience and let it be known that this was not a thing for daughters' meddling. Something in the set of her face and the steel in her voice told me that I did not, indeed, know the sum of her case against my father, and that her years of stubborn refusal to leave Stratford, even to visit him somewhere, were not simple spite. Spite they may have been, but the spite was not simple.

I had too much to do with the untangling of my own life's knot to try to undo hers. So I did not urge her further.

Still, his letters were so imploring and pitiful that Susanna and Aunt Joan and I sent a parade of family members to see his new plays, in the hope that it would make him feel loved at home, as certainly he was. First Susanna went with John, and then Susanna went again with John, and then one April day I decided that it was time, at last, for me to return to the city of my father's dreams. Within a fortnight I was seated with my aunt Joan and her husband in a hired carriage that was, sadly, not much more comfortable than the one that had bounced me from Coventry to London when I was a scant fourteen. And we set forth.

My father met us in the center of the city, and gave us the expected mingle of welcome and disappointedness when Joan proved the last to disembark.

"She's not in there, as I take it," he said.

"Well—no. But *we* are here." I kissed his cheek.

"Excellent."

He had lodgings with a Huguenot hatter in Silver Street. These were no grander than his old rooms in Southwark, but they were much more homelike, and this I was happy to see. We did not stay there, though, but in a comfortable inn very close to the King's Men's second theater. The new playhouse, said my father, pleased the finer folk of the city, who paid higher prices for night performances by torchlight and a roof to keep rain off their heads.

"And yet I prefer the Globe." He sighed. " 'Tis not the heat and the cold and the yardlings' oniony breath that draw me there, but another thing."

"The stage trees," I suggested.

He pondered it. "Aye," he said. "The stage trees."

"I like the Globe better, too."

"We'll go back to it," he said happily. Then his anxious look returned. "But not tonight. 'Tis the new playhouse tonight."

That night we would see a play at the splendid Blackfriars, which was noisy enough despite its lofty patrons, my father assured me. He proudly displayed before me and my aunt a copy of a complaint lodged against the King's Men by citizens who dwelt near the theater. It was full of the direst legal invective against the shouts and shrieks of the players, and the lewdness of their audiences. "So you see, it is almost like Southwark," my father said, rolling the document up with some satisfaction.

"But in Southwark the neighbors were as bawdy as the audiences, so there was no conflict."

"True enough. But conflict is the soul of drama. My dears, I will see you after the play."

BUT my father's mood was not so merry when *Cymbeline* was done.

My heart felt torn in sympathy for him.

"I do not like roofed public playhouses," he said. "I do not *like* roofed public playhouses."

"But this is not public," said his sister Joan. "The finer folk come—"

"Oh, they are not finer folk just because they pay *money*." He was wrapped in a cloak in the corner of our carriage, bound for Silver Street. "They can be vile enough when they choose. Yet 'tis not the audience I damn; they did well enough. 'Tis the poxy windlass and the cursed *notion* of lowering a god on the stage. A god should walk on the ground. 'Tis much safer. I have tried to tell Burbage that since the beginning, but my vote is now one in twelve."

"One in twelve? They think you a Judas," my aunt's husband said cleverly.

It startled all of us, because until that moment he had seemed to be sleeping in a far corner of the carriage.

"Aye!" said my father, pointing at him. "You have hit it! But now they see. It's the curse of that clown Kempe! It still haunts us." But my uncle's eyes had closed again.

Joan laughed. "My husband is not for poetry," she said. "He came for the love of me, and slept through the play."

"The better," my father muttered, wrapping himself more tightly in his cloak and shrinking back into his seat. "The better."

THE play had indeed been disastrous.

The blame fell on the new machine that the King's Men had installed in the roof of the theater. It was a windlass, with a rope to be used to lower fairies and gods and swing them through the air. Richard Burbage had thought it perfect for my father's *Cymbeline*, wherein the Roman god Jupiter visits the paltry humans, and strikes fear into watchers' hearts. Burbage had persuaded my father to mount Jupiter on an eagle and let him address the audience from above. But the pulley had broken and Jupiter nearly plunged to the stage and broke his neck before one or two men grabbed the ropes from above and halted his fall with main force.

The result was that Jupiter, played by my old house-host Henry Condell, looked something more terrified than majestic.

His fear didn't lessen when the ropes pulled him up with a jerk and then let him drop again, this time two feet closer to the stage floor, and then got twisted so he went whirling around the place like a child's toy. I will say he carried it as well as he might have, shouting his lines out from this or that corner of the stage where they swung him. But the effect of his bravery was marred when his plaster eagle hit a wall and its head came flying off into the lap of a gallant who sat at the stage's corner. That one shrieked like a lady who had seen a mouse and threw the thing behind him, while Condell rose jerkily up to Olympus mounted on his headless bird.

"You once counseled me to avoid romances, Da," I jested in the carriage. "Perhaps *you* should."

"Leave me be, Judith," he said, and threw his cloak over his head.

THE next day went better.

We saw a play at the Globe, which lacked the swinging harness for the gods, and none of us missed it. The crowd was the same raucous mob I remembered, but I was no longer a plainly clad lad in the midst of it. I was myself: a fine young woman in a satin gown, watching from one of the lord's rooms that my father reserved for our use.

Joan and her husband and I sat with a beautiful lady named Elizabeth and her husband, Henry Wriothesley, the blond and blue-eyed Earl of Southampton. He was my father's old patron, and a man I had oft heard him praise, not least for his loan of the stake he had once needed to buy a share in an acting company. Glamour and a sense of risk surrounded the earl, for he had been caught and imprisoned nearly ten years before for his part in Lord Essex's attempt to unseat old Queen Elizabeth, at the tail end of her reign.

Indeed, my father himself had encountered some trouble in that scandalous affair.

Though he had always professed that he held *no* views and took *no* sides and did nothing but stage some foolish plays, still, the play he and his fellows had chosen to stage on the eve of *that* famous revolt nearly landed them all in the Clink. They wouldn't even have been granted the dignity of a Tower lodging, like the great blond earl. After all, *they* were not nobles, but only poor players. They were saved at the last by an actor's cleverness, and my father was happily spared.

I was prepared to hate Henry Wriothesley for the trouble he'd pulled my father into, not only in the Essex revolt back in 1601, but in the time before that. For I knew well that it was the earl's house, and not our home in Stratford, to which my father had fled from plague-ridden London the year I was nine. And it was his long stay in that palace that had first sent Hamnet despairing that he would never come home again. I well remembered what tragedy followed.

So the earl was a monster in my mind.

And indeed, on first view of him, his long curly locks and sky-blue cloak did little to recommend him to me; they seemed like styles that would better suit *me* than a gentleman of thirty-five. But his charm and his open enjoyment of the play were such that I could not sustain my dislike of him, as valiantly as I tried.

"Thy father is the greatest of stage poets," he charged me at the end of the comedy, as though I would argue the point. "He brings *life* to the stage."

"Some would say all playwrights do the same." I smiled at his excitement. "Players *are* alive, after all."

"But look you, dear lady," he said, pointing to the boys on the stage who were sweeping the leaves that the wind had shaken from the ash trees. "Those trees! Who but he would have thought of *that*? And I will tell you another thing. I saw the play we saw today the first day it was staged, and do you know what your father did in it?"

"I think I have heard the tale."

"Yes! All England has heard it by now! A live bear, taken from the bear-baiting pits, and given work as a player! Fed fish every day, and his only task to chase an old man off the stage!"

I laughed. "*I* heard that the old man was my father, and that the scene did not go well."

"Ah, well, it did not go as planned," the earl conceded. "But the spirit of the thing was well applauded!"

The earl and his wife left us with an invitation to dine with them on the morrow in their house in the Strand. We met my father outside, and he and Joan's husband departed in a boat for the Thames' north shore. Joan and I were to follow.

We walked east along the river paths, Joan and I, watching the bobbing boats and the anglers on the shore and the fine anchored sailing vessels and the palaces upriver. If we kept our gaze trained right we could almost think ourselves in a pastoral world, an Arcadia. We tried not to look closer at hand, at the bleached skulls and rotting heads that crowned the spikes on London Bridge, or the bobbing heads of the prisoners chained in the water that ran by the Clink; or to hear, behind us, the shrieks of the mad in Bedlam and the howls of the bears in the pit.

The cool nave of Saint Saviour's Church was a haven from the welter outside. We sat for a while in a pew, then rose to walk to the graveyard.

Joan found it first.

She placed some violets at the base, then crouched to brush dust from the stone. I stood behind her, silently, as she prayed.

Then she stood, and I looked at her awkwardly.

"You will want to be alone here," I said, hit by a sudden thought. "I should not have come."

"Oh, no, Judith. Why would you think it?"

"Because—he was your brother, after all."

"And your uncle. No. We'll visit him together."

" 'Tis well, then," I said, and crouched to trace the carved name of Edmund Shakespeare with my finger.

But it wasn't well, I thought. It was not well at all. I rose and looked at the stone with some malevolence, not for Edmund, but for whatever player's fate had put him there.

"Twenty-seven," I said. "A scant two years older than I am now. 'Tis a pity."

"All of our years are lent to us," Joan said. "And he had more years than some. His babe preceded him to the grave."

I looked at her in surprise. "His babe?"

"Yes." At first she hesitated, seeing that I had not been told the story, but I pressed her. "What is this, Joan?"

"Edmund had a babe. He was handfasted to the child's mother; they hadn't yet wed, Will said. But the child was born lifeless, or didn't live long; I am not sure which. And then Edmund's death came soon after."

"What became of his wife?"

"Will gave her money after his funeral, and tried to look after her, but she vanished from view."

"Who was she, then?"

Joan smiled sadly. "A girl of Southwark. Ned found her in a tavern hard by, the Bishop's Hat or some such—"

"The Cardinal's Cap."

Joan looked at me with raised eyebrows. "I had forgot what a London adventurer *you* were as a young maid."

"It seems years ago now."

"It *was* years ago, Judy."

"Oh. Well, that's what it seems."

I looked pensively at my uncle's grave, trying to understand what sort of God would smite a young man down for playing on the stage, or a young boy for playing in a river, or a babe for having the audacity to be born.

"God's ways are mysterious," Joan said, as though she'd read my thoughts.

"To that I say amen."

THE next day we dined with the Wriothesleys.

Until that day New Place was the finest house I'd seen from the inside. The home of the earl was enough to humble me. The largest Turkish rug I had ever seen stretched over the floor, and the windows were hung with heavy damask curtains. Embroidered cushions were scattered everywhere, and a trio of musicians played for us, on oboe and flute and viol. Dozens of servants scurried between the carved oaken pillars that supported the roof of his great hall, a place big enough to seat two-score guests, though we were only ten or so that day.

From gold plates we lifted our bites of roasted pheasant and swan and our scallops and ices and cakes, and we did it not only with knives and spoons but with a fancy three-pronged thing that Henry Wriothesley called a fork. We drank Italian wines from crystal glasses, all but my father, who avoided the wine and bade me, with a warning look, shun it as well, though I could not forbear a sip or two. It was much better than the rot I had swilled at the Shottery Phoenix.

"This is a fine finish to our last day in London," Joan said. She and her husband and my father and I had ransacked the Globe's tiring-house and made a great sport of dressing as fine lords and ladies for this occasion.

"I cannot abide this wear," my father had said, "but I think of it as a play." He wore three-piled velvet trunks and pale yellow silk stockings and silver-buckled shoes, a purple peascod doublet ornately cut with eyelet holes, a high-crowned hat, and a ruff so wide that on it his head stood like a cake on a plate, which is what I told him. "Marry, and I had hoped to affect John the Baptist at Herod's feast," he said.

Joan wore a green satin skirt pushed out with a bum roll, and a cape of green velvet. Her husband at first looked as though he felt foolish in his fine black galligaskins, his French hood, and his ornamental rapier, but all that passed after his second goblet.

Myself, I had striven to look as grand as the earl's wife had the day before in our playhouse box. I wore a peach-colored Italian gown—cut so low that my father's eyebrows had shot near to his hairline when he saw it—and, underneath, a three-foot Spanish farthingale, from which my skirt flared out in a hoop about my waist and fell in folds almost to my feet. I wore heeled satin slippers and white silk stockings so fine they were nearly sheer. My cape, of which I was proudest, was of purple velvet, and my hair was pushed back from my forehead with an amethyst-studded band. It hung down my back in the unmarried style, and curled around the glittering stones that hung from my ears.

"Paste," said my father, as he rubbed the earring-stones between thumb and forefinger. "But uncommonly good paste. Rosalind wore them, you know."

The feast and the songs and the games prolonged themselves into late afternoon and I covered a yawn, and saw Joan looking closely at me.

"Thou art tired of this company," she whispered to me. She pushed a stray curl behind my ear. "But look about thee. There is a young lord near the table's end who has made sheep's eyes at thee since we arrived. And that other, with the Spanish ruff. You have twice refused his offer to dance."

"Because I cannot dance as they do here!" I complained. "Besides, Aunt, I am no lady. What should those prick-me-dainties want with such as me?"

"I thought you liked play-acting," she said, smiling.

"I do," I said. "Or indeed, I always have. 'Tis only that . . ."

"What?" She waited.

"This is a wondrous game, but I find I want to go. To see the London streets while the sun sets."

"Alone? With dusk approaching?"

"The earl has been good enough to put carriages at our disposal." I looked over at Henry Wriothesley, who with my

father was enthusiastically laying out cards for a game of pri-
mero. "Perhaps he would not mind if I took my leave in one,
while the three of you stay to enjoy his bounty."

She looked at me hard. "Where are you going, Judith?"

"Only make my excuses to our host and the rest. I'll see
you at the inn anon."

She sighed.

"Be not *worried*." I took her hands. "I am twenty-five, Aunt.
I am no green girl, unsifted in perilous circumstance."

She frowned. "Un*sifted*?"

I dropped her hands. " 'Tis from *Hamlet*. I know not why
he chose that word; it has the right syllables. Marry, only make
my excuses, may it please you, Auntie Joan. I tire of this scene."

I left in a carriage pulled by two magnificent bay horses. But
I did not go back to the inn. There was someone I wanted to
see.

Chapter Eighteen

Or, more truthfully, there was someone I wanted to see *me*.

He had his own acting company now, the Lady Elizabeth's Men. Tonight they played in a fine private playhouse in Drury Lane. I had gleaned this information from among the odds and ends of theater chat that had flown about my wide-open ears since we'd come to the city three days before.

The company's patronage was royal, and though its actors, like my father's men, often played to a lower-born crowd, tonight their audience was weighted with heavy gowns and pearl-encrusted capes and even a diadem or two. I was one glittering bird among many, though I still drew interested eyes as I stepped haughtily from my borrowed carriage, which stood choking the streets with the rest. I held my own bejeweled head high and rented a low box seat, where I sat back, away from the light.

Like the Blackfriars Theater, this playhouse was furnished with blazing torches and comfortable seats and a formidable harness for lowering gods on stage. But the harness saw no use during this night's performance, a tragedy in which the deaths of the innocent mocked the gods' vacant perch.

It was called *Bussy D'Ambois*. He played the lead, in a jet-black doublet and a Spanish cape and spurred leather boots that came up past his knees. He was a good four inches taller than when I'd seen him last. His beard was slight, but his voice had matured fully, to a deep, mellifluous, honeyed timbre any player would have envied.

Eleven years past he had held me in his hands.

Now he held all of us there.

He commanded our eyes and our ears, speaking soft and low and then suddenly harsh as he spit out the syllables of his revenge. I had seen his grace in action before. But in this play, when he burst across the stage in fast swordplay, I saw the force and power his women's roles had made him contain.

WHEN the play was done I asked the coachman to pull our carriage to the rear of the hall. It took us fifteen minutes to push through the crush of conveyances that blocked the streets, while the drivers swore and the silk-clad passengers drummed fingers within, and I regretted I hadn't walked the short distance. But the proud Southampton crest on our coach made other drivers pull back, though they fumed, and finally we reached the end of the building and the rear door.

It stood half-open, and light and laughter spilled forth from inside; I guessed it must lead to the tiring-rooms. Again I stepped from the coach, pulling my cape close around me. Two players came out the door as I entered. They bowed and let me pass. I saw them glance with interest at the earl's coach, then shrewdly at each other.

Nathan Field was slouched in a chair in an inner room. He had loosened his doublet and linen shirt and had just finished wiping the sweat and greasepaint from his face with a rag. His hair was tousled, and the torchlight caught the single gold earring in his ear and made it glint.

"Till tomorrow, then," a man was saying as he slipped from the room. "We're back at the Fortune."

"Aye. Bring what we owe Henslowe."

"Ah, I had forgot me. Till the morrow." The man walked past me in the hall, eyeing me with curious admiration.

I stood at the door, my heart beating rapidly. But the player gods were with me, and when I spoke my voice was as calm as a smooth sea. "A marvelous performance, Master Field," I said quietly. "A great pleasure."

He turned, and no sooner caught sight of me standing there than he was on his feet catlike and bowing deeply, a hand at his chest and one arm extended. "And a pleasure to entertain thee, my lady." He straightened with one fluid motion. My eyes met his, and I gave him a smile of infinite suggestion.

"Will you grant me the pleasure of hearing your name, lady?" he said, with a courteous smile. "It surprises me that I noted you not from the stage."

"And why would you, sir?"

" 'Tis my custom to note any thing of great beauty. But 'tis well you hung back from the light." He smiled. "My part asked for full concentration."

Ah, he had learned the tricks of courtesy, had Nate Field.

No more was he the rough stone of Southwark who had bought my virginity at such a high price. I was sure he'd had hundreds of chances to practice this sweet speech, since it was words that smoothed the paths to success for lowly players, and not least the words that flattered fine ladies. And seeing him close, all even-featured and green-eyed and now three inches higher than I even in my heeled slippers—seeing him thus, I was sure he'd had ample success.

"Do you not know my name?" I asked, looking straight at his eyes. "I'faith, we have met before."

"If that is true, then you must forgive my weakness of mind. What madness that *your* face should pass from my recall!" His voice was smooth as glass, but I saw a twinge of uncertainty flicker in his eyes.

"Do you know nothing of me?"

His eyes looked past my shoulder. "I know you have powerful friends."

I turned. The Earl of Southampton's coach was clearly visible where it stood in the street, its crest emblazoned on the door.

I turned back. "I am very good friends with a very good friend of the earl."

I could see, under the mask of his courtesy, the old wariness enter his face. I could almost read his mind at work. He thought me a great man's mistress, and was weighing his desire against the risks of an unwanted duel. For I saw that he did desire me—desired the benefits that came with a rich woman's favor, but also wanted *me*, as he had wanted me before. I saw that greed in his eyes, and it filled me with a sense of power.

"You would know my name, then?" I said. "That same good friend sometimes calls me Viola." And I looked at him pointedly.

At first he only frowned in puzzlement. Then his eyes went wide. "Nay," he said. "Not—" Hesitantly, he reached out his hand and touched my face with his finger. I felt again the decade-old flame in my blood.

"Christ and all the saints, it *is* you," he said. "By God, it *is!*"

"Aye, Nathan, 'tis," I said. "And I'm pleased to see you have tempered your wilder playing gestures." I smiled. "You did not once spin your arms like a windmill tonight. I'faith, you've found yourself as a man on the stage."

"By God," he said slowly. "By God. You are beautiful."

That undid me. I had come to show off my glorious borrowed carriage and silks and to nettle him in some vague way. But he'd suddenly put me at sea. Now I did not know what I wanted.

Well—perhaps that is not quite true.

"But who *are* you?" he said. "What became of you, those—eleven years past?"

"Come, Master Field." I held out my arm, and he took it. "The poor coachman's been waiting for hours."

"I'll give him a pound. I've money enough now."

"So I see."

He took his cap and we went out to the street. God knew where the footmen had gone; no doubt they were tippling and singing catches in the tavern across the way. But the coachman jumped to my service, straightening his fine blue livery and swinging wide the carriage door. "Will we be gone now, Mistress Shakespeare?" he said, bowing low.

That was a moment of glory.

Nathan halted in mid-step, and looked from the servant to me and from me to the servant. Then he loosed my arm and stepped three paces back. "You," he said, incredulous. "You are Will—Shakespeare's—*daughter*."

"I wonder you think that a crime," I said sweetly. I produced a mock-pearl-studded fan from the folds of my cape and waved it at my face. "Shall I take you to your dwelling, Master Field?"

He shook his head slowly, watching me carefully, as though he expected some new and more frightening surprise— or as though I were a tiger poised to spring at him. But he stayed his ground. "I'm not such a fool as to—" He stopped, glancing at the coachman, who remained frozen in position, wearing a mask of studied indifference.

I stepped close to Nathan and whispered, "Hang it, Nate! 'Tis a poxy fine carriage; you've never *seen* the like. Velvet upholstery and cushions, and torches fixed to the windows! Come for a ride, before this poor fellow drops in the mud."

"I—" Suddenly he laughed. "Well enough, then. Have at you, mistress!" And the coachman handed us up.

Inside, he stretched himself against the plush seat. "Marry, we could do *much* in here!" He sat up. "But do I dare? Mistress *Shakespeare*? And he found you out back then, didn't he? Found you and sent you back crying to your dam."

"Not crying."

He leaned toward me. "He did find you out, I'll stake money on it! I came across John Rice in the Knavish Loon, four days after you played your Viola at the Globe. He said you'd vanished into thin air, and the only one who pretended to know anything of it was Shakespeare. First he said you'd joined the fleet, and then that you were in the Clink, and then that you'd fallen into the Thames or some such thing. A different tale every time." He studied me closely, and I grinned at him. "By God, you even have a trick of his face."

"I am sorry to hear it."

"Ah, it favors *thee*. Even if *he* looks to have been bashed by a runaway ox-cart."

"Take care! 'Tis my father you speak of."

"Nay, I honor him!" Nate took off his hat and leaned back against the seat. "So I do. He's the only King's Man who'll speak to me. The only one who forgave me for all the thieving I did from their company."

"I am sure *that* was more than a bag of nails."

"And you may be right, but I'll confess no crimes to *you*, my fine lady."

"Ah, the old secrecy."

"*You* talk of secrets!" He shook his head, laughing. "*You!*"

"I am passing good with secrets, I'll admit."

I sat primly across from him, while he placed his boots on the seat next to me. "*Vi-o-la*," he said. "Lady *Vi-o-la*." He put his hand outside and rapped his knuckles on the roof. "Golding Lane," he called through the window. "Three houses south of the Fortune." We started smoothly off.

I pushed his boots away. "Look you, Nathan," I said. "You can bounce on this seat." I showed him.

"I'll bounce *you* on this seat."

"No you won't. Marry, let's not go home! Show me some of London."

"No." He shook his head. "I'll not be seen anywhere with you, now you've told me who you are. I told you, Vi—what *is* your Christian name?"

"Judith. And my friends call me Judy."

"I am not your friend, because you played me an ill trick and I have not forgiven you. But I will call you Judy, because it reminds me of the puppet shows, and I might like to give you a punch."

"Then best beware my rolling pin. A punch! Fie. What have you got to reproach me with? Stealing your foolish herbs? Acting your play-part better than you could? You deserved what villainy I could devise." I assumed a wounded look. "So do all rough fellows who ravage innocent maids."

He laughed in sheer amusement. "You were as innocent as a pit-viper, and as for ravishing—now, Judy."

I hoped the dim light did not reveal my blush. "What did you think of my performance?" I said, to change the subject.

"In the tiring-house, on the pile of clothes?"

"*Nay!* As Viola."

"Ah, you will not let that lie, will you?"

"My father thought I was not as good as you."

"Then listen to him."

"If I listened to my father I'd not be here, I assure you."

"Well, there's the rub, Judy." He shook his head doubt-fully. "As I began to say, I may be fool enough to tangle with thee, but I'm not fool enough to tangle with him. He bears some authority in the circles I—circle in."

"Like a shark," I said. "Look you, I know that. But fear me not, Nathan. I have not spoken of you to him or anyone these long years. Why should I break silence now?"

He twirled his cap with his fingers and watched me with wary gaze.

"These fellows," he suddenly said, and gestured over his head and behind him to where the coachman sat, invisible outside the carriage. "They see all, though they play blind man. And they talk."

"Then give him a pound, and another when next you see him drive by. You've money enough, did you not say?"

The green eyes again. Gazing, they drew the heat into my cheeks. But I did not look away from him, and slowly, he smiled.

HE dismissed the driver with two pounds and a slap on the shoulder, and the fellow's eyes went wide with surprise at his good fortune. He drove off not toward the Strand but back toward Drury Lane, to search for his two wayward footmen, I guessed. Nate took my hand and pulled me inside a two-story wood house. Inside, I found myself tripping in the dark over strangely shaped objects until he suddenly lifted me and carried me up the stair to his bed.

He laughed when he pulled at my hoops. "Did you borrow this gear from the Globe tiring-house?" he said, thinking he made a great jest.

"Of course. Dost think I'd waste money on such frippery?"

"Why not? It becomes thee, and great Shakespeare's daughter must have gold enow."

"Had you ever tried to walk in a Spanish farthingale, you'd know why not." I wrinkled my brow. "But perhaps you have."

"My days in skirts are long over. But I've done other things inside Spanish farthingales."

"Rude!" I tried to roll away from him, but he had me about the waist, and tickled me. "Many Spanish farthingales, I doubt not," I wheezed.

He stopped his torture. "Ah, you'd not credit the number of highborn minxes who'll creep from the lords' rooms to throw themselves at a player—" He stopped. I was looking at him with wide-eyed interest. "The devil," he said. "I had forgot you were not a fellow. Shall we speak of new topics?"

"As?"

"The bend in thy knee."

Hours later I lay, almost sleeping, in his arms, when he whispered, "Judith. There is something I want to say in the dark."

I propped myself on an elbow. "What is it, then?"

He reached up a hand to smooth my hair. Then he kissed me, and said, "You were better."

"Better at what?"

"At playing Viola."

"That matters not," I said, though it did. I was warmed all over with that praise.

"I will say it. When I heard you speak the lines by yourself on the stage, that night in the dark, when no one else was there, it full chilled me. I listened longer than you thought. You *were* Viola. How did you do it so well?"

I was quiet, thinking. Then I said, "Well, there is this. I am an actual woman."

"Ah."

"And to add to that, I lost a brother—"

He put a finger to my lips. "I know."

I was sure he didn't know all of it, but I didn't want to say more. I knew the past would be back, and haunt me again later, but at that moment, as I snuggled in the crook of Nathan's arm, it did not hurt me a whit.

"I am sorry I am a better Viola," I said. "But not very. And sorry I stole your part." I buried my face in his arm, muffling my voice. "But not very."

"It did no harm in the end. I'sooth, it did me good. I had to scrape for money and a company, but I got what I wanted."

"And that was . . ."

"Men's parts."

"I like your men's parts, too."

"You are the bawdiest of wenches, and now you will suffer—"

But I pushed him from me, laughing.

A cathedral bell had chimed the hour, and I knew I had to go.

Chapter Nineteen

I had much ado explaining to my aunt Joan why I was not back at the inn before half past three. Though her husband snored, she had lain awake, worried to the point of sickness, and she demanded to know where I'd been. I told her as much as I was willing to tell.

"So you've been to a play. Well enough. And you've been with a man. That is *not* well, Judith," she whispered, clutching her nightgown close to her body. "Will you not think of your safety?"

"Fear me not, Aunt. The man was not unknown to me."

"Not unknown to you. Then you know him to be of good family?"

"He is the son of a Puritan pastor," I said hopefully.

"Joseph and Mary, those lads are the worst of all! I'll say

nothing of this to your mother, but only because we'll be gone from this town tomorrow."

"But dear Joan, I had thought to ask you to stay with me another week."

"Stay with *you* another week! What you want is for me to give some color to your—to your dalliance!"

"Oh, but Joan! Think of the plays, and the bookstalls in Paul's Yard and on Fleet Street; you've only begun to taste of them, you were telling me yesterday. Send your husband back to Stratford, and we'll stay another week, and we'll—"

"We'll what? I know what *you'll* do. Marry, you want me for a Pandarus, a bawd, and what would your parents think of me?"

"They'll not know of it, Joan. And I told you, I'm not a green girl. I'm a woman. Why, my sister was a mother at my age!"

She gave me a meaningful glare. "Aye. A married mother. I see you want to be the other kind."

"Nay, I do not."

"You think you are different from the rest of us, then? You think you cannot conceive a bastard? It's easily done, you know."

"I am different in one thing: I know herb lore and I know the phases of the moon, and I know when to plan a—visit to London."

She looked at me doubtfully.

"Fear me *not*, Aunt. I will not conceive. Listen. Have you never loved beyond the bounds of reason?"

Her eyes grew cloudy. "That is not something I wish to speak of, Judy."

"*Aunt!* Well, no matter. Keep thy secret. But I mean to say that *I* do not love beyond reason. I know what I do." She was looking ever more grim, and I threw up my hands. "I have one great adventure every five or six years! 'Tis not so very much to ask."

"One of *your* adventures is more than most women have in a lifetime."

"I cannot help them. But I can help myself. If *you* will help me."

I looked at her pleadingly, with my hands clasped before me. She looked back, uncertain and worried. Then, sighing, she relented. "We will stay, then. You are crazed like a hare, niece."

"No. Crazed like a fox."

So Joan's husband returned to Stratford alone, bearing a message for my mother, and Joan spent a pleasant week poring through books at the stationers' shops and in Paul's Yard.

To my blame, I kept her small company, just as she had foreseen.

I had claimed to have hold on my reason, but in that week it was hard to keep my grip, so many fathoms deep in love was I. When I was with Nathan it was as if we were glued together, and when he gazed at me I thought I would drown in his eyes. When I was alone I tripped and walked into walls, dreaming of his last caress, and I was sure every London citizen I passed must grow hot from the radiance of my passion.

It was my great fortune that my father was madly busy that week, preparing for a performance at Whitehall Palace. Our great king James expected not only the new play, *Cymbeline,* but his old favorite, *Macbeth,* a play that gave my father tremors. Whenever it was staged something terrible happened in the course of it, such as hanging light-fixtures falling on watchers' heads or high winds blowing in windows and destroying stage sets. Once Dick Burbage accidentally stabbed Sander Cooke in the final scene, when the two of them were fighting as Macbeth and young Siward. It was several long minutes before the players noticed that the red seeping from Cooke's body onto the scaffold wasn't the usual pig's blood. Cooke recovered from that fracas, but my father never did. He went pale with horror whenever he told the tale of it, saying, "That clown Will Kempe's curse *still* haunts us!" Therefore, when rehearsal of *Macbeth* was in the works, my father could spare little time for his family.

Which, for the nonce, was just as well for me.

By daylight I discovered that the odd objects over which I had stumbled on the first night Nathan brought me to his house were stage properties. He had wooden battle-axes and tables bearing false food and a huge tin throne in the middle of his parlor. "They are borrowed," he told me, as he lounged on the throne.

"Borrowed!" I laughed. "Borrowing's not your way."

"Ah, Judy, think better of me. I'm not the rogue I was, I swear it."

"I care not if you are! Be not better for my sake."

On the days when Nathan did not play until night, we walked the London streets, and he bought me foolish things, like pincushions and a mechanical bird that chirped the tune to "Greensleeves." He showed me the stage at the open-air Fortune, and then he brought me onto the stage, and we read comic parts when no one but the groundskeeper was there to applaud us.

"You play well, Judy," he told me that night, as we lay with our fingers entwined. "You would have done well in Italy, where women perform the commedia dell'arte."

"Oh, the shame of it, to my mother!"

"And your father? What thought bald Will of thy stage-playing?"

I pondered. "I believe he was more worried for me than shamed. That is my father."

He gave a short, bitter laugh. "Would he were mine."

"Rebel, don't pity thyself. Had a player been your father, you'd have taken orders to spite him. You'd be a zealot, waving your pocket Testament. Or a Jesuit."

"Not a Jesuit," he said, running his hand along my hip.

The next day he took me for a long walk to Lothbury Street, by Angel Court. He stopped me in front of a small stone church. "Saint Margaret's," he said.

" 'Tis not your parish."

"No, 'tis my father's. He draws great crowds these days,

preaching much in favor of God's love, and against lechery, dicing, drinking, and plays. He's a fair speaker. I've heard he even mentions me by name."

"Do you see him?"

"Nay. Not for years." He looked at the chapel front, brooding. "Plays are the enemy of life. He writes this in a penny pamphlet. I bought one and have it at home; I will show you."

"No. Tell me."

"Plays draw folk to spend passion in a false temple—that is the Globe, mark you, or the Fortune, or Blackfriars—and not to give Christian care to their brothers and families and neighbors."

"Ah. Well, he's not wholly wrong, is he? Consider my father, slaving over his *Macbeth* while his daughter runs riot in London."

Nathan laughed. "Marry, Judith, I thought you would take my part in this."

"I ne'er take sides."

He pinched me. "Thou *art* thy father's daughter. He is forever saying that. Come, let's walk."

When we reached Drury Lane he said, "I must go on to the theater. I will hire you a carriage."

I frowned. "I want to sit in a box and see the play."

" 'Tis *Bussy D'Ambois* again."

"I care not. I will catch your mistakes tonight, and tell you of them later."

"Do not waste three hours here, Judy."

I looked at him closely. "Does a mistress await you in one of the tiring-rooms?"

"Nay," he said, as though the question were not unreasonable. "Nay. But—" He sighed, and held my hands. "I would have you come to me tonight. But you must know that I—"

I shook him off angrily. "I have one more night in London. Do you want me back at the inn with my aunt? Sitting like Patience on a monument?"

He smiled a little bleakly. "You remember your *Twelfth Night*. So do I. You should have regarded the next lines."

"I know them. *We men may say more, swear more, but indeed, we prove much in our vows, but little in our love.*"

"So it is." He sighed. "Judy, you know my heart, and some of it's rotten. You are like no other woman to me. You are the one I'll not lie to. I will never be faithful, and I don't plan to marry."

"Nor do I. And I will not haunt thee in London anymore after this."

He looked hurt, and so good an actor was he that to this day I know not if I saw real pain on his face or mere stageplay. "Ah, I see," he said bitterly. "The daughter of a player thou art, but a player's not grand enough for thee. Thy father's a gentleman now."

"Stow thy nonsense! I care nothing for that. But I'll never live torn in two as he does, betwixt country and city. Whate'er I do, I *will* find a way to be whole."

I suddenly felt ten years old, and stamped my feet in frustration. "Whence comes this? I did not ask you to marry me, or to be true to me for more than the space of a week. And I did not want to be speaking of this on my last night here!"

"Forgive me." Freed from the threats he'd imagined, he let

his tenderness spill forth. He gathered me into his arms and whispered endearments to me, holding me so tight and so long that folk going into the theater stared, and I pulled away, ashamed.

THE next morning, before dawn, he stood in the shadows of the street, watching while I pulled up my woolen hood. "Thank you for keeping my secret all of these years," I whispered.

"What secret?"

"That Castor the player was a she."

"Ah, that." He laughed softly. "It was only that I thought I'd dreamt what passed between us."

"As did I, sometimes. Fare thee well, now." I took a step toward the darkened inn where my aunt lay sleeping—or worrying. Then I turned back to him. "I had me a brother," I said. "But *you* were my true twin, Nathan. Is't not so?"

For answer he drew me back and kissed me, not like a lover, but chastely, on the forehead, as a brother would do. He held me close to his heart for a moment, and then he let me go.

Chapter Twenty

I thought of Nathan often in Stratford. But I did not miss the thrill of Southwark and Drury Lane as much as I might have guessed I would. I found I was glad to be home and wandering the fields, collecting herbs and simples for good Doctor Hall, or jesting with patients, or pounding with mortar and pestle in the surgery. The excitement of that one week was enough to feed my dreams for years. Over time I came to think of my two visits to London as episodes, in the nature of a play, or a story. There was the chapter wherein I'd played a player, and the one where I'd loved Nathan Field. These chapters had turned out neatly enough, so I did not wish them to continue.

For I could see with my own eyes what became of life's real entanglements, the ones that went on and on, day after day.

Susanna and John seemed to think they were happy, but

their life was marred by petty quarrels and occasional deeper rifts, as well as the exhaustions of child-minding. Aunt Joan was content, but I did not see how, with a husband so sweetly dull. And as for my mother, she had lived far from my father for so many years that hers was barely a marriage at all.

She seemed now satisfied with this arrangement, and although my father had always planned to return to Stratford, saying he'd give up plays to angle on the Avon, I came to doubt that she wanted him there. And so I was shocked when one day, as I was caring for an ailing cousin in Snitterfield, I had word from Susanna that he was home for good, and that it was my mother's doing.

I had been gone from Stratford for two weeks. I hastened back to find my father slumped in a chair in our huge garden, watching the birds feed on mulberries dropped from the limbs of a tree. He looked placid enough, and it was a moment before I realized what was so strange in the picture of him there.

He held no pen in his hand.

"Look ye, Jude," he said, as though he had seen me that very morning, though in fact it had been nearly a year since we'd spoken. "That sparrow gorges and tries to peck to death any other that hops by. A fit image of a greedy landlord, would you not say?"

"Then learn from it, Da. Thou thyself art a landlord now."

He gestured toward the fat bird. "God uses great Nature to teach us our faults, is't not so?"

"Da! What happened to your hands?"

He looked down at the thick bandages, wrapped tightly

from his wrists to his fingers so that only the tips protruded. "There was a fire, Judy," he said sadly. "A very bad fire."

"A *fire*! Where? Did any die?"

"None, by God's grace. Though I nearly did. Thy mother brought me home."

"She came to London?"

"She did," he said in a wondering tone. As an afterthought, he added, "The Globe's burnt to the ground."

"*Nay!*"

My mother bustled into the garden with a tray. "Good morrow, Judith; are you back with us? And how be Cousin Catherine?"

"Yes, and how be Cousin Catherine?" echoed my father.

"Hang Cousin Catherine! I mean, she's mending; she's well. The *Globe!*"

" 'Tis burnt well enough. You may imagine what capital the Puritan pastors make of the happening," my mother said scornfully, placing the tray on my father's knees. "Wages of sin and so on."

"But my mother, *you* always spoke the same—"

"Hsst, girl. Now let thy father sit."

"And contemplate his sins!" he cackled, as she went back into the house.

THE burning of the Globe was a spectacular incident, and yet within my family we inclined to my father's view that the truly colossal event was my mother's visit to London.

What amazed us was that after twenty-three years she had put aside her stubbornness. It was that sacrifice, and not the loss of his playhouse, that changed everything for my father, and made him content to live with her at last. Once that great move was made, she even went back with him to London more than once, and saw one or two of his plays performed there, although he himself had lost interest in them.

And how had the Globe burned down? Well, that was a mystery. My father said something about a cannon blast firing the thatch, but then another time he said that Sir Walter Raleigh was smoking pipeweed in a lord's room and dropped the bowl, and still another that a bolt of lightning shot from the sky to the scaffold just after Richard Burbage vilely misspoke one of the best lines in *Henry the Eighth,* and that it had narrowly missed Burbage's shoes. It all put me in mind of the tales he had spun to put a good color on Castor Popworthy's disappearance from Southwark, and I judged I would never know the truth. And since I could not derive from either of my parents whether my mother had broken her steely resolve and visited London before or after the fire, I will never know whether she herself sneaked into the cellarage and started the blaze with a tinderbox. The Globe had been fourteen years her rival.

It would have been motive enough for me.

The two of them lived peacefully after that, and more so, no doubt, because of the sad passing of Uncle Gilbert the very next year. Doctor Hall tried to save him, but his liver was rotted and none of our medicines would do any good. My mother wept buckets at the loss, and the last day of his life my father stayed with him long hours as Gilbert moaned on a pillow. I know not what they said to each other, but when my father came out of my uncle's room his eyes, too, were swollen and red with sorrow.

We buried Gilbert near Hamnet in Holy Trinity graveyard. After the rest of the family departed I stood for a long time looking at the lilies and hollyhocks that covered the graves of my brother and my grandfer, by the mound of new earth over my uncle. I thought about all the times Gilbert and I had planted such flowers in the New Place garden and weeded their beds, in wordless harmony. I thought of my father and his funeral elegies and dark tragedies and sad comedies and how his grief and regret had always blossomed forth on the empty space of a page.

And then I went home and took paper and quill and began to write.

SUSANNA came to me as I chopped hyssop in John's surgery. She looked sad, and I thought she had been thinking of our uncle, remembering the three-year anniversary of his passing. I myself had been recollecting the times he had played with us and taken us to the May Day celebrations, once upon a distant time when we were children and had such things as May Day celebrations. I thought perhaps she was thinking on his big, callused hands, and on his melancholy smile.

"What is't?" I asked, hoping to jest her out of her dumps. "Hath good Doctor Hall insulted your gown?"

"Marry, Judith, enough on it," she said tiredly. "I know well enough that you hate me."

I looked at her in complete surprise. "Hate thee? Thou art my sister! Hate enters not into the thing."

"It is to your regret that I am your sole sibling. You'd rather have a—another to share your gibes with, and mock at me."

"I—would not. You suit me well enough, Susan."

She sat by the window, and I kept at my cutting, feeling a little ashamed. In a minute she said, "I deserve you to hate me. I've not looked after you as I should have. All your wild doings since you were a child! I might have stopped it. I might have stopped—Why do you laugh?"

"You do not remember how often you tried. You tattled on us at the least opportunity."

"That was to prevent scandal and—"

"Whatever your motive, you tried. And failed. You could not have succeeded. And dost thou know why?"

"Why?"

I raised my knife menacingly above my head. "Because I am the great witch of Arden!"

I meant her to laugh, but she frowned. "Judith, such jests are not—"

"Seemly?"

"Seemliness has naught to do with it. I myself am not as seemly as you might think."

"Truly?" This was interesting news, but Susanna did not unfold her meaning. She only shook her head, saying, "Most folk are not as you think. We're not characters in a play, to be read and understood. But I'm speaking of thee. 'Tis not thy conformity I hanker for, but thy safety. Marry, and my husband's, if it comes to that. The two of you run close enough to the border of the law, with your herbs and your moon-study and your magical mixtures. Jesting about witchery is not wise in a town that lately hanged three for practicing it. We may not believe in sorcery, but the town council does."

I knew she was right, and I was abashed, but, little-sister-like, I argued. "There's none here but us. These walls have no ears."

"You are merry, little Jude. Only take care to curb thy merriment *beyond* these walls."

Little Jude. She rarely called me that, and the name warmed me. "Fear me not," I said. "And do not waste time in idle self-reproaches. There was nothing you could have done to alter me. I am—" I stopped chopping, seeking words, but I could only lamely say, "Different. I am a burr on your petticoat."

She rose and pressed my shoulder, then went to the door. When she reached it she turned. "Tom Quiney would not be the *worst* of husbands, Judith."

I threw down my knife in irritation. "Stop that, now! He's a sot, and he sings under my casement. Off-key."

"He is no sot, no more than was Uncle Gilbert."

"Well, there you have it."

She sighed, and opened the door. "Good morrow, sister."

"Why should you be so anxious to pair me off?" I called after her. "Is another Noah's flood on its way?" But the door had shut behind her. "I do well enough alone," I grumbled at the hyssop.

.   .   .

Tom Quiney indeed would not cease pestering me.

He came to New Place on any excuse—with a crate of wine, or a message from his father to mine, or something else utterly transparent. His tread was so heavy I could always tell it was he, and would flee to the garden, but he would follow me there and corner me at the bottom of the orchard and try to look deeply into my eyes.

But he had nothing witty to say.

"I am able to marry now, Judith," he told me. "I'm no longer an apprentice. And I made good profit selling wine last year."

"Because you watered the Rhenish."

He colored. "Not overmuch," he said. "Not beyond what others do."

"I suppose you will say that anyone who wastes his money on wine deserves to be so cheated." I laughed. "Or that you did the tipplers good, giving them weaker spirits to creep into their brains and steal their reason."

"No."

"Hm. Well, if you can think of nothing better to say, I'll be gone."

He held my arm with a very strong grip. "Judith—"

"What?"

He looked at me helplessly. He was sturdy and tall and could have cracked a walnut in his fist, but, God forgive me, his tongue was tied. All he could say was "I love thee. I'd be glad to have thee as my wife."

"I am flattered, Thomas. Truly I am. But I wish you to a better wife than me."

For truly, my heart was something torn in those days. I had had a letter from London. It was the first in years, and was signed "Bussy D'Ambois," perhaps for fear of my father's o'erlooking it.

But of course it was from Nathan Field.

I had never wanted him to write to me, and he had honored my unspoken wish, in the main. But now and again he would send me a message full of private jests and railleries, and news of the playhouses and his successes there. These letters would be replete with absurd boasts and exaggerated mocks at the theater owners, and rival players, and the lords and ladies who flocked to see him now. His stories made me laugh for days, and lit me inside with London fancies.

But they also disturbed my sleep at night, and all in all I did not welcome them.

Two years before, he had written to say that he had rejoined my father's old company, the King's Men, who now gave him the parts that Burbage had played when that great actor was young. They would be performing in Oxford in the summer, he said, and he made it plain that he would welcome the sight of me there.

The days before their playing date I could get no rest for the hurly-burly in my blood. I had a friend in Oxford; it would be a small matter to make the day-long journey to see her, and little to explain. I went as far as to stop in the Swan Tavern to inquire when Oxford-bound coaches were likeliest to travel, and went home dreaming of the gown I would wear in the hall where the play was performed. I plotted what I would say to Nathan, and how we would escape the eyes of the wardens of the college that housed the players, and of the King's Men who would know me by sight. I told Doctor Hall and my parents that I would be gone for a week, and since my visits to friends were frequent they said little enough on the subject.

But on the morning the coach was to leave I lay in bed and could not budge.

What stopped me was not fear of discovery, but the thought of the long days after my return, when I'd lie in the mornings in that same bed with naught but the memory of Nate to warm me. It was better not even to go. And though my stomach ached with love's agony all that day and the next, I felt better the following week, when my father made the stray remark—I think it was a stray remark—that lead players such as, ah, hum, Nathan Field traveled with strossers unlaced on their summer journeys, since they had trysts in every town.

"I was never a lead player, my dearest," he said to my mother, who only laughed.

After that I had no word from Nathan for a very long time, and was sure he had forgotten me, but then this new letter came. I could tell he had written it in a mood of tearful melancholy, which players are often prone to. Amid his witty gibes was a confession that he had done himself wrong not to keep me in London years before and set me up in his house in Golding Lane with a wardrobe of furred capes and jeweled slippers and satin gowns from the Fortune's tiring-house.

And there you would be, my fine lady, he wrote. *Home I would wend to you, from a court performance, sick to the teeth of the knee-bowing and off-capping a fellow must do to keep favor with his patron, as though speaking Hamlet's verse were not enough. I'faith, I am tired of this player's life, Judy. In two months' time I will leave it. I am done. I will set me up as a merchant in Shoreditch. I have earned enough from my King's Men share to stake me amply, and my father would well approve. And then you may come to me there and we will live as others do, but merrier.*

I walked about Stratford for days with that letter in my bodice.

My father had left the plays in the end, I thought. Might not Nathan do the same? And yet the cases were different; all cases were different. My father had stayed decades in London, and had only come home when his theater burnt to the ground. Nathan was young, and at the height of his fame. And Nathan was—Nathan.

I desired, and I doubted, and I sat by the Avon's rocks and was miserable.

Finally I wrote him. *I had sworn never to marry*, I said. *But send to me from Shoreditch when your plan is well underway. If your purpose hold, you will see me again.*

It was the first letter I had ever sent him. I gave it for delivery to a trusted traveler, and I waited, like Patience on a monument.

．　　．　　．

Six months later Susanna and John, just back from a visit to London, described to me the plays they'd seen there and the great stir Nathan Field had made as Ferdinand in *The Duchess of Malfi*, and the greater stir he'd made afterwards, riding off in a carriage pulled by two bay horses. Through its windows they'd seen the coach's other occupant, who looked to be the bejeweled wife of the Earl of Southampton.

"Be thy golden-haired earl handy with a rapier?" I asked my father that night.

"His hair is not so golden now. But for rapier, he was handy enough in his youth. He fought with Essex at Cádiz, and captured a Spanish frigate. I would not want to tangle with him, for all my stage-fighting skills. It may be he's stayed in practice."

"I hope so," I said, to my father's puzzlement.

Then I went out, humming, to gather my simples for the next day's drying.

Chapter Twenty-one

I was pushing onions into the earth. My mother came out to the garden and knelt to work by my side.

"I am sure you miss Gilbert," I said, after a minute.

"I think not overmuch of him now," she said. "That was in the past."

"He would bend his back out here till an hour after sundown."

"And then he would tipple till midnight in our parlor, or in the Bear Tavern. Much good did it do him."

"How can you speak so harshly of him?"

"Because I speak of what's real." She stopped planting and looked at me hard, brushing her old hands on her apron. "Your help in the garden is good. But things will not keep from happening because you pretend they are not."

"I know not your meaning."

"We age, Judy. Time flows on, like that cursed river."

"That is what Da would call a moldy conceit, but *cursed* is good, Ma. *Cursed* is purely thine own."

She smiled. "Your humor would cheer him. You should go to him, Judy. You've busied yourself elsewhere too long. If you don't see him now you'll be much aggrieved later, and I know what manner of thing you do when your melancholy hits."

"Fear me not," I said. "To bear out what you've said of time's flow, I am now an old woman of thirty-one. I am not the wild harlot of days gone by."

"I never thought you harlot."

"Because you do not know all." My mother looked at me with a questioning frown. "I jest," I said. "But perhaps Aunt Joan will reveal my deep secrets, if you bake her a currant pie."

She shook her head at me. "I gave up the reins o'er you long ago, Judy, but I will play the strict mother now and order you in if I must. See him. There is not too much time left."

I rose and went into the house.

THE room where he lay was April chilly, and I pushed up the fire with the tongs. I went to his bedside and adjusted the blanket on his knees. He smiled as well as he could, a lopsided hoist of one corner of his face.

"How . . . goes . . . it . . . Jude?" he said thickly. His words were slurred and carefully said. Speech had been arduous for him since his stroke of the month before, when we'd found him under the ash tree at the base of the garden. Now he avoided the long and curly words and chose simple, short ones.

"I am well, Da," I said, unconsciously adopting his idiom. "Most well."

He grinned the crooked grin again, and gestured weakly toward my belly. "Name . . . it . . . for . . . me."

I smiled at his request. It amused me, his thought that he needed any son I might bear in order for his name to live on.

IT was what he had asked me the winter before, on the path by the frozen Avon. Then his voice was still as strong and quick as the river's waters in spring, though his heart was weak enough for him to need my steadying arm.

"Do you think Master Hall will keep me alive with his quicksilver and boiled dragon tongues?" he'd teased, with his cackly laugh. "Will he cool me with a baboon's blood?"

"What's it to thee? I know you pour the medicines in the hedge. I have seen you."

He stopped suddenly and reached down to tap the river's ice with his stick. "Do you think I might walk on the water today?"

"I will not come to fetch you when you fall midway."

"Oh ho, we are rhyming."

"I did not mean to rhyme, Da. Come, walk. 'Tis shivery cold."

He shot me a keen glance as we started off again. "Methinks you are something sour today, Judith. I know what would sweeten your disposition."

I sighed. "A husband. God's death, I've heard it before."

"Still spilling salty tears for a dead brother."

I frowned. "You *do* think I am Olivia. But she is a ninny."

"I thank you. My lovely creation. A ninny."

"Well, not entirely a ninny, but—"

"A headstrong. In charge of a houseful of men whom she thinks she can order here and there. But i'truth, she can't control a one of them."

I drew in my breath. "What's thy parallel?"

" 'Tis this. Since thou hast raised the topic of thy departed brother—"

"*I* did not—"

"Hush. Since thou hast raised the topic of thy departed brother, I will continue in the vein." He adopted the tone of a stage narrator. "Once there lived a little girl who thought she led her brother on a string, but he was not as stupid as she imagined."

I was growing hot with anger. "I ne'er said—"

"List, Jude." He abandoned his storytelling voice. "I'faith, thou rememberest him wrong. I tried to tell thee once before. I see thee scribbling all Montaigne-like in the garden, scarring pages with the tale of thy life for thy grandchildren, and I'll warrant thou hast thyself as a young witch and thy brother an innocent lamb. And as for that night—"

"Sir, as for that night, I was there and you were not. You were far from home that night, and 'tis because you were far from home that the thing happened, is't not?"

He stopped in the middle of the path. Abashed, I grabbed his arm. "Da, I don't mean what I say."

He waved me off. "You can be cruel, Judith."

"I did not mean—"

"Hush. I have stirred you up, I see, though I meant to comfort you. I know what a long shadow his death has cast o'er your life."

And yours, I thought, knowing he was thinking it. But he would not say it, for fear of the hurt it would cause me.

"Nay, I am worth your blame, God knows." He still stood brooding. "Some things time cannot make right, whate'er I may say in a play."

Heartily sorry to have saddened him, I touched his gloved fist, which leaned on his walking staff, pressing it to the hard earth.

Then, inexplicably, he brightened. "But perhaps I am wrong," he said. "Now." He pointed with his stick. "Look at that." I followed his gesture. Ahead of us a robin pecked at the snow on a tree branch, scarlet breast against white.

"The robin and the snow," I said. "And the metaphor is . . . ?"

"Nothing at all. 'Tis a fine display of color, is all." He patted my hand, and said, "I'll say no more, to keep you from bolting from my side and leaving me to hobble home alone, now that your legs are faster than mine. I'truth, your bustle outstrips me." He gestured. "I would like to rest on this rock."

"Oh, Da. Forgive me." I sat him down and knelt by his side. "I won't run away. Say your foolish piece. I am listening now."

"Marry, 'tis this," he said, settling himself. " 'Tis said that it is a wise father who knows his own son. I am a wise father—though perhaps I have not always been—and I knew my son. He had the Shakespeare blood, and you know what that means. He was mad for fantasies."

His mind was all Hamnet. Perhaps it was because we were so close to the part of the river where he'd died. I tried to shift his course. "Grandfer had Shakespeare blood, and he wasn't mad for fantasies."

He smiled mischievously. "Did Grandfer ne'er tell you of the story he designed about his ancestry, to make good his application for a coat of arms?"

"Nay!"

"Ah, well. A tale for another time." He sat pensively for a moment. "Hamnet. He did like the plays—"

I sighed heavily.

"And the pretending, as you did, and much of his mad thought and melancholy was play. There is a character I made after him."

"Sebastian in *Twelfth Night*, was't not?"

"No. Another." He fell silent, looking at the sky.

I clapped my hands once. "Father. You are back in London, on the boards of the stage."

"Ah, no, not there." He laughed, a little sadly. "That world is gone. When I go to London now it is to see friends." I was quiet, not wanting to say what both of us knew, which was that he would not be making the two-day journey to London anymore.

"Well, then." He struggled to rise, and I pulled him up.

"You will marry." He said this as though concluding an argument.

"*What!*" I shrieked.

"Of course thou must. I have a husband in mind who will suit your turn."

"Be not bawdy!"

"Thou art thirty-one, and must think hard on what men still hang on the branch for the picking."

"I reckon you think I must sell when I can; I am not for all markets," I said, a touch bitterly.

"Daughter, I think you are for the Royal Exchange. But you have chosen a life in Stratford, and here you must make your bed, in a manner of speaking."

"That I have chosen to live here, in this town, near this river, does not mean I need knit my soul to that of a fool man."

"He need not be a fool man. Indeed, I would not recommend it."

"I want no man to master me!"

"What you mean is you want to master a man. But you would not love a man who would let himself be mastered, and there's your paradox."

God forgive me, he was starting to anger me again. I did not want to hear these views, but I had sworn I would not run away and let him topple, and so I stood and fumed and listened.

"You are like your mother in this," he said. "She wanted mastery in marriage, and thought she could have it because I was younger than she. Ha! She did not get it!" He shook his staff in the air triumphantly. "And thou, seeing this, art—though a very great fool—wise enough to know that a man may be four years thy junior and perhaps less clever, and furthermore smitten dumb with adoration, and yet be sturdy enough not to be ruled by thee. Ah, 'tis hard to bear, my Judy."

"You think you know all, but you know little of the case!" I said. "Why do you rail at me?" I was very close to tears.

"Then tell me thy mind," he said, in a gentler tone.

"If thy candidate knew me full well he'd not adore me, that's certain."

"Ah, poor Jude. Yet from what I have heard of it, he's seen thee at thy worst."

This was my father's first indication that he knew something of my merry drunk in the Shottery Phoenix, now a decade past. I jumped us quick to a new topic. "He is not even witty!"

"It is true my plays teach nothing, then. The most trustworthy men in my comedies protest that they are slow of speech, and know not how to woo."

"But they protest it most cleverly."

Now he looked at me with frank exasperation. "Because my dialogue is meant to *entertain*. Words are not everything, Judith. And life is not an unbroken stream of entertainment."

"For some folk it seems to be." I thought of a green-eyed fellow in London.

"That only seems. There is more to life."

"As?"

"The having of children. Our line falters, my girl. Susanna

cannot seem to have any more, despite the good doctor's remedies."

"Or because of them?" I murmured. It was a thought that had worried me. But he did not hear me. He was striking the ground with his stick. "Marry!" *Thump.* "Have a son!" *Thump.* "Name him for me!" *Thump.*

"I want no puking swaddled babe named Shakespeare," I said firmly.

"Thou hast a lion-heart, my girl. Be not a coward to thyself."

I bristled. "Who calls me coward?"

He laughed. "That is Hamlet! Ah, a good one. Here's another." He made me a frightening face. *"Be lion-mettled, proud, and take no care!"*

"By the rood, do you want me to kill the king? That's said to Macbeth, is't not?"

He laughed, but darted a look behind us. "Soft you now, daughter."

I lowered my voice. "But how am I cowardly?"

He waved a dismissive hand. "Ah, you think yourself valiant, all running to London and being a boy, and now stitching up gashes in an apothecary's shop, as bold as a surgeon. But you could dare more than the odd adventure. It takes real courage to promise thy care and life's company to another. I've learned that at my cost." He coughed. "And then to do it! Ah, ah."

I could see he was full tired, and I turned him toward home. "What is the good of such pledges between folk, anyway?" I said desolately. "Folk die."

"They do." He coughed again. " 'Tis why we get new ones."

"*Children* die."

"They do, sometimes. All life is lent. The world goes on."

"You give me the roundest banalities. From thee I want wisdom!"

"Nay, you don't. You want poetry, and I'm stripped of it. Wisdom is something else again."

So I married Tom Quiney to honor him, and I kept my doubts to myself. I moved to a house on the High Street, and while no New Place, all in all it is comfortable, of a size more in keeping with a family sized two or three. For a wedding gift my parents yielded us their best bed, with its carved oaken head showing Adam and Eve and the devilish snake, staring from his perch on the tree. My mother warned me to keep my own eye on the devil by day, since he'd be watching us both by night.

"THAT."

Weakly my father's good hand gestured toward the table in the center of the room. I looked; saw papers scattered over its surface, a quill, and a cup of water. I picked up the water and brought it to him, but he shook his head. "That." I went back to the table and picked up the quill. He nodded.

"But you cannot work it now," I said.

"I . . . hold it."

I brought him the pen and placed it in his right hand, then curled his fingers around it. It seemed to content him.

"Da," I said, kneeling. "Will you tell me a thing?"

"Ah."

"Two things, and here is the first. All those years ago, when I played the part of Viola, you said, after, that I was adequate. Not as good as Nathan Field, you said. Not very good, is what you seemed to say. Did you mean it?"

He struggled, and I laid my hand on his shoulder. "Not if it hurts. It does not so much matter."

"Nay," he said, and paused to breathe. Then, "You . . . best. Best!"

I shook my head. "Then why did you say what you said?"

"Save . . . you . . . from . . . plays."

I bowed my head to hide the tears that were slipping down my cheeks. "Then here is the other," I said in a low voice. " 'Tis a far more important question. If our lives are lent to us, does that mean that when they leave us they go off to where they began? That they came from a place, and go back there?"

His eyes were closed, and for a moment I thought he had fallen asleep, and not heard me. But then he spoke.

"I . . . will . . . find . . . out."

.   .   .

THAT was the last thing William Shakespeare said. I have toyed with it, and can find in it different shapes of meaning. Perhaps it was "I will find out," or perhaps again it was "I, Will, find out!"—less hopeful and more determined. Or maybe he meant that he, Will, was finding an out, an exit from our worldly stage.

But being himself, he probably meant all three of those things at once, and possibly more besides.

I visit his grave with Thomas, and find to my surprise that my husband knows just what to say while we stand there, which is nothing at all. We place our flowers on the flat stone and then we go through the churchyard and put new blossoms on the graves of Hamnet and Gilbert and my grandparents and his, and I think of poor Uncle Edmund in his London grave, so far from the rest of us.

I fare well with Thomas, who bears with my strangeness, and speaks in ways that are not so much worded as acted, which is a thing I am sure my father has in a play somewhere. There are times when he drinks himself stupid and nights when he's gone till all hours with the dicing, but early or late he always returns, and then it is love, love, love, till I think I must flee his embrace or be crushed by it.

He carries my sacks of herbs now that my back tires easily, and each morning I drink my chamomile brew, and if ever I have a fleeting thought of the wild raillery of a leather-booted London player, then I weigh it against the warmth in my bed and the weight of my belly and the square-jawed face that is really quite kind, and I tell myself that my town is a town of hard bargains.

YESTERDAY I walked far into the Arden Forest, for the first time in twenty years. I came to the fork in the path and then to the spreading oak tree where my brother and I danced long ago and cast foolish spells.

I knelt by the tree and looked about me, surprised to find myself tearless. All of those years I had feared that the sight of that place would plunge me back, willy-nilly, into a past that I could not bear. Yet it didn't. Familiar as the clearing was, it was smaller and tamer than the place in my mind. There were the same path and the same tree and perhaps the same rocks that I'd piled to mark our buried box of poetry, but all of it was an image of what I remembered, and not the thing itself. I think I could have dug for Susanna's old tin and opened it and seen the crumbling paper inside, all spidery with my father's runes, and still the box would not have been the tin box of our game, because that one rested within me, sacred and immovable.

I sat still, straining against the kick of the babe in my belly.

Then it struck me.

Philosophy teaches true.

The memories we bear inside are more real than the things we touch.

Chapter Twenty-two

THE godly say that the dead are not dead, but stored up somewhere, and that one day the parts of ourselves we have lost will be gathered and bound like the leaves of a book. Whole and perfect we will be, they say, their eyes lifted up to that other world that sent us here and lent us to ourselves.

I am down here, in the valley of the shadow, where I walk by the river and at times skim a stone to the bank on the other side.

And I hope very much they are right.

ACKNOWLEDGMENTS

For this book's existence I am indebted
to four friends. I thank my sister,
Amanda Tiffany, for her enthusiasm;
my agent, Carolyn French, for her
faith; my editor, Allison McCabe, for
her skill; and my colleague, David
Daniell, for his generosity.